Th
be
tel

16

23

HAPPY BIRTHDAY, MR SHAKESPEARE

Will Green drives a coach for Welcome Tours out of London. He spends his days taking tourists around the sites of traditional England, extolling the delights of Stratford-upon-Avon, Stonehenge and Windsor. But when he returns home each evening it's to his grim two-bedroom flat overlooking the M1, which he shares with his growing family and a growing population of dustmites. How he wishes he had the money to buy the Climbing Rose Tea-room and Gift Shop, and live happily ever after in the shadow of Anne Hathaway's Cottage. 'You've got to follow your dream,' says Alice, the lovely tour guide, as she partners him on a series of overnight excursions to Bath, York and Beatrix Potter Country. But following his dream is the hardest thing Will has ever had to do, and his schemes for financing it are hopelessly flawed. His quest for the Climbing Rose begins to obsess him, until he realizes there's only one person who can help him: Robin Hood.

HAPPY BIRTHDAY, MR SHAKESPEARE

Mark Wallington

CHIVERS PRESS
BATH

First published 1999
by
Michael Joseph
This Large Print edition published by
Chivers Press
by arrangement with
Penguin Books Limited
2000

ISBN 0 7540 1434 7

British Library Cataloguing in Publication Data available

Printed and bound in Great Britain by
REDWOOD BOOKS, Trowbridge, Wiltshire

For the grandfather, father and son

Love's not Time's fool, though rosy lips and cheeks
Within his bending sickle's compass come;
Love alters not with his brief hours and weeks,
But bears it out even to the edge of doom.

The Sonnets, CXVI

To be or not to be: that is the question:
Whether 'tis nobler in the mind to suffer
The slings and arrows of outrageous fortune,
Or to take up arms against a sea of troubles,
And by opposing end them?

Tea towel, Stratford-upon-Avon

CHAPTER ONE

JACK THE RIPPER WITH A FISH-AND-CHIP SUPPER OPTION

The Jack the Ripper tour was the turning point. After that I knew things had to change.

I remember it was a cool April evening; I was still not used to the longer days. I was sitting behind the wheel of my coach reading the newspaper while Frank the tour guide stood at the bottom of the steps collecting tickets. A German led his young family on board and said to me: 'I understand it will stay fine and then deteriorate on Thursday. Is that correct?'

'Yes,' I said.

'Good,' he said, and hurried his children to the back.

A half-page advert for Turbo Vac vacuum cleaners caught my attention. *Three million dustmites live in the average mattress,* it warned. *You swallow three this size every day!* And there was a photograph of a family of fat tics magnified 438 times so they looked the size of Volkswagens. *Call Turbo Vac today and let its unique filtration system help you in your battle against allergens.*

'Good evening . . . Will.' A woman was peering at my name-tag through sunglasses. She was wearing a Sherlock Holmes deerstalker and cape; she had to be American. 'Barbara Scott from Pittsburgh,' she announced. 'I'm a single traveller.' Her shoulder sagged under the weight of her camera bag.

I smiled reassuringly for her. She was only in her fifties but her legs didn't look too good. 'We'll look after you, dear, don't you worry.' I got up to steer her to a seat, and as I did so a coin fell out of a hole in my trouser pocket, bounced off my shoe and rolled down the aisle. A blonde woman picked it up and handed it back to me. She was probably Scandinavian. The coin was a twenty-pence piece.

Barbara Scott sat across the aisle from some other Americans and introduced herself. 'Pittsburgh, eh?' I heard the man say. 'I once knew a Walter Friel from Pittsburgh.'

'Don't know him,' said Barbara Scott.

The coach quickly filled. The Jack the Ripper tour was a good seller. It had the kind of dark edge other excursions like the World of Legoland could never match. Frank jumped on board and did a head count. He polished his glasses with a grey hanky then blew his nose on it. The doors hissed shut and I drove off into the brown evening.

*   *   *

The first thing I noticed about tourists when I started working with them was the way they showed more enthusiasm for the places they had already been to, and those they were going to next, than for the one they were actually at. They seemed to be uneasy in the here and now; it made them grumble about their jetlag and their sore feet; it had them glancing at the sky wondering whether to put on their waterproofs. The present was best recorded on camera and viewed at a more convenient time. It was simply a place to use the facilities and then back on the coach.

This attitude always appealed to me. It was the part of being a tourist I envied the most, because my life was all present. I was stuck in the present, stuck in the driver's seat of a Welcome coach, stuck now behind a number 25 bus in Whitechapel with Frank whispering into the microphone: 'The autumn of 1888 was an autumn of terror. There were eighty thousand prostitutes in London, a city soaking in cheap Dutch gin. Five women were horribly murdered in ten weeks.'

The clients were itchy. They had paid to be comfortably horrified before their optional fish-and-chip supper, and they wanted their money's worth.

'Their throats were cut,' continued Frank softly, enjoying himself. 'Their bodies were mutilated. The first victim, Mary Ann Nichols, was found brutally murdered in an alleyway on the site of the building to our left.' Everyone turned to face the anonymous glass and steel headquarters of Pearl Assurance where a window cleaner was suspended three floors up. A number of people took pictures. The window cleaner waved cheekily.

We continued down the Mile End Road. Frank was sounding like the voice-over on a *Crimewatch* re-creation now. He was trying hard, thinking of the basket of tips at the end of the trip. 'Whoever the Ripper was he knew how to disembowel a victim and had the equipment to do so. Maybe he was someone from Smithfield meat market, or a doctor from the London Hospital.' On cue we passed the London Hospital. More cameras buzzed and clicked.

'And now,' announced Frank, suddenly upbeat, 'it's time to sample the ales of a local London pub.

Let's call in and have a quick one at the Duke of Devonshire.'

Ah, refreshment. They all sighed with communal relief. As they filed down the steps the pub-stop took on the breathing space of a commercial break.

I always thought the Devonshire was a strange choice for Welcome to make. It wasn't the normal sort of place you took tourists to. It was, in fact, a fairly good example of a local London pub: pool table, fruit machines, mucky carpet and patched seats. There was even a local clientele playing pool, although the landlord always shepherded us into another side of the bar away from them. I caught his eye and he glanced at his wife and she put the kettle on for me.

'Have you ever been on the Boston Strangler tour?' the big German asked a little Canadian woman. She shook her head. 'You have to fly Northwest Airlines to Boston,' said the German.

I sat in the corner. I knew my role. As the driver it was my duty to be sober and serious, only to speak when I was spoken to, like to the American woman in the Sherlock Holmes hat whose name I had already forgotten. She made her way over to me and asked in a whisper, 'Will, should I tip the barman?'

'No, dear.'

'Thank you so much.'

'You're welcome.'

She drifted off, her video camera at the ready, safety catch off. She raised it to her eye and focused on the range of optics above the bar, then panned round to me reading my paper. I kept my head down, but then I could imagine her showing the film of her holiday to her family back home, so

4

I looked up and gave a little wave.

Frank was happily discussing gibbets with the Germans. A phone was sitting right in front of me on the bar. It seemed a shame to waste such an opportunity so I called Turbo Vac's twenty-four-hour information line and asked them for help in my battle against allergens.

I was trying to remember my postcode, and didn't really register the shriek when it came from the other side of the bar. I looked up to see one of the men from the pool table running through the tourists, and then there was the woman in the Sherlock Holmes hat screaming, 'Stop him. Stop him!' She was reaching out helplessly for her handbag and camera, but he'd ripped them off her arms. Frank and the rest of the Welcome passengers were blocking his exit. 'Stop him,' she cried again, and as one they neatly parted and gave him a straight run for the door. It crashed open and closed and he was gone.

There was a moment's pause as everyone waited for someone else to do something. I noticed Frank edge backwards. And then I just charged. My stool tumbled; the phone receiver bungy jumped towards the floor; my cup of tea spilled. I launched myself through the crowd as if I were being propelled. I remember thinking: This isn't like me, but by then I was out of the door and sprinting down the Mile End Road. I hated this man for robbing tourists. Tourists were such easy targets; tourists were my livelihood. I had no idea what I was going to do if I caught up with him. I just didn't want him to get away with it.

Catching up with him wasn't difficult, as it turned out. I was fitter and faster, and I quickly gained on him. He glanced over his shoulder once, saw me and tried to speed up. He darted through traffic across the road, past a parked British Telecom van, through a queue at a bus stop, but he knew he was beaten. As I reached out to grab his shoulder I caught a glimpse of his other arm swinging. He pivoted, and something black and heavy hit me on the head. I heard a crack, and I went over as if I'd been shot.

Maybe he stunned me, I don't know, but I hit the pavement very hard, and the black object clattered by my side. I remember lying there, hearing his running steps fade into the distance.

More running steps, but these getting closer, and then people all around me—people from the bus stop, people off the tour, a crowd of assorted accents. A jacket smelling sharply of aftershave was laid over me; hands touched my face.

'Is he all right?'

'He's been hit.'

'What an appalling thing to do.'

'My camera!' And I looked up then to see the woman in the Sherlock Holmes deerstalker— Barbara Scott, her name suddenly came back to me. She picked up the black video camera and checked it for damage.

'He got away with the bag,' I said.

'My camera. Thank you so very much.'

I heard someone say: 'Do you want an ambulance? Better call him an ambulance.'

But then Frank was standing over me, looking at me as if all this was my fault. 'Are you bleeding or something?' he said.

'No,' but when I touched my head my finger came away wet.

'I thought it was part of the tour at first,' said an Australian woman.

'It's just a scratch,' said Frank. 'You won't need an ambulance. Everyone back on the bus.' He wanted to get going. He was thinking of his tips again.

I sat up. There was a tiny red splash on the pavement.

'Blood!' said the Scandinavian woman.

'And only half a mile from where Jack the Ripper slaughtered his first victim,' said the big German.

*   *   *

There was no fish-and-chip supper that night, optional or otherwise. The police were called and the tour was aborted. I wasn't allowed to drive the coach back. Roy, another Welcome driver, came out to take everyone home. He said to me, 'You should tap her for some kind of reward, that American bird.'

'I tried to grab him as he ran out . . .' said Frank, blushing.

Roy laughed at him.

Back at Welcome, Graham the manager met me off the coach and ushered me and all the passengers into reception. A journalist from the *Standard* had arrived. 'She just turned up,' protested Graham when I asked him what she was doing there. 'Nothing to do with me.'

He took me by the arm and announced so that everyone could hear: 'We're going to have you checked over by a doctor, Will, whether you like it or not.' Then he led me into his office, gave me a plaster and told me he wanted me to do an interview, and I was to mention Welcome Coach Tours as often as I could. 'No such thing as bad publicity.'

He pushed me back out into the foyer, but then whenever the journalist asked me a question he would answer. 'Everyone at Welcome Tours knows that London needs to look after its tourists, don't we, Will?'

'That's right, Graham.' I had felt awkward with the attention to start with, but I was beginning to feel pleased with myself now.

'Everyone at Welcome wants visitors to go home with a good impression of the city. Don't we, Will?'

'We do, yeah.'

'Does this the kind of thing happen often?' the journalist asked.

'No no, not often,' answered Graham. 'But when it does happen it's nice to know that at Welcome we've got drivers like Will around. Show her your cut, Will. He chased that bloke right down the Mile End Road. Welcome Tours likes its drivers to be fit.'

'How do you keep fit, Will?' asked the journalist.

'I go swimming,' I said.

'He goes swimming,' said Graham.

I was taken outside to have my picture taken with Barbara Scott. She was asked to put her Sherlock Holmes hat back on. Graham made sure the background of the photo was filled with a Welcome coach. Frank combed his greasy hair and tried to get in the picture, but Graham told him to get lost and go home.

Barbara Scott reminded them repeatedly how brave I had been. 'He saved my camera! My whole holiday is on here.' Then she admitted her bag had five hundred pounds in it, and almost three hundred in dollars. I felt terrible for her.

'That's a lot of cash to carry round,' said the journalist.

'I'm a tourist,' explained Barbara Scott.

The journalist thanked me for my time. 'He should have the day off tomorrow,' she said to Graham.

Graham looked appalled that anyone should think otherwise. 'You bet he's going to have the day off tomorrow. I'm going to call him a taxi now.'

But he never did. Everyone went home or back to their hotels, while I was left sitting on my own in reception for half an hour. When I went to see what was happening Graham said, 'What are you still doing here?'

'I'm waiting for my taxi.'

'Oh, I couldn't get one. You're all right for the tube, aren't you?'

'Yeah, all right.'

And he called after me, 'Tell you what, you can come in at midday tomorrow. Do the Leeds Castle run.'

I wasn't bothered, I told myself; I didn't want special attention. I sat on the Underground as the train rattled north and gazed at my reflection in the opposite window. I walked from the station saving forty pence bus fare. I listened to the hum of the motorway grow louder the closer I got to my flat. I tried to ignore the dog turd on the pavement outside my front door. I slapped off the stairwell light switch left on unnecessarily. I noticed my life sliding back to normal.

And that was where I probably would have left

9

it, had it not been for my brother-in-law Ted. He was round with his wife Rita when I got home. I sighed as I climbed the stairs and heard his voice. All I wanted was to slump in a chair and have Kate make a fuss of me, but as I came into the kitchen he jumped up: 'Where have you been?' He was annoyed he'd missed drinking time.

Kate was emptying the washing machine. She saw my plaster and said, 'What happened to your head?' and she gently touched the wound.

'Come on,' said Ted. He was edging me to the door.

I explained what had happened. Kate was amazed. 'What did you want to do a thing like that for?'

'It was a spontaneous reaction. I don't like people who steal from tourists.'

'I cut my head like that a fortnight ago,' said Rita. 'On a cupboard door—wasn't 'alf painful.' She was sitting there with her cigarettes and lighter stacked on the table in front of her.

'You could have got yourself badly hurt,' said Kate.

'Don't go on at him,' said Ted. 'He was defending the good name of his country. He deserves a drink.'

'Will someone make me a cup of tea?' I was having to raise my voice.

'You don't want tea, mate,' said Ted. 'I'm taking you for last orders.'

'I've still got a scab, look,' said Rita and she lowered her head to show Kate.

Ted marched me down under the motorway to the George. It was packed as usual. The carpet was crunchy with broken glass. Ted found a way

10

through to the bar and grabbed the attention of the barman who still refused to recognize us even though Ted had been dragging me here for five years. Ted drank the top inch of each pint to make sure he didn't spill any, then fought his way back to me, a cigar still in its cellophane wrapper gripped in his teeth. He carefully placed the drinks on the table and was gone again, back to get the other two pints he'd ordered, so we didn't have to go to the bar again when they called time. I would never drink my second, and so Ted would have to say, 'No point in wasting it,' and he'd pour it into his glass. Three pints in twenty minutes and he was a happy man.

He settled in his seat, calmer now he had a semi-circle of glasses around him. A man rushed past us to the door and vomited on the step. Ted lit his cigar and a beam of relaxation spread across his face. 'It's not like you to go attacking muggers.'

I shrugged. 'People like him piss me off.'

He looked at me, blowing smoke just past my ear. 'How much was in the wallet?'

'Five hundred quid!'

'What! Well, she deserves everything she gets.'

'And another three in dollars.'

'You're kidding. So the mugger still gets away with nearly seven hundred quid?'

We both took swigs of beer. Ted shook his head. Nothing made him fall silent more than the thought of someone making a lot of money for no effort. It was what he had done all his life.

'But there's a problem here, Will, isn't there?'

'What problem?'

'The trouble is, see, looking at it from a financial point of view and everything, what's interesting

11

about this whole incident, this robbery that you so bravely semi-thwarted, is the way everyone came off very nicely . . . except you.'

'How's that?'

'Well, there's the mugger—a good night's work as far as mugging goes, I would say. There's Welcome Coach Tours—they did all right too, big picture in the paper, name splashed all over, hundred thousand pounds' worth of free publicity. And there's the American lady—well, you can bet your bottom dollar if she lost a grand she'll claim for two on her insurance. That's the easiest way of all to make money. That leaves little old you, the one who acted out of a sense of moral injustice, the one who put his life in danger, the one player in this drama who, let's face it, could really do with a nice little bonus, and what did you get out of it? You got fuck all, that's what.' He downed the rest of his pint, puffed on his cigar, and gave me his am-I-right-or-am-I-wrong face, the face I can't stand.

I said nothing. I'd never thought of it like that. It occurred to me I didn't even get the chance to collect tips. I had actually lost money on the night.

'You should complain to someone,' said Ted, and I thought: Who?

Ted took Rita home and Kate went to bed. I slumped at last in front of the TV. I had begun the day in this two-bedroomed second-floor flat overlooking the M1 which I shared with my growing family and a growing population of dustmites and this was where I was going to end it again. It was the inevitability of it all that I found so exhausting.

The weather forecast came on, a holiday forecast. A Scottish weatherman informed me what it was like in Italy and Greece. It was raining. Good. I couldn't stand it when they gave you the foreign weather and it was sunny all the time, just rubbing it in for those who weren't going away.

I went to check on the kids: Stephen asleep with a smile on his face; Martin surrounded by his asthma prevention equipment. He needed good air to breathe and I was making him live yards away from the nation's busiest road.

Then I went to bed and watched the headlights move across the ceiling. We lived this close to the motorway and yet there was no way on to the thing for miles.

Martin coughed and Kate stirred. We both listened for a minute. She saw I was awake. 'Are you all right?'

'Yeah.'

'Are you sure?'

'Sure.'

'You don't look all right.'

'I'm all right, really.'

But I was lying there thinking: I'm being left behind here.

CHAPTER TWO

STRATFORD-UPON-AVON AND A VISIT TO ANNE HATHAWAY'S COTTAGE

I was reading a lot of those lifestyle columns at the time: *Fridge File; A Day in the Life of; My Hols.* I'd search for them in the papers and magazines that lay around the waiting room at Welcome. I enjoyed reading the detail of other people's existences, not because they were celebrities—often they weren't, they were charity workers perhaps, or lighthouse keepers—but because they always appeared to be people in control of their lives. They had obstacles, but not insurmountable ones; they had stress, but a healthy amount. They were all doing what they wanted to do, working happily towards their goal. I found that irresistible. I wanted to know if there was a formula.

I imagined myself being interviewed—it was something to do in traffic hold-ups. To begin with I told the truth: how the most exciting moment of my twenty-four hours was at breakfast when I opened the milk bottles and, with all the family watching, checked under the tops for a letter H to see if we'd won a family holiday to Hawaii. I'd tell how I relaxed in the evenings by looking under things for the TV remote control; how the most comforting moment of my day was my regular visit to the bottle bank; how I went to bed and dreamt of dustmites.

But that wouldn't have done, of course, so I began to invent alternative versions of my life, more of what readers expected. I made up details of the holidays I took on a perfect corner of a Greek island (not revealing the name, or everyone would go). I listed the contents of my fantasy fridge: Australian white wine, free-range eggs, mange-touts, Marks & Spencer's stuff. I described my typical day: how I got up at six and checked my e-mail, then went out for a run over the hills above our Cotswold house; how I brought my wife breakfast in bed—a half-grapefruit on a tray with a freshly picked flower—then spent the morning

14

hard at work running my business: a guest house or restaurant, or maybe a shop that specialized in imported handicraft. I always made time in the afternoon to pick up the kids from school, and in the evening we'd sit down to a family meal with my father at the table—he'd be living in the annexe we'd had built for him at the bottom of the garden. I had no time for TV except the news. I went to bed early and read biographies and was asleep the minute the light was out.

They were the details of a parallel existence, the one I expected I'd be living by now, the one I was beginning to think was sliding out of my reach. Everyone assumed I reacted the way I did on the Jack the Ripper tour out of a sense of duty, out of fair play, but the more I thought about it the more I became convinced I had responded to a growing desperation, a need just to make something happen. When, a few days later, I saw the Climbing Rose Tea-rooms and Gift Shop for the first time, I recognized that same sense of frustration surfacing, the feeling that I was running out of time.

It was 23 April, Shakespeare's birthday, and I was driving a coach up the M40 in the rain, bound for Stratford-upon-Avon and the birthday celebrations. 'Battle of Edgehill, 1642...' chirped Monica the tour guide, and fifty-three visitors from around the world looked out of the window expecting to see hostilities raging on the hard shoulder. 'Invention of the steam railway, 1804...' And they turned to look out of the other side where a rainbow curved over the services at the junction with the A43.

Coaches were everywhere that day. A Frames Rickards set the pace in front; a Wallace Arnold filled my mirror; an Evans Evans overtook me with a Japanese-language tour. We were part of a convoy heading for the Heart of England, and by the time we got to Stratford the town was a scrum. I dropped everyone off in the centre and let Monica lead them away with her multi-coloured umbrella held high. They didn't really want to leave their seats; they were happier in the warm. They followed her in a huddle, yawning, clutching their Harrods carrier bags, waterproofs zipped up to their chins. After they'd gone the bus smelt of dry cleaning.

I parked up in the coach park. Other drivers were gathered round a Golden Tours coach, eating sandwiches and drinking from flasks, moaning about the number of continental vehicles that took up all the parking space. They were miseries. I never made any effort with them, but then I never thought I'd be doing this job for longer than six months. I normally went for a swim or studied my French grammar during this free time, or I'd walk around the attractions. It was the idea of spending the day touring round classic England and being paid for it that made me take this job in the first place. Three years later I still got a kick out of the sights.

I decided to go and watch the birthday parade. I needed to go into town anyway. I had something to celebrate myself that day and I needed a gift. The birth of Shakespeare wasn't the only memorable event to take place on 23 April. Another occurred 416 years later in the Blinking Owl night-club in Barnet, North London, when, to the sound of Squeeze's 'Up the Junction', I met Kate.

I remembered this anniversary every year. It

16

always seemed more important to me than our wedding day. Whenever I see that column *The Difference a Day Makes*, where people describe the day that had most impact on their lives, it's that evening in the night-club that comes to mind. I can remember every detail, every cliché: the drink she was holding, the first thing she said to me, the clothes she wore, the song. She remembered nothing, but that didn't bother me. I was the memory in our family, the one who passed down the verbal history. Kate had other skills. Tonight we'd get the kids to bed early and have a bottle of wine. We couldn't afford Paris in the springtime, but I would read her a sonnet and we'd make love in the sitting room. I headed into town riding a wave of optimism. Nothing was going to spoil my day. I was determined.

The streets were lined with spectators as the birthday parade approached. Yellow placards, each bearing the name of a play, had been tied to lampposts and now one had broken free and was being blown down towards the canal. 'There goes Julius Caesar!' called out a tall woman wearing a West-Coast-Tall-Persons-Club-Tour-of-Great-Britain T-shirt.

The parade consisted of a troupe of strolling players and musicians, followed by boy scouts and girl guides and the Band of the Corps of the Royal Engineers. A party of local dignitaries brought up the rear, waving like royalty. The Tall Persons Club tour had hogged the front rank and everyone else strained for a view. 'I can't see the show,' whined a woman in a South African accent behind me, so I let her in and then her friend, and then her friend's husband who had an umbrella. I could see this any

17

year. This might be their only opportunity.

The crowd followed the procession past the Bard's Walk shopping centre. I crossed the road to a greeting card shop where I found something suitable for Kate on the blank-for-your-own-message shelf. I just needed a little gift now, a thought, a Terry's Chocolate Orange would have done the trick. But then I passed Broomfield and Whitton estate agent's, and there it was in the window, the thing I really wanted to buy her.

I was unable to resist estate agents, particularly in towns like Stratford. I'd try to look away and walk past them, and with the first one or two maybe I'd succeed, but then I'd turn a corner and one would sneak up on me, and before I knew what I was doing I'd be leering at the photos in the window like some pervert, wanting to finger the details. The Climbing Rose Tea-rooms and Gift Shop caught my eye immediately and it was enough to make me drool. A rambling, old brick building, a jumble of gables and chimneys and crooked windows, and what was most appealing was the way it was almost surrounded by greenery. Trees framed the building like a hand shading a face. In the photograph it looked empty, but it was advertised as a going business, with accommodation above, and a playground and car parking for customers, all 'in the shadow of Anne Hathaway's Cottage'. There was no price underneath, of course. I should have just walked on, but I couldn't stop myself.

Inside the office was a peaceful and warm haven. A young woman looked up from the telephone and cupped the mouthpiece: 'Be with you in a minute.' She looked as if she'd just come back from a

Spanish holiday. She handed me a card. 'Maybe you could fill in your details.'

I strolled round, hands in pockets. They even had exposed beams in the estate agents here. I wanted a house with exposed beams. I wondered if the Climbing Rose Tea-rooms and Gift Shop had exposed beams. It must have; every house in Stratford has exposed beams.

'Swimming pools are very expensive to maintain,' she said down the phone, and I felt a little thrill. I wondered if the real reason I enjoyed padding about estate agent's was because I was able to make them think I was someone with money, someone who was considering packing up what he was doing in the city and buying a place in the shires. The walls were lined with those sort of properties, grand houses with grounds and stables and guest wings. The truth was I didn't want anything vulgar like that. I just wanted what I had worked for. And I didn't want to start thinking this way either. I didn't want to spoil today. I closed my eyes and tried to relax. I saw dustmites on my eyelids.

She put down the phone and rose from her desk; she was taller than I expected. 'Now, how can I help? I'm Clarissa.' She had no idea I was a coach driver; they never did. I always removed my name-tag.

Just looking at the Climbing Rose Tea-rooms and Gift Shop,' I said.

'Oh, lovely,' and she bent to a filing cabinet. 'A lovely situation in the shadow of Anne Hathaway's Cottage. Perfect location for a business, with a three-bedroomed flat upstairs, and very historic. Apparently it's on land that goes back to the time of the Domesday Book.'

The M40 was on land that went back to the time of the Domesday Book, wasn't it?

She handed me the details. I was thinking what I'd put in the blank-for-your-own-message card to Kate: *Eighteen years since we met and as a little memento of my my love and affection I would like to give you these tea-rooms and gift shop in the shadow of Anne Hathaway's Cottage.*

'Just out of interest, how much is . . . you know, just out of interest?' and I looked away.

'Two hundred and five.'

I nodded positively, but she must have seen my shoulders slump.

'They are willing to sell the leasehold, of course, with a view to selling on the freehold in a few years.'

'How much is the leasehold?'

'Forty thousand.'

That was better. That was cheap, in fact, for somewhere that size, but still about thirty-five thousand pounds beyond me.

'I'm sure they'll listen to offers,' said Clarissa. She edged closer and added, 'Don't tell them I told you, but it's a divorce. It's been on the market for six months. It does need some work.'

I could work.

'Would you like to view?'

Anne Hathaway's Cottage was our next stop. I could call in while they all looked round the house. 'No thanks,' I said. There was no point.

*   *   *

A Morris dancer had had a heart attack outside

Burger King. A number of Welcome passengers had been watching at the time. When I picked them up at the meeting point they were breathless. 'Everyone thought it was part of the dance,' said Carl from Atlanta. 'But I knew.'

'He knew there was something wrong,' said his wife.

'Had one myself in '92,' said Carl.

'In the cocktail lounge of the Spice Island Hotel in Jamaica,' added his wife.

'A good hotel,' said Carl. 'A good holiday.'

The other passengers all wanted details. The Morris dancer had collapsed in a jingle-jangle of bells. His fellow dancers had loosened his many scarves and removed his glasses, and he'd been sped away by ambulance. Carl had offered his tweed jacket purchased in Edinburgh to keep the poor man warm. I wondered if anyone had caught the incident on video.

But this brush with mortality had bonded the bus. There was a camaraderie now as we drove the short distance to Anne Hathaway's Cottage. An Australian man introduced himself to Carl and his wife. 'We're going to France at the weekend,' I heard him say.

'We're going to Scotland,' replied Carl. 'We took a trip to France already.'

'Where'd you stay?'

'Oh, downtown somewhere.'

'Spanish Armada, 1588,' announced Monica the guide, and they all happily stepped down and followed her at heel on a tour of the house and garden.

I parked up again and took out my French grammar book. *Le jardinier a retourné le sol*. The gardener turned over the soil.

What did I want to go and see the Climbing Rose Tea-rooms and Gift Shop for? I'd looked at too many places I couldn't afford.

Le gangster a sorti un revolver. The gangster pulled out a revolver.

Places like the Climbing Rose just put me in a bad mood.

On cue a French coach pulled in next to me, an address in Strasbourg on the side. I watched the driver as he unwrapped a sandwich, then lifted up the bread and stared at the contents. I stepped down, stretched my legs, wandered over to him. *'Bonjour,'* I said through his open window, and he switched on his radio.

I'd just go and have a quick look. You never could tell.

It took a while to find. The estate agent had said it was set back from the road, but she didn't say you had to beat a path through undergrowth to the entrance. I was thinking: This is brilliant, a woodland theme to the place. The vegetation smelt so damp and rich, and there were bluebells right up to the door. But then I realized it wasn't a theme, it was neglect. If I thought about it I must have seen the building before from the road, but I'd never known it was a teashop. It had the gables and eaves of the photograph, but it also had peeling paint and last winter's leaves still littering the pathways. As I approached the door the smell of the woods gave way to that of a chip fryer.

One of the many business schemes I'd had over the years was to open the first café you came to as you emerged from the Channel Tunnel, the first teashop in England. It would be the standard by which all other teashops were judged. It would give visitors their first and last taste of the nation. It would offer a bright welcome and a fond farewell. It would have home baking and a sign outside that said *Families Welcome* and it would mean it. It would be the start of a teashop revolution that would have put places like the Climbing Rose out of business.

As I stepped inside I was reminded of the days of black-and-white television. The gift shop was a little counter that sold faded table-mats with scenes of Stratford, a few key-rings, some pencil and rubber sets, and a few mugs printed with Christian names. The café had the sort of chairs you pile in stacks in church halls. The menu covers appeared to have been chewed.

There were about twenty people in there and they all looked on the point of leaving. Turnover should have been brisk at this time of day, but no one had any food. This was because there was only one person working, a young waitress who was hovering over a table with a face like a dishcloth, a face that said, 'If you want serving you're going to have to put up with me being rude to you.'

Her customers were looking to order. They said, in Italian accents, 'We would like some cottage pie . . .'

'Lunch is finished.'

'Excuse me?'

'We don't do lunches after two o'clock,' and she looked out of the window.

'We would like cottage . . . ?'

'We don't do lunches after two o'clock,' she repeated, slowly, loudly, because that was how you spoke to foreigners. They grew indecisive, so she walked off. I wanted to apologize for her.

I sat and watched a while. There was no danger of being served. The estate agent had said the place needed work, but more than that it needed to breathe. I wanted to peel off the old skin and reveal the true potential beneath.

As the waitress hurried past I said, 'I've come from the estate agent's. Is the owner around?'

'I don't know where she is. Try in the back.' And she waved towards a double door that led off into the kitchen.

I went through and called, but there was no one there. A kettle boiled away, the on-off switch broken, the room filling with steam. The floor was sticky, littered with miniature tubs of jam that had spilt from a box and been crunched underfoot. The cream for the cream teas came out of an aerosol. There were stainless steel teapots everywhere. I decided then that if I ever got to run a teashop I would use only old china teapots. They wouldn't have to be expensive; they wouldn't even have to match. You saw some lovely old ones down the car boot sale. In fact, the idea of them not matching would give an informal charm. It just took a bit of thought; all it needed was the right person in the job.

The waitress came rushing through: 'She's probably having a fag somewhere. Go on up if you want,' and she threw some scones in the microwave to defrost.

I climbed the stairs to the flat and called out again on the landing, but there was no sign of life; even the goldfish tank was empty. I peered into the rooms. They were all built into the roof and had attractive, odd angles, but the woodchip wallpaper

24

was stained and the corners were peeling off the walls. The carpet was embedded with what looked like cat litter.

In the living room was a huge TV and a dented couch that smelt of cigarettes. In one bedroom I saw an unmade bed, and around a waste-paper basket was a ring of rubbish. Then I glanced out of a window, down into the garden, and there was a woman sitting in a burst of sunshine, smoking and reading *Hello!* magazine. She had fat arms and ankles and a blotchy, crimson complexion. Beyond her through the trees you could just see the chimneys of Anne Hathaway's Cottage. I looked around and thought: This place could be wonderful. I could fill that café. I could do something with the gift shop. I could turn that garden into a play area. I could make this flat home. I could turn this place into the best tea-room in the country, but I'm never going to get the chance.

She took a long draw on her cigarette. I saw her cough, and I had the urge to go and squash her like an insect.

*   *   *

The clients filed back on to the coach. 'Some house, eh?' said Carl from Atlanta.

'It is, isn't it?' I replied, although I'd never been inside.

'You live in a thatched place, Will?'

'Yes. Yes I do. Nice old beams, inglenook fireplace, cottage garden. We've even got a hen that lays breakfast eggs.'

He smiled knowingly, then said grandly: 'You

know what I like about this country? You got history. We don't have history.'

It rained most of the way home. Monica said, 'Battle of St Albans, 1455,' and signed off. We cruised down the motorway, everyone sleepy. There was a hold-up just outside Beaconsfield; an accident had blocked two lanes. It hadn't happened long ago. A police Range Rover was parked across the carriageway; an ambulance was in attendance. I could see two cars horribly entangled and a limp arm hanging out of a smashed window.

No one spoke. I wanted to shield the passengers from the horror outside, as I would have done my own children. They had had a good day. They had all enjoyed themselves. They'd been surrounded by medieval buildings and history. That should have been the impression they took home, not this. Something like this could have a huge effect on tips.

As we hit London and the rush-hour the rain became torrential. I looked over to the Australian on the front seat and said, 'Oh to be in England now that April's here, eh?

' "There",' he replied.

'Pardon?'

'Not "here", "there". Browning wrote that poem in exile. "Home Thoughts from Abroad". He was in Rome I think. The line is: "Oh, to be in England Now that April's there."'

I hated it when tourists did that.

*   *   *

There was another dog turd outside my flat when I got home. Vinod from the grocery shop

26

underneath us came out to warn me. 'I would have moved it for you, but it doesn't look good to see a grocer handling dog shit.' He wrung his hands and gestured to his fine display of fruit and vegetables.

We stood looking at it, a big hard turd curved like a signature, happy to be there on my doorstep. I could either ignore it and wait till someone trod in it and smeared it all over the pavement—probably one of my children—or I could clear it up.

'I'll give you a piece of cardboard,' said Vinod.

I tried to scoop it up with the cardboard, but it kept falling off, so I just steered it towards the gutter. A double-decker bus pulled up. A line of faces looked blankly down from the top deck, watching a thirty-seven-year-old man roll a dog turd across the pavement. My life isn't really like this, I wanted to explain. I had Further Education; I have a business studies diploma upstairs. I once had a thriving sandwich shop. This is just a bad patch I'm going through.

My plan had been to trot up the stairs, put my arm round Kate and say, 'Happy Shakespeare's birthday!' and enjoy her surprise. But two things distracted me as I came in. The first was an envelope on the doormat that said *Crisis in Sudan*. The second was a complete stranger in the living room, a man watching *Peter Pan* on the video with Kate and the kids.

As soon as I saw him I knew he was a vacuum-cleaner salesman. He had shiny trousers and a dusting of dandruff on his shoulders. He jumped up: 'Good evening. You must be Mr Green. Toby Jones, from Turbo Vac.' He grabbed my hand but then shook it limply. 'You phoned,' he said when I looked at him dimly. 'I've just been demonstrating the Turbo Vac to your good wife.'

Stephen pulled himself away from *Peter Pan* and slammed the door shut behind me.

'I want you to have a look at this,' said Toby Jones, and he switched on his demonstration model and started to vacuum around the children. This didn't bother them, but then a juggernaut rolling off the motorway and coming through the window wouldn't have bothered them if a video was on. They just turned up the volume.

Toby Jones spoke above it all: 'Being incredibly lightweight the Turbo Vac is easier to push, pull and lift. The air-glide system does the work for you. Watch.' And he glided round the room in such style it was difficult not to sit down and watch him like you would the European figure-skating championships.

'Your wife tells me one of your children suffers from asthma. Dust can trigger off an attack with ease. Are you familiar with dustmites, Mr Green?'

'Yes, I am.'

At least I thought I was familiar with dustmites, but compared to Toby Jones I was a novice. He spoke sincerely: 'You see, it's not the dustmites that cause allergic reaction, it's their excrement.'

On the TV Peter Pan took Wendy by the hand and sailed away over Big Ben to a better place. Kate sighed at me like: Who is this man?

'I'll show you something in the bedroom,' said Toby Jones as if he knew some awful secret, and he was off vacuuming down the corridor.

'He won't leave,' said Kate. 'And the car won't start either.'

My shoulders slumped again.

'Don't look at me. It just won't start.'

28

I followed Toby Jones into the bedroom. Stephen slammed the living-room door behind me. Toby Jones whipped back the bed covers and started to vacuum the mattress. 'Actually it's our anniversary,' I said and gave a laugh.

'Just have a look at that.' He had unscrewed the dust compartment of the Turbo Vac and now offered me the result of his one sweep across the mattress, a greasy little pile of something. 'Look what came off the bed! That's what you sleep on every night.'

'What is it?'

'Dead skin.' He was gloating.

'Whose dead skin?'

'Yours. As you turn over in bed you shed dead skin; you can't help it. And you lose a pint and half of liquid each night. Perfect breeding ground for *Dermatophogoides pteronyssinus*.'

'For what?'

'That's Latin for dustmite. Literally translated it means: skin-eating spider. Your bed may appear clean on the surface but under a microscope it would look like downtown Tokyo.' He passed me the Turbo Vac. 'Have a test drive.'

I went into the kids' room and ran the Turbo Vac over Martin's bed. It produced the same mound of dead skin and dustmite shit.

'No need to be embarrassed, Mr Green. There's nothing you could have done. There's no vacuum cleaner on the market that could have shifted that except for the Turbo Vac. Tests have proved it.'

'How much is it?' I sort of asked.

'Tell me: are you satisfied with the vacuum cleaner you use at the moment?'

'No.'

29

'Why not?'

'It's broken. But how much is this?'

'Feel this handle. It's orthopaedically designed.'

'I want to know how much it is.'

'How much do you think it is?'

'I don't know.'

'It's seven hundred pounds.'

For the second time that day I tried not to register shock at the cost of something, but this time I failed: 'Seven hundred fucking quid!'

Toby Jones was used to that sort of response. 'When you buy a vacuum cleaner the cost shouldn't be your main priority. There are other ways to save money apart from paying less.'

'Seven hundred quid for a Hoover!'

'It'll last you fifteen to twenty-five years. That's thirty-five pounds a year for a completely dust-free house. And it's not a Hoover. It's a Turbo Vac.'

'Listen, I've got to fix the car.' I grabbed the hairdryer and the extension cable and started off down the stairs.

'Good,' said Toby Jones. 'The Turbo Vac is really impressive in the car.'

He followed me outside, and while I tried to breathe some life into the tired plugs with the hairdryer, he cleaned the inside of the vehicle, a job that hadn't been done since we bought it. 'You wouldn't believe what I'm getting up here,' he called gleefully. 'Look, a fifty-pence piece,' and I banged my head on the bonnet as I went to grab it off him. 'See, the Turbo Vac is saving you money already.'

The car wouldn't start. I'd used all sorts of tricks over the years, but it had gradually built up an immunity to them all. It went through a period of

30

starting only when the windscreen wipers were on. Then and only when someone was sitting in the passenger seat. The hairdryer method had worked for a few months, but the last couple of attempts had failed. I know very little about cars.

'So, are you going to treat yourself?' said Toby Jones as I closed the bonnet.

'I'll think about it,' I said and headed inside.

'This machine will change your life!' he yelled above the traffic.

*   *   *

Kate made a meal while I put the kids to bed. '"The story of Robin Hood",' I read to Stephen. '"First published by Kingfisher 1994. ISBN 1 85697 2542".' Stephen liked to have all of the book read to him. There was no skipping the publisher's address in Australia or the ISBN number. He listened intensely, occasionally interrupting with questions: 'If you drink poison and don't brush your teeth, do you die?'

'Yes.'

'Oh.'

Stephen was a spirited child who was interested in death and didn't like doors to be open.

'"Text copyright, Robert Leeson. All rights reserved. Printed and bound in Italy."' It usually took so long to read him the imprint page of a book he was asleep by the time we got to the story itself. I was convinced Stephen was a six-year-old genius.

Martin was three years older and introspective by comparison. He showed me the picture he had drawn at school, another in his alien series: a

31

drawing of a whole planet with just one person on it. I'd shown all his pictures to the asthma counsellor when she asked to see us. 'He's a genius,' I had enthused.

She studied them carefully and said, 'You have to understand, asthma can isolate a child.'

I switched their light off and joined Kate in the kitchen where she was grating cheese into a saucepan of macaroni. She looked exhausted. 'Are you all right?' I said. The washing machine kicked into spin and the room began to vibrate.

'Yeah,' she sighed. 'I'm all right.'

I didn't want to ask her what the matter was. I didn't want to start talking about work or something. I wanted to get into the wine and the chocolate orange and enjoy the evening.

I told her the cost of the Turbo Vac and she shrieked: 'Seven hundred pounds for a Hoover! You could provide water-purification units for fourteen Mozambique villages with that.'

'I know.'

'You could give cataract operations to eighty people in Ethiopia.'

'I know.' I was thinking: We could buy a new car.

She took the food into the living room. I sneaked the wine out of the fridge and followed her, and when she was sitting down on the couch I came up behind her and pressed the cold bottle against her face.

'What's this?'

'Don't tell me you've forgotten.'

'What?'

'It's Shakespeare's birthday!'

Now she smiled and made an effort. 'Oh dear,' she said, and sat back and ran her hand through

32

her hair, then pulled me down and kissed my head. 'Happy birthday, Mr Shakespeare.'

I gave her the card. It was still blank for my own message. 'You always do that,' she giggled.

We ate the macaroni on odd plates and drank the wine in odd glasses, sitting on our couch that was made for romance inasmuch as it sank towards one end so steeply that when two people sat on it they always ended up on top of each other.

'This time eighteen years ago we were just getting ready to go out to the Blinking Owl,' I said. 'We never even knew each other existed.' These anniversaries had a pattern. It was the same conversation every year. 'I was putting on my dark blue shirt and those white trousers that used to show up in the ultraviolet lights.'

'What was I wearing?'

'Black jeans and a low-cut brown T-shirt with short sleeves that made your arms look sexy. I saw you as soon as you walked in the room.'

'What song was playing?'

'"Up the Junction" by Squeeze. You drank a vodka and bitter lemon without any ice because you didn't like it diluted. And your friend Yvonne drank Pernod because she didn't like the taste and so she wouldn't drink it so fast.'

She looked away and tried to remember. She was paler and had lost weight since those days. Her eyes were dimmer, but she looked beautiful when her cheekbones rose in a smile.

I took her plate and kissed her. Her hair still smelt of the archives where she worked. I pulled out my copy of *The Sonnets* from my back pocket, and I was about to read the one I read to her every year, comparing her to a summer's day, when she

33

said something that wasn't in the anniversary script, something that took me by surprise because she'd never said anything like it before. She settled back and said, 'Eighteen years ago . . . Is this where you imagined you'd be in eighteen years' time?'

And suddenly I was splashing about in a pool of disappointment. For a few minutes I'd been able to forget the motorway outside the window and the dog who crapped on the doorstep. I'd been able to enjoy this once-a-year moment, but she'd gone and unplugged it.

'What do you mean?' I didn't want to answer her.

'You know, did you think this was how your life would pan out?'

Of course this wasn't how I thought my life would pan out. I stalled: 'Is this how you thought your life would pan out? Are you happy where you are?'

And she shrugged and said, 'Yes.'

'You're telling me you don't want anything to change?'

'I'd like the men in the house to put the toilet seat down after they use it.'

I pulled a face. She could see I was being serious. 'Oh, come on,' she laughed. 'All right, I used to want things, but I'm not bothered now. I mean, I had plans, but there was never time to do anything about them. I left all that to you . . .'

That was the killer blow. The raising of our standard of living was my department, and this was how far I had got us. I fell silent. She amazed me sometimes, the way she was so unconcerned with what I was so concerned about.

'Go on, then, read me a sonnet,' she said in her

jolly voice. But I had to turn away. I would have choked if I'd read a sonnet. I glanced at the TV, asleep with the standby light on. I had the sudden urge to watch a Disney film, *101 Dalmatians* would have done the trick.

To the rescue came the telephone. 'Don't answer it,' she said.

'It might be Dad.'

It wasn't my dad. It was her co-ordinator from Amnesty International. By the time he'd finished with her I'd drunk all the wine and was yawning.

She crept back to me: 'It's that time of the month, you know.'

By which she meant it was her most fertile time, that window when everything was in place, eggs cast adrift, uterine walls pumped up and waiting, her body temperature raised.

We made love on the couch. She looked deeply into me, urging me to make this one count. I couldn't get *101 Dalmatians* out of my mind. I'd been trying to work out recently if making love when you were attempting to get pregnant was better or worse than when you weren't. That night, with my head full of spotted dogs, I decided it was worse. I thought: How come, with all those puppies everywhere, there wasn't one turd in the whole film?

Afterwards Kate went to the bathroom and I took the empty bottle of Soave round to the bottle bank. The night was starless and smelt of wet cardboard. A lamp high above the motorway fizzed. At the bottle bank I met the man with the ponytail who lived on Hamilton Road. He stood holding an empty blue bottle of Virgin vodka. He didn't look at me, he just said: 'If that Richard

Branson is so clever, what hole do you put his blue bottles in?'

I lobbed my empty Soave into the green. The bank was almost empty and it made a pleasing hollow thunk and then a smash. 'I don't know. Shove it in brown.'

'It's not brown.'

'Shove it in green then.'

'It's not green either, is it?' He looked worried.

'You've got to make a decision, or you'll be here all night.'

'Then there's Optrex bottles,' he sighed, 'and Milk of Magnesia.'

I went home to bed, and lay listening to Martin wheeze across the corridor. I tried to imagine him playing in that garden behind the Climbing Rose, but the fat woman with the blotchy arms kept blocking my view.

Kate turned over. 'Are you all right?'

'Yeah, I'm all right.'

'You don't look all right.'

'I'm all right . . . I was just thinking of this place I saw today for sale. A tea-room and gift shop. It would be perfect for us. We could really make a go of it.' And I closed my eyes and saw the gift shop with jewellery from Mexico. In the teashop area I saw roses everywhere; a fresh one on each table. I saw Kate baking fruit cakes. I saw myself being charming to families from Japan. I saw us making a success of it. That was where, eighteen years ago, I thought I'd be now—making a success of it.

'Wouldn't you love to move out?' I said.

She didn't reply. I moved closer to her. 'Wouldn't you?'

'What?' She was almost asleep.

36

'Love to move out?'

A siren wailed. A dog howled. I wondered what a crisis in Sudan looked like.

'I bought a chocolate orange,' I said. 'I forgot.' But she was gone.

*　　　*　　　*

The next morning when I got to work Graham handed me a letter. *To Will the Coach-driver* was written on the front. 'Who's it from?' I asked.

'I don't know,' he said. 'A bike brought it.'

Inside was a letter written on Piccadilly Palace Hotel paper:

> *Dear Will,*
> *I'm afraid I was not able to thank you adequately for the service you did me the other night. Please visit me at my hotel. This evening at 6.30 would be good. I want to reward you more appropriately.*
> *Best wishes,*
> *Barbie Scott, Room 203*

I folded it up and put it neatly back in the envelope, then took the tour to Oxford and Blenheim Palace. But every so often, throughout the day, I opened the letter and reread it, running my fingers over the embossed letterhead, examining the signature, interpreting the way she'd used Barbie instead of Barbara, the way she'd written 'best wishes' instead of 'yours sincerely'. And how was, she going to reward me appropriately? She was a rich woman. She carried large amounts of cash around. She was alone, staying in a five-star hotel. And I had saved her holiday, she'd told me as much. 'How much would you say is just reward?' she'd ask as she looked at me across a glass-topped table with her pen poised over her cheque book.

'Guess where I'm going,' I said to Roy when I got back to the depot.

When I told him he made a face and asked, 'What kind of reward?'

'I don't know. An appropriate one.'

'I should be careful. Accept money and nothing else.'

'What?'

'You never know.'

I caught the tube down to Piccadilly and read the results of *Which?* magazine's tests on vacuum cleaners. The Electrolux Power System 1720 is the first vacuum cleaner with two ways to collect dust. Conventional bag, or reusable canister. I found it hard to concentrate. What had Roy meant? Be careful. What did I have to be careful of? This was the break I'd been waiting for. This was the luck I had made for myself. What could Barbara Scott possibly do to me? The thought that she might want to reward me with anything other than money was ridiculous. It was also hideous—all that jewellery, that wig, the way her painted toenails squirted out of her sandals. Miele is the most reliable make of cylinder vacuum cleaner. AEG is the most troublesome.

*   *   *

The lobby of the Palace Hotel buzzed with tourists dressed in blazers and bright tracksuits, doing

38

business in the reception and souvenir shop. They bought model taxis and buses, policemen's helmets and Big Ben head scarves. They booked theatre trips and hair appointments, the sort of activities that never entered my life.

I went to the Gents, washed my hands and straightened my tie. The place was a disgrace. Cigarette butts clogged the urinals, chewing gum was stuck to the basin and it smelt like a drain. I ripped some toilet paper off to blow my nose and saw skid marks on the wall. Tourists couldn't have done this, surely.

At reception I asked for Mrs Barbara Scott, and when the receptionist looked me over I told her, 'She's expecting me.'

She rang the room and announced me, then said, 'Take the lift to the fifth floor. She'll meet you outside.'

I shared the lift with a French family. There were adverts for expensive watches and perfumes on the panels. The woman said something in French which I tried to understand but couldn't, although she did mention Princess Diana three times.

My armpits had become sticky. What would I do if Barbara Scott tried to kiss me? I looked at the ceiling; the very idea made me squirm. The lift stopped. The doors opened and there she was, wearing a long dress with a shawl and a tiara in her hair, her huge sunglasses still on.

I stepped out and she took me by the hands like an old friend and said, 'Am I glad to see you!' I stiffened, hoping she wasn't going to hug me. I was conscious of the French family watching me as the lift doors slid to.

She led me down the corridor. 'Going out?' I asked.

'Why do you say that?'

'You're dressed, you know ...'

'Oh this,' and she flicked the flimsy shawl. 'Do you like it?'

'Yes. Well ... it's ... all right.'

'I thought I might change into something else. I've booked a theatre trip but I'm not sure I want to go.'

'What are you going to see?'

'Oh ... what's it called ...? A play, that's it.'

Her door was ajar. She pushed it open and led me into a vast, bright suite with long curtains at big windows. Through a door I could see the corner of a big white bed and beyond that a gleaming white bathroom. For all the time I spent with tourists I rarely went near hotel rooms, and whenever I did I was always impressed by their luxury. They made me feel self-conscious; I didn't know where to put my hands. I folded my arms and stood there, trying not to look too closely at anything, but her belongings were everywhere: underwear strewn over chairs; make-up peeking out of the bathroom; I could see bottles of pills by the bed. She went to the window and said, 'London is such a beautiful city. You must love living here.'

I didn't reply. She turned and grinned and showed her gold teeth. Then she took both my hands again. 'I expect you're wondering why I asked you here.'

'Well, I thought I'd just come along, you know,' and I whipped my hands back.

'I said I wanted to reward you and I meant it. I've spent thousands of dollars on this vacation and you rescued it for me. If I'd lost my video camera, do you know what I would have had to do?'

'What?'

'I'd have had to come again. Next year. Imagine that? Do the whole thing over. I don't know if I could have managed that. Being a tourist is pretty boring you know, Will. Why don't you sit down?'

I sat down at the writing table, as far from the bedroom door as possible. She was looking at me, not saying anything. I couldn't stand the silence. 'It's just that I don't like people stealing from tourists. It's unfair, you know. People come here for a holiday. They've earned their money. I want them to get a good impression—'

'Listen to me,' she interrupted. 'I want to do something for you that you will never forget.'

'Right. Good.' I uncrossed my arms, trying to appear businesslike. My leg started to shake. I had a feeling illegal substances were going to be involved here. I noticed that every light in the room was on. Bedside lamps, wall lamps, bathroom lights. I wondered what the Palace Hotel paid for electricity a quarter.

She sat down at the table with me. 'Whatever it is that is important to you I am going to give you.'

'What are you going to give to me?'

'Everything. From now on everything is possible for you. You are a good man, Will, and you deserve it.'

I thought: What the fuck are you talking about, you silly bitch? Just give me the cheque and let me get out of here.

'I've travelled a lot, Will. South America. Australia and the South Pacific. I've got lots of money!'

41

'Yes,' I mumbled.

'But what I'm going to give you, money can't buy.'

Oh no.

'I'm going to invigorate you, allow you to reinvent yourself.'

'Thank you.'

'I want you to remember this day for ever. So concentrate, Will. From now on your life will be split into two halves—the half before this moment and the half after. What I'm going to give you will redefine you.'

'What exactly?'

And she opened a suitcase by the side of the desk to reveal a pile of books. She took one out and closed the lid. The book had a crucifix on the front cover. It was a bible. I really thought I was going to burst into tears.

Now she was on her feet, so I jumped to mine. 'You're a good man, Will. You deserve to know about God. I don't let everyone I meet on my travels know about him. I don't want you thinking I'm one of those evangelists who goes round telling everyone, "You can be saved; God loves you." Because I don't think he does love everyone.'

She had her arms outstretched. She was spitting as she spoke; a blob landed on my shirt.

'I don't think he loves that guy who tried to steal my camera the other night. Why should he? I don't think he loves Saddam, or the President. And that's good, because I don't want those people up there when I get to heaven. I want people like you. I want to meet you in the afterlife, Will.' And she thrust the book at me with such force I stumbled backwards.

42

'Right. Well, thanks for the book. I've actually got to . . .'

'I want you to come with me to the play,' she insisted.

'I can't.'

'I've got good seats.'

I opened the door and stepped out into the corridor. 'Thanks for the advice about God. I'll read this . . . on the train home.' I hurried away; she hurried after me.

'But I want to show you how to read it, Will.'

'Enjoy the rest of your holiday.'

'You can't do it without my help.'

We got to the lift. I could hear it coming. I pressed the button and kept it pressed.

'We need to spend time together.'

'You should try to get to the West Country, it's very nice down there. It's my favourite part. Ah, here's the lift.'

The lift doors opened and I stepped in among a family of smiling Scandinavians. Barbara Scott wouldn't let go of me.

'Trust in God, Will. God can help you, you must believe that.'

I tugged my arm away from her. The doors closed. We descended in silence for three floors, then the Scandinavian man coughed and asked me if I could direct him to the London Palladium.

*   *   *

I walked most of the way home. By Cricklewood I was over the embarrassment of what had happened, but then I started to get angry. I put my hand out to stop a bus and it went straight past. I

43

yelled at it. I carried the bible as far as Brent Cross, then dumped it in a bin.

I told Kate I'd been working late. She said, 'You could have phoned.' I didn't want to tell her what had happened. I felt naïve.

I switched all the lights off and sat in the grey living room. Grotesque shadows of long vehicles moved across the bare walls. I felt shipwrecked in this flat. I couldn't understand how we had managed to get stranded here. It was only ever meant to be a starter home; like the job at Welcome, it was a temporary measure. I never meant to raise a family here—I still didn't. When are you going to decorate? Kate would ask. When are you going to put up some shelves or something? And I'd say there was no point, we weren't staying here much longer. But I'd been saying that for five years now, and there was no sign of rescue.

In the bedroom Kate was asleep with *Middlemarch* on her chin, a picture from the TV series on the front cover. She'd been reading it for six months and was only a third of the way through. I picked it off her sleep-creased face and kissed her lightly. She started to snore. I needed to take her on a holiday. A bit of sun, a laugh in a restaurant on a warm Mediterranean evening and her eyes would turn blue again. It was up to me. Her life had become a routine.

I checked the kids. The traffic noise was like a lullaby to them. It would be the sound of their childhood, like some people have the sea. Watching them sleep I knew I couldn't rely on good luck any more. 'Trust in God,' Barbara Scott had yelled after me. 'God will help you!' She didn't know how

44

wrong she was. Only I could help myself, and that night as I slid into bed, and the dustmites surfaced for another night's munching on my dead skin, I made myself a promise. When Shakespeare's birthday next came around I would not be in this flat. I would not be in this bed. I would not be listening to the sound of the M1. I would be somewhere else. We all would.

The next morning I had a phone call from Clarissa at Broomfield and Whitton in Stratford. She wondered if I had reconsidered the Climbing Rose Tea-rooms, whether I could be persuaded to view and see the true potential. When I told her I had already viewed and already seen the true potential she seemed put out.

'What did you think?' she asked.

'I liked it very much.'

'Oh,' and she gave me her yes-swimming-pools-are-expensive-to-maintain purr. 'Well. Maybe you'd like to put in an offer?'

And before I could stop myself I'd said, 'Yes, I would like to.'

'Oh good.'

'I would like to put in an offer.'

'Good.'

'For the leasehold. With a view to buying the freehold in the not-too-distant future.'

'Good.'

She was waiting for me to give a figure, but I said, 'I just need to arrange the finance. I'll be in touch.'

CHAPTER THREE

A CELEBRITY TOUR

'I have this dream.'

'I've heard your dream.'

'No no, this is a different dream.'

I was having a meeting with Paul, my BBM, my Business Banking Manager. I was trying to appear inspired, but not finding it easy. That morning I had read in the paper that a girl from Redhill had found a thirty-thousand-pound jackpot voucher in her crisp packet as she walked to school. That sort of news could ruin the whole day of a man in my position.

Paul fingered my business plan as if he might catch something from it. I leant forward and showed him the palms of my hands. I wanted to assure him there was nothing up my sleeve, that this was as honest a proposal as he was likely to get. 'It's in the shadow of Anne Hathaway's Cottage,' I enthused. 'A wonderful location, a little gold mine, Paul. But it's run by people who have had enough. They've let it go. Between you and me, it's a divorce. But we could make it work—my wife and I. There's a flat on top and everything, so we could live there for a while. It's on the main tourist route, all the coaches stop there. They're willing to sell the leasehold to start off . . .'

I was talking too quickly, trying to overpower him with my conviction. I wanted to tell him about the exciting menu I had in mind, about the range of scented candles I planned to sell in the gift shop. I wanted to win him over with the idea of the nature-trail tea-garden I would create. I wanted him to respond with a: What! The current owner uses instant coffee instead of fresh? Outrageous! Here's the money; go and turn the place around.

But instead he tried to slide the business plan back across the desk to me. He looked at me with heavy eyes: 'You see, Mr Green, I've got to be realistic about this.'

The problem with Paul was he was about ten years younger than me. It was like asking your little brother to lend you money. I said, 'I know you have to be realistic, Paul, so do I.'

'I mean, you've talked about this sort of thing before, haven't you?' He glanced at his notes. 'This time last year. You had another . . . dream.'

'Did I?'

'Sexy Sausages.'

'Ah, Sexy Sausages.'

Well, that was all his fault, or the bank's anyway. They kept sending me statements, and across the top they'd splash: *Thinking of buying a boat?* Or, *Thinking of buying a holiday home?* Or, *Starting your own business? Come and speak to one of our advisors about a loan.* So I had, and I'd seen Paul, and told him I wanted to start a restaurant that sold sausages and nothing else. Not just any old sausages, of course, sausages from around the world: wild boar and Stilton sausages, venison and apricot sausages, designer sausages. It was a good idea and Paul had listened enthusiastically until he looked at my accounts and realized I was only twenty-two pounds and forty pence in credit.

'We missed out on a golden opportunity with Sexy Sausages, Paul. A very similar sort of place

47

started up in town. Doing a bomb.'

He swivelled in his chair. 'But the problem now is the same as it was then, Mr Green. You have to be prepared to put in capital of your own. We'd also be unlikely to lend you money without security.'

I looked him in the eyes. He looked at his shoes. I thought: Don't talk to me about security, sonny, you have no idea. People like me have come through the bad times. We're survivors. We deserve more respect.

'Paul. I know your hands are tied. I know you're doing your best. But you know and I know that I am just the sort of person you should be lending money to. Not only do I have a sound idea, I also have a huge will to succeed.'

'You also have no money.'

'I've got a property.'

'Worth what?'

'Sixty thousand.'

'How much equity?'

'A bit.'

'How much?'

'Three thousand. But it's rising, everyone knows that.'

'I have to be realistic, Mr Green.'

I wished he wouldn't call me Mr Green. I called him Paul. I bet he called the people he was going to lend money to by their Christian names. 'And I'll tell you something else, Paul. Tourism is the boom industry. It earns more than North Sea oil. Everyone is looking to it as the big millennium earner.'

He didn't even look up from his files. 'I'm sorry, Mr Green. I don't really see how the bank can help you at this stage.'

'I'll tell you how you can help me. You know those actors and writers who are always being interviewed when their blockbusters come out, and they always talk about how they struggled for years with no money but, fortunately, they had a bank manager who liked to sponsor the arts . . . well, I want you to be one of those, but one who's into tea-rooms and gift shops.'

He blushed. I'd embarrassed him—a moral victory. I got up to go and a coin slipped through the hole in my trouser pocket and fell on to the beige carpet. We both looked down at it: a ten-pence piece. The hole in my pocket was getting bigger. I said, 'While I'm here, any chance of a seven-hundred-pound overdraft?'

'What?'

'I need to buy a new vacuum cleaner.'

'Seven hundred pounds for a vacuum cleaner!'

'A special one. My kid's got asthma, you see, and this deals with dustmites like you wouldn't believe. You think your carpet's clean, but if you ran this vacuum cleaner over here you'd be amazed at the results. You'd want one yourself. Did you know how much dustmite excrement you inhale every day? Have a guess.'

'I can't help you, Mr Green.'

'Lend me three hundred and fifty quid, then. I'm prepared to put the rest in myself.'

'Mr Green . . .'

I bent down and picked up my ten-pence bit. I had a horrible feeling that the schoolgirl from Redhill who had found thirty thousand pounds in her crisp packet was, at that moment, putting together a business plan to buy the Climbing Rose.

49

I had to move quickly.

Paul shook my hand and said, 'I think what you need to do, Mr Green... is generate more income.'

*   *   *

I'd never bought a lottery ticket before. I always thought the lottery was the easy way out. It was what you resorted to when you couldn't achieve what you wanted through ingenuity. I had planned to save the lottery for the day when I really needed it. That day had come.

I called in at the newsagent opposite the bank. I'd try it once and if it didn't work—if I didn't win the five million first time—then never again.

Pick any six numbers, the instructions on the back of the ticket read. But it wasn't a case of picking just any six numbers. It was a case of picking the right six numbers. If I was only going to do this once I wanted to use a more scientific method. And there it was, on a shelf next to True Romance, a book entitled: *How to Win the Lottery.*

And it was just as I thought. Only a loser chose his numbers by combining how many children he had with his age and his house number. The formula to winning lottery millions lay locked away in your dreams, or so the Chinese mystic who had written this book claimed. The secret was being able to interpret them. The book cost three quid, but what an investment if you won twelve million! *Guaranteed*, it promised on the front. I bought a copy. I also bought one of those packets of crisps with the thirty-thousand-pound vouchers inside.

I read the book on the bus home. People looked

50

at me and smirked so I folded the cover under. The numbers to pick depended on which animal you dreamt of on the nights leading up to the draw. If you dreamt of a cat you chose one specific sequence of numbers. If you dreamt of a goat another sequence applied. There was one for every animal. The reasoning behind this wasn't explained, but who needed a reason if it worked? The only problem was I couldn't remember dreaming of any animals recently except dustmites, and they were about the only creature on earth that didn't feature on the list.

'Tell me what you dreamt of last night,' I asked Kate when I got home. She was hanging laundry over the radiators. Every room in the house was limp with damp washing. A tumble-dryer would have changed our lives, but there was simply nowhere to put one except to use it as a TV table. At least damp helped keep the dust down.

'I dreamt I was in a cell with a man with a gun standing over me, and he picked me up roughly and hauled me off to a firing squad.'

She'd been out to an Amnesty meeting the night before.

'No animals anywhere, then? No rats in the cell or anything?'

'No. Why?'

'Just wondered.'

How did you get to dream of animals? I scanned the TV listings for wildlife programmes that might inspire me. There was one about ants on at six o'clock. Ants were on the list. I'd get the kids to watch it with me. It would be something educational for them to watch.

'We're watching *Batman*,' said Martin when I

went to change channels.

'No we're not,' I said firmly. 'Where's the remote? Stephen?'

'On top of the fridge,' replied Stephen. For all his obsessive compulsive behaviour, Stephen did have one unusual and amazing skill: he knew instinctively where any lost object was. There was the remote on top of the fridge.

I switched to Channel Four and ants littered the screen. They all looked so determined, so focused.

'Dad?'

'What?'

'Is it still today?' Stephen was bored already.

Just watch the programme, will you!' I snapped at him.

He sulked. I hated myself when I was impatient with the kids. I became unreasonably apologetic. 'Yes, Stephen, it is still today. Let's watch the ants.'

Millions of them marched across the jungle floor, holding up chunks of leaves. Every one of them had a goal and a means of achieving it.

Martin said, 'Have you ever been on Concorde, Dad?'

'No.'

'Neither have I.'

'Didn't think you had.'

The Cuna Indians of the Panamanian rain forest would use the jaws of a soldier ant as a stitch if they cut themselves. A Cuna Indian was shown hiking through the jungle. His life looked blissful.

'If it's still today what day is it?' said Stephen

I smiled lovingly at him. How wonderful not to know or even care what day it was. 'It begins with a F,' I told him.

'Fursday,' he said.

'Let's watch the ants, eh?'

'My tooth has come out,' said Martin, and he opened his mouth to reveal a bleeding gum. He held a bloody tooth in his hand.

'I want a go,' demanded Stephen, grabbing Martin's hand. Martin held the tooth in the air so he couldn't reach it.

'Will you sit still and watch the ants?' I snapped at them again.

'It's my go with the tooth,' yelled Stephen.

'It's my tooth,' screamed Martin, running round the couch.

'Shut up!'

'He's got to share.'

'Give me the damned tooth!'

We all chased Martin round the room after his tooth. I shouted, 'Sit down! Just shut up and sit down.'

They flinched, suddenly frightened of me, and they stopped instantly. Stephen started to cry. 'It's my turn with the tooth,' he sobbed.

I held out my hand. 'Give me the tooth. Now!'

Martin gave me his tooth. I opened the window and traffic noise burst in. I threw the tooth out over the motorway.

Kate came in. 'What's happening?'

'He threw my tooth out of the window!' cried Martin, and buried his head in her.

'I thought you were watching ants.'

'Forget the ants! Watch bloody *Batman*! Jesus!'

I stamped down the stairs and all the way to the swimming pool. A cool, cool swim. My body was a sharp edge slicing through the water. I turned and kicked and stretched, and stayed under until my lungs hurt, then surfaced feeling calm again. I loved my children. I loathed myself when I shouted at them. I did fifty laps, then afterwards, in the shower, I stood next to a man whose stomach had swallowed his genitals. I looked down at my leanness and my well-shaped feet, and I felt better about myself.

*   *   *

Generate more income. Well, that couldn't be so difficult. It was Sunday, the day I took my dad to the car-boot sale, and I did my usual trawl of the flat. This time, though, there would be no room for sentimentality. This time I was going for the clearance sale.

Kate was on the phone talking to a friend about fertility. That would take her out of action for an hour. The kids were occupied with a three-hundred-piece jigsaw of Waterloo Station. They were both on the floor under the table hunting for the piece with Platform 8 on it. This was a good time to raid the house.

I started in the cupboard no one dared open because of the deluge that followed. I pulled the door open and stood back, and out fell an electric fan, a car rust prevention kit still in its Halfords box, some curling tongs and a fondue set. Perfect. I slammed the door shut again.

The fondue set was a wedding present and had never been used. Best not ask Kate if she wanted to keep it; she'd just say yes. The same went for boxes of stuff in the kids' room: toys, books, stuffed animals that collected dust and should have been thrown out anyway; clothes hardly worn but grown out of. 'Keep them for the new baby,' Kate would joke, except she wasn't joking.

In the kitchen I found a set of coasters featuring birds of Africa; a cookery book entitled *Cooking with Kiwi Fruit*, which contained a hundred standard recipes all with a slice of kiwi on the side of the plate. In the living room I found a CD of yodelling songs which we'd got free and was useless because we had never owned a CD player; a set of liqueur glasses marked *A Gift From the Channel Islands*; and a pack of playing cards with a picture of a matador on the back. This last item was the only one that had any emotional value for me, and it was a painful emotion at that. The cards were a souvenir from the last proper holiday we'd had, to Spain, the summer the sandwich bar went bust. Just looking at the packet made me feel sad. We shouldn't have gone; we couldn't afford it; it just added to our woes. I knew the business was going under. I was a misery the whole time, and then Martin had his first asthma attack in Fuengirola and we all ended up in Casualty. We never talked about the trip now.

I stuffed everything into a box and headed for the door. 'Where are my car keys?'

'By the biscuit tin,' called Stephen.

Brilliant. His was a talent that kept me awake at night as I desperately tried to think of ways to harness it. If he could find murder weapons or sunken Spanish galleons we'd be in demand. We could take him to the Wash and say, 'Stephen. Concentrate. Where are the crown jewels King John so carelessly lost with his baggage train? Away you go.'

For now we had to make do with mislaid remote controls and car keys, but he was still young.

55

My dad lived in the lost suburb of London Colney, where I grew up in the days before orbital motorways, when the city was some distant land you rarely went to.

'Where the hell is London Colney?' was the only remark people made when you said you came from there. 'North,' you replied, and it sounded like somewhere dark and frozen, rather than a nicely ignored piece of country with woods and fields and streams, and a mental hospital every few miles. My dad lived there in the council house that had been the family home for thirty years. 'See us out, this will,' he said proudly, a phrase he began to use for all sorts of things when he retired. My mother proved him half right when she died five years later.

Our outing each Sunday to the car-boot sale on a nearby playing field had become my regular visit. He expected it of me and I'd grown to enjoy it. His routines were slowly becoming my routines. To begin with I had looked around the field of stalls littered with junk and thought, What am I doing here? But now I knew: I was spending time with my old dad.

I let myself into the house. 'It's me.'

'I'm in here,' he called from the toilet.

Of course he was in the toilet, it was twenty past one. He was always on the toilet at twenty past one.

He called out, 'You said you'd be here at one o'clock.'

'Sorry.'

'There's a cuppa on the table.'

56

If you told my dad you were coming round at one o'clock that was when he poured your cup of tea. If you weren't there, hard luck. These were the rules of life. There was no room for interpretation. Rules were all he had left.

I drank the cold tea, and stood with my back to the fire that had two bars but had never been known to have them both on at once. The cistern flushed and Dad emerged clutching a copy of Delia Smith's *Complete Cookery Course*. The day after my mother died he took an interest in cookery in general and Delia Smith in particular. Now he couldn't separate the two, and he was never far from one of her books. Left on his own we thought he'd fossilize. Kate and I even talked about having him move in with us, although God knows where we'd have put him. But that was nearly four years ago and he'd coped just fine. His routines kept him happy.

'I've brought you some old yoghurt pots,' I said, and dumped a plastic bag full of them on the table. I couldn't remember what he used old yoghurt pots for, but I knew he was always pleased to have them.

'I'll hang my laundry out and be with you.'

I stood in the kitchen and watched him work his way down the clothes line. He had economy down to such a fine art that he even saved money on clothes pegs. No piece of washing got two pegs to itself. They all overlapped, so that one peg secured the end of a shirt and the start of a pair of pants. If you asked him why, he'd look at you as if you were simple, pointing out that if you hung your laundry up his way not only did you need to buy fewer pegs, but you also saved wear and tear on the ones you owned. It was frightening the ways he could think of to save money, although what was more frightening was the way his traits surfaced in me. No matter how hard I tried to rebel against it I knew I had the economy gene. Just the other day I looked in my wardrobe and felt uneasy with the number of clothes-hangers supporting only one shirt. Hangers had to work a lot harder in my dad's household. They had to strain under the weight of two shirts and a pair of trousers before they were considered to be doing their job. Spare hangers were put in a pile at the bottom of the wardrobe, and when there were twenty of them they'd be tied up and sold at the next car-boot sale under a sign: *Twenty coathangers. Twenty five pence.*

'I'm going to have chicken in a paprika sauce with spring greens tonight,' he announced as we headed round the dual carriageway. 'So we need to do a bit of shopping.'

'Which supermarkets?'

'Tesco's, Gateway and Sainsbury's.'

You never got away with just one supermarket when you took my dad shopping. He had to go to three different ones because he'd researched the prices in the local paper. Tesco's for chicken, Gateway for rice and Sainsbury's for greens. I said to him, 'Any money you save is spent on petrol.'

'But I don't pay for the petrol, do I?' he replied, and you couldn't argue with that.

In Tesco's I watched him push his trolley up the aisles. 'Forty-five pence for Birds' custard? That's a good price,' he exclaimed, genuinely excited. I enjoyed watching my dad in the supermarket the way I enjoyed watching my children on a climbing frame. He made me want to tell him how proud I was of him. I never did of course. We never had too much to say to each other. He didn't waste words in the same way he didn't waste clothes pegs. The only subject he liked to talk at length on was my elder brother Colin.

'I heard from him again last week,' he told me as we set up stall in our usual spot on the playing field. He laid out his collections of dishcloths, elastic bands and empty cassette cases.

'Yeah, you told me.'

Colin who had gone to university, then to America. Colin who was earning a fortune working in a laboratory in Georgia. Colin who had an ex-wife and three children to support. Colin who only came home for funerals.

'He's doing well. Goodness me,' and he shook his head in admiration. When Colin had come home for Mum's funeral Dad was overwhelmed. 'He flew all that way.'

'He's bought a new house, you know.'

'You told me.'

'With a double garage.'

Long ago I had promised myself that when my boys grew up, the one thing I would never do was go on and on to one about how well the other was doing.

'Why don't you go and stay with him in America?' I suggested.

'No.'

'Why not?'

'Much too expensive.'

'He'll pay!'

'I couldn't let him do that. He's got those kids to support.'

'He's just bought a house with a double garage!'

But he wouldn't consider it; he didn't want to be

a burden. And Colin didn't encourage him.

'Says he's got another girlfriend.'

'Good for him.'

My dad sold everything, even his plastic bag of twenty-five biro tops for fifteen pence. I sold the electric fan for two pounds and the fondue set for two pounds fifty, but then I went and had a look round the other stalls and blew the money on a bright yellow and white ringed teapot to start my collection for the Climbing Rose, and a kid's tennis racket.

'How could you go and waste your money on a tennis racket?' moaned my dad as I drove him home. 'Your kids have got too many toys.'

'It was only three pounds. I'll teach Martin how to play. I remember you buying me a tennis racket when I was a kid. We used to play. You used to buy us all sorts of things like this.'

We motored on in silence, but my extravagance had unsettled him. As we pulled up outside his house, he said, 'You need to look after the pennies and the pounds will look after themselves.' It was this message, or a version of it, with which he left me each week. In fact this was the lecture he had given me all my life: I shouldn't get carried away; I should do things slowly and methodically and I would get there; I shouldn't be too ambitious, I wasn't the sort. It never seemed to occur to him I was thirty-seven now, that in effect I was in charge of him. I wanted to say, Actually, Dad, your advice is hopelessly outdated. These days one's standard of living isn't increased by simply looking after the pennies. You need to generate more income.

But instead I said, 'What did you dream of last

night?'

'The chimney sweep. Why?'

'Why the chimney sweep?'

'I need to get him round. He's one pound fifty cheaper at this time of year.'

'You didn't dream of any animals, then?'

'No.'

'The chimney sweep didn't come with his dog or anything?'

'The chimney sweep doesn't have a dog as far as I'm aware.'

I helped him get his stuff out, his cardboard boxes and bags. There was something Third World about him at the end of a Sunday boot sale. 'Shall I come in?' I asked, knowing what his answer would be.

'Don't you worry about me.'

I watched him walk up the path, and saw myself and my boys in his stride. A tear came to my eye in the way it did whenever I watched a Disney film these days.

*   *   *

Kate had fallen asleep putting the children to bed. The three of them lay wrapped up in one another. It seemed a shame to wake her. She seemed to get so tired and I could never understand why. How could working part-time in a library get anyone so tired?

She sensed me there and woke with a mad look. 'I'm going to bed,' she mumbled.

Stephen opened his eyes and said, 'Close the door on your way out.'

I lay on our bed as she undressed. 'Why does he

like doors closed all the time?'

'Why do you turn out lights all the time?'

She was in a bad mood. I'd cheer her up.

'Were you ever really good at anything?' I asked.

'What?'

'I just wondered if you were ever good at some sport or something; whether you had some talent that you never told me about. I mean, it would really surprise me if, say, you turned out to be a really good violinist, and it had just slipped your mind to tell me all these years.'

She didn't reply. She smelt her socks and put them in the laundry basket. I pressed her: 'I mean, you never took a course or anything?'

'In what?'

'I don't know. Pottery, fabric design, furniture-making. Could you, for instance, illustrate a children's book?'

She screwed her face up. I was trying to be cheerful. She was determined to be downbeat. I said, 'I could write a book and you could illustrate it. Children's books make a fortune.'

She sighed. 'Is this what all those packets of crisps in the kitchen are about?'

'What?'

'And why the tooth fairy only put ten pence under Martin's pillow last night? I can't cope with you when you get like this. Why do you get like this?'

'I'm just trying to improve our standard of living. We've all got to chip in. This is a family effort.'

'A fifty per cent reduction in tooth-fairy prices isn't going to improve anyone's standard of living. It's going to do the opposite. He was very upset.' She looked at me hopelessly, then padded to the bathroom. I could hear her brushing her teeth in that way, the way that said, 'This is what I have to bear.'

She came back to bed and switched out the light. I put my arm on her shoulder in the hope she'd turn and bury her head in my chest, but all she said was, 'Have you seen the fondue set? I can't find it.'

I turned all the lights out and went to watch TV, the end of some film about the Mafia. The trouble with crooks was they didn't know when to stop. Why didn't they have some sense and just do the one job then invest the loot in a limited-access account at the building society and live off the interest?

A famine appeal for Sudan followed. I rummaged for the remote control. Kate could hear these things in her sleep. She'd be taking down the address and writing out a cheque before the adverts were on. I used to put up with her donations to anyone who asked, but then one day, shortly after the sandwich shop closed, she bought all the tickets for the Amnesty Christmas raffle herself because she didn't have the time to go out and sell them. She said, 'They need the money more than we do,' and I thought: Hold on a minute, I'm not so sure that's true. And from then on I always got to the post first and intercepted any appeal. If I heard the rattle of a tin I steered her down a side-street. My justification was that if we looked after ourselves and got richer, then think how much more money we'd be able to give away.

Phil Collins came on asking for people to send money. So why didn't he just write a cheque and feed the lot of them?

I switched the set off. I felt mean. Before I went

to bed I put another ten-pence piece under Martin's pillow.

* * *

'He's right, Will. You've got to generate more income, no doubt about it.' That was Ted, a couple of nights later in the George, after I'd told him about the Climbing Rose. 'How much do you need for this exactly?'

We stood squashed together against a wall that was sticky with something. I said, 'Forty grand. The bank says it won't begin to take me seriously unless I put in twenty-five.'

'And how much have you got?'

'Nothing.'

'I mean, I could lend you a lump sum, but that's not going to do anyone any good, is it?'

He often said that to me. I could never understand it.

'See, your trouble is, you're not thinking creatively.'

'Did you dream of any animals last night?'

'That's a strange thing to ask.'

'There's this Chinese mystic written a book on how to win the lottery. You pick a sequence of numbers depending on what animal you dreamt of.'

'My point exactly. If you want to make money out of the lottery, don't go buying a ticket, write a book that tells other people how to win the thing. You've got to have a scheme. You can't gather together twenty-five grand switching the lights off and going to boot sales.'

He emptied his pint. At a nearby table a woman

threw a glass of lager over the man she was with and walked out. He picked up his car keys and followed. 'There's a free table,' said Ted.

We sat down. A fight had broken out by the dartboard. 'You don't get pubs like this in Totteridge,' he sighed.

I said, 'What happened to all the stuff they dug out of the ground to build the Channel Tunnel?'

'What stuff?'

'All the earth. Where did they put it?'

'I don't know.'

'Neither do I. But once I thought: Why don't they put it in bottles and sell it like souvenirs?'

'Like lumps of concrete from the Berlin Wall?'

'That sort of thing.'

He looked me in the eye. 'That's brilliant.'

'Or I thought if you bought the whole lot you could have turned it into a dry ski slope in Kent.'

'Why Kent?'

'It's nearest. Save on transport costs.'

'I prefer the bottle idea. More simple; less outlay.'

'But I didn't do anything about it. It was just an idea.'

Ted belched. 'That's the difference between success and failure, see. The rich man acts on impulse.'

We meandered home round the houses—down Hamilton Road, one of the few nice streets in our neighbourhood. It had good-looking semi-detached Victorian properties with three storeys and bay windows, and decent-sized gardens. No sound of the motorway here. These places had been done up one by one and now they sold for a lot of money.

Ted smacked his lips. 'It's all about boom and

bust, see, Will. You have to ride out the bad times and cash in in the good. You were unlucky with that sandwich shop, that was all.'

I could never believe that he and Kate were brother and sister. Kate was clothed from Oxfam; Ted from Marks & Spencer's leisurewear. He was overweight; she was underweight. He had bad teeth; hers were good. His nose flared at the edges; hers was prominent but cute. If only she could have been the one who made a fortune out of the property market, and he the one so keen to give to charity.

We stopped outside number fifty-six as we always did, and Ted looked up at the man with the ponytail who worked all hours on his house, carting barrowloads of rubble out to a skip. 'That was me fifteen years ago,' said Ted, nostalgia tilting his voice. 'Me and Rita. We never stopped.'

'I often see him down the bottle bank. He used to drink German wine, now he drinks Virgin vodka.'

'. . . And look at us now, offshore bank account, part owners of a golf course, critical illness insurance up to our ears. If I lose my thumb I get a hundred grand.'

I imagined myself with an axe poised over my thumb, willing myself to bring it smashing down.

The man with the ponytail was up a ladder working on a ceiling, plastering with style and rhythm, a roll-up in his mouth. Ted looked up at him and sighed. 'But I'll tell you what. I'd give it all away just to have the eighties again. Happy days.'

When we got near to our flat I turned to him and said, 'Don't mention this to Kate will you? About the Climbing Rose and everything. She's a bit . . . you know.'

'I know what you mean, mate.'

'I want it to be a surprise for her.'

'You can rely on me. I know you've got her best interests at heart.'

That was the thing I liked about Ted: for all their differences he really cared about his sister. They cared about each other. They were family. And he was right of course—I did have her best interests at heart. I wanted this for both of us, for all of us.

* * *

I was parked up on Abbey Road NW6, outside the legendary recording studios. A little further up a group of four Japanese tourists waited for a gap in the traffic, then ran on to the zebra crossing made famous by the Beatles to have their picture taken. Frank arranged them to recreate the photograph on the back of the *Abbey Road* album. But they giggled too much and took too long. Frank started to lose his patience. A 139 to West Hampstead scattered them.

Should you win the £60,000 jackpot how would you like your money paid, cheque or direct deposit?

Cheque, I think.

I was sitting in the coach filling in the form that would win me sixty thousand pounds in the *Reader's Digest* Grand Draw. It had conveniently dropped through the letter box that morning.

Should you win the £60,000 jackpot we will come with balloons, flowers and a cheque. If you agree to let us film the moment you will receive an additional payment of £3000.

Someone has to win the thing, I kept telling myself. It came with an endorsement from Mrs Ivy Sheringham of Brockenhurst, after all: *I couldn't believe it when the white envelope informing me I had won second prize of £30,000 arrived on the doormat. My retirement will now be a happy one.*

I'd spent the morning at home combing the magazines and newspapers lying round, entering competitions to pay off my mortgage, to win a new car, to send us all away to Florida. I'd tried everything from spot-the-ball contests to 'design a new arts centre for Peterborough'. There were money-making opportunities everywhere if you looked for them. On the motoring pages were adverts from agencies wanting to buy your car licence-plate number: *up to £2000 paid. You may have the number we are looking for.* On a lifestyle page an advertisement read: *Father-and-son lookalikes needed for interesting work.* Martin and I qualified for that; everyone said we were the spitting image. On the TV pages researchers offered cash for stories of failed businesses.

They were rolls of the dice that could just as easily send you down a snake as up a ladder, but the attitude, I had decided, was to be up for absolutely everything. I left my car registration on Personalized Plates' answer machine. I posted a picture of me and Martin off to a box number. I sent a brief outline of the story of my failed sandwich shop to a production company.

Should you win the £60,000 jackpot would you be willing to take part in a celebratory luncheon where a celebrity from a soap opera will award you your prize?

Sure.

Frank led another four Japanese out on to the

crossing. One of them lit a cigarette and took his shoes off. Another stuck his hands deep in his pockets. Frank stood in the middle of the road and took the picture, the sun shining off his lank hair. It looked like he got the council to cut it. I wondered if he had any money-making scheme going, like everybody down at Welcome claimed they had. Money was all they talked about because they got paid so little. Barry behind the reception desk had been writing a sitcom for ten years. 'It's beautifully simple,' he happily told you when you asked what it was about. 'It takes place in this sort of reception area in a coach-tour company, and the drivers and passengers come in and go out, and it's about their lives and loves and all the funny, sort of quirky things that happen to them. It's called *Coach*.'

Then there was Roy, who was always moaning about the maintenance he had to pay his ex-wife, and how he topped up his earnings with 'my little cottage industry'. He came to work once with a van full of new microwaves for sale. He once said to me, 'If ever anything like a video camera, or some foreign currency, or a nice piece of jewellery should come your way, I'll give you a good price. Know what I mean?'

But I didn't know what he meant, not at first, so I said to him, 'If I found a video camera I'd hand it in, wouldn't I?'

'Well, course you would,' he laughed. 'So would I, but just say . . .' and then I understood and I laughed, although I felt angry with him.

Frank climbed back on the coach. He was sweating but he wouldn't take his anorak off. He poured himself some tea from his flask and crunched on a biscuit like a rodent, his Hitler

69

moustache rising and falling on his lip like an extra eyebrow. I said, 'So, Frank, do you have a nice little earner on the side?'

'I beg your pardon?'

'You know, something you do to raise a bit extra when you need it.'

He blew on his tea. 'Look how hot that is and I made it'—he looked at his watch—'five hours ago now. Such a good Thermos.'

He wasn't going to answer such a personal question. But then when I turned back to my entry form he said, 'I do have a nice little earner actually, yes.'

'What?'

'I take glamour pictures of my wife.'

Outside, four more tourists ran out on to the crossing. A pick-up truck full of scaffolding and scaffolders went past and yelled abuse. I said to Frank, 'What do you mean? I mean, how does that earn . . . you know?'

'I sell them to men's magazines.'

'Nude pictures?'

'Yes.'

'Nude pictures of your wife?'

'That's right. I send them to the *Readers' Wives* pages. I'll bring some in and show you if you want, or you could buy one of the magazines of course.'

He finished his tea and screwed up his flask. 'What do you do?'

'What?'

'To supplement your income?'

'Nothing.'

We were on the Celebrity Tour, a drive round the homes and haunts of London's rich and famous, and the next stop was Sir Paul

70

McCartney's house, even though he didn't live there any more. I pulled up outside, but I kept the engine idling. An Australian woman said, 'I've heard he's very friendly.'

Frank said, 'On hot summer nights he used to open his top window and play "Blackbird" to the fans waiting below.'

Someone else said, 'Poor Linda.'

Another Australian, Sid, wanted to stop and knock on the door. 'Hey, last night we had dinner with Lord and Lady Salisbury at Hatfield House.'

We headed on up to Hampstead. 'More and more American stars are coming to England these days to buy homes,' said Frank into the microphone, 'attracted by the countryside, the lower crime rate and the public-school system. Madonna has a house here now, and I heard Tom Cruise and Nicole Kidman are buying a property in Berkshire.'

I never failed to get a little thrill of pride when I heard that, for all her money, Madonna would rather live in England than in America.

'Michael Palin lives on the left,' said Frank.

We continued on up to George Michael's house. 'He often comes out to take his dog Hippy for a walk on the heath,' Frank informed us. And we waited for a while, and watched, but there was no sign of George Michael, just a black Range Rover with tinted windows in the driveway. Everyone took a picture of the Range Rover.

At Keats's house they all got out again, this time for tea. Frank poured himself another cup from his flask. I said, 'So these pictures of your wife?'

'Yes.' He seemed rather proud of it all.

'She's quite happy to do it, is she?'

71

'Oh yes. It's an artistic thing. She has an excellent body.'

'Where do you take them?'

'Round the house, or on the patio on garden furniture. Sometimes in a blow-up paddling pool.'

'Where do you get them developed?'

'Boots.'

'You're kidding!'

'No.'

'How much do you get paid for them, then?'

'It varies. We earned enough to pay for our fly-drive holiday to Portugal last year.'

We headed back to base via the former homes of Sigmund Freud and Sting. 'They were neighbours, that's nice,' said someone behind me. And then past Boy George's house with its neat lawn. 'I like his curtains,' said Sid.

I was having trouble driving straight. I'd never met Frank's wife, but I had this image of her sun-lamped body sprawled over the kitchen table, and Frank, with his Instamatic, kneeling over her, wearing his anorak, saying, 'You're looking good, baby!' I felt distracted—I had to watch carefully for red lights. Then I started to get angry—I drove much too fast through Paddington.

Back in the belly of the Welcome garage I climbed down and slammed the door of the coach. Even Frank, the company joke, had enough imagination to finance an annual foreign holiday for his family. I marched into Graham's office and said firmly, 'I want to do some overnights.'

'So do lots of drivers,' he replied with a snort. Overnights guaranteed overtime. You could add thirty pounds to your weekly wage without any trouble.

'Listen. I did you a big favour with that mugger. You can do me one now,' and I turned and walked out. I didn't wait to see what his reaction was; I didn't care. Everyone felt good when they shouted at Graham.

*   *   *

I put Martin on a stool in front of the mirror and stood next to him. 'Smile.'

He smiled. I smiled. I said, 'Do you think we look alike?'

'No.'

'Course we do.' I flicked his hair over the same side as mine: 'Same blond wavy hair, same sort of nose. We both look like Grandpa.'

Everyone said we looked alike. We were a good-looking father and son. I was on a down escalator the other day and got a nice look from a woman on the up.

Kate came in. I said to her, 'We look alike, don't we?'

'The washing machine's broken,' she replied. 'It won't drain.'

I took Martin to the park with his new old tennis racket. 'You're lucky. If you want to a be a tennis star you're halfway there if you're good looking.'

'My trainers are too tight,' he said.

'They can't be, we only just bought them.'

The park tennis courts were rectangles of scabby and cratered tarmac that had moss creeping over them like a disease. There was no one to pay so we just walked on, and swiped our one ball to each other over the ragged net. I hadn't played tennis since I was about ten. I called to Martin, 'You

73

know, Andre Agassi's dad had a tennis ball swinging from his boy's crib, so the baby Andre would learn to keep his eye on the ball from an early age.'

Martin hit it back hard. He was pretty good; he had natural timing.

'Agassi's dad tied a bat to his hand when he was three.' Not that I'd ever behave like that. I wouldn't be one of those pushy parents. And I wouldn't look for tax dodges like Steffi Graf's dad either. I mean, Martin might not even want me to be his manager; I'd understand that. However, if he did want me . . . 'When Agassi started to play in junior tournaments his dad threw away second or third-place medals.'

Imagine us all at Wimbledon. Kate and me up in the competitors' stand wearing sunglasses and looking anxious. Sitting next to us would be Martin's girlfriend, an actress/model. He'd have to outgrow his asthma before then of course, or get it under control at least, but they said that would probably happen. No reason why he couldn't lead a perfectly normal, active life, they said.

A voice boomed behind me: 'I don't seem to remember anyone booking a court!'

I turned and there was the park attendant: hands on his hips, mobile phone clipped to his belt, bald sun-tanned head. He looked like a great white hunter.

'There was no one here. And no one was using it. We thought—'

'You haven't even got proper shoes!'

He had caught me on a bad day. I walked slowly to the wire, mirrored his poise, and spoke with a great deal of control. 'Do you know something? It's people like you who are keeping British tennis in the wilderness.'

'What?'

'The theory is that the next British Wimbledon champion is not going to come from the ranks of the elite, or the academies of sporting excellence, he or she is going to come from the street, from the underprivileged. Basically, he will be a natural, with an ability so potent no amount of environmental disadvantage will be able to suppress it. If you took the trouble to watch this boy, you would realize he is a prodigy; he just needs a corner of his urban surroundings in which to develop. If you kicked out the vandals who smash bottles in the playground; if you did something about the dog owners who encourage their animals to come in here and shit at random; if you did something about the wankers who hit golf balls about like missiles, then maybe we could play tennis out on the grass. As it is we're playing on the court 'cos it's the only area in this godforsaken dump called a park where you can run around without risk of serious injury or infection.'

He looked at me with narrowed eyes, so I looked back at him with even narrower ones, and he said, 'OK. Play on.'

'What?'

'Play on. You're right. There's nowhere else in this park to play. Have a good game,' and he marched off.

I felt nervous after that. I had a vision of him returning with an automatic weapon and leaving us hanging over the netting, our rackets forced down our throats. We knocked a few more balls over, but we'd lost enthusiasm and we walked back to our car, our car with registration number G30 BOY. I started to laugh when I thought: Boy George would buy that.

*   *   *

I laughed again when I told Ted in the pub, but he didn't see the joke, he was very serious. He paused with a pint pot between table and mouth. He said quietly, 'That's brilliant. That's wonderful.' He moved closer to me as if someone might listen in and nick the idea. 'Now that is what I mean by thinking creatively. Not only is it clever, you're cutting out the middleman.'

'What?'

'Well, you don't have to go through the agent, do you? Who would give you next to nothing and do exactly what you're going to do.'

'What am I going to do?'

'You said you know where Boy George lives.'

'Yeah.'

'So you can go straight there.'

'I was only joking, you know.'

'What?'

'You don't seriously think I'm going round his house? I was joking.'

Ted looked disappointed. 'What did I just tell you about the rich man acting on impulse?'

'I was only joking, all right!'

Half an hour later we were in a nice pub in Hampstead, and Ted was very excited. 'All you got to do is knock on the door and say, "Good evening, Mr George. I just wondered if you would like to buy my licence plate." It's the easiest thing in the world.'

'For you maybe.'

'What have you got to lose? It's not twenty-five

76

grand but it's a start. Ask him for two. Show him the newspaper, show him the bargain he's getting. He might just say yes.'

'What if he says, "piss off, I'm calling the police"?'

'Then you come down in price. One thousand eight hundred.'

It was a nice pub. Nice bar snacks, and you didn't pay for sauces. I would have been enjoying myself normally, but my heart was thumping because I knew I was going to have to do this just to show Ted I was serious; and because if I didn't, in two years' time when I was still living in my box by the motorway, he'd be saying: 'Things might have been a lot different if you'd knocked on Boy George's house that night.'

'Oh for Christ's sake.' I downed my pint, thumped it on the counter and strode out to the car.

We drove to Boy George's house and parked across the road. Ted peered at it. 'It's not much to look at, is it? I'd have thought he lived in something a lot grander, you know. I mean, he's supposed to be making a comeback and everything, isn't he?'

'Yeah, well.' My mouth was dry. I knew I was about to make a fool of myself.

'Nice curtains, though,' said Ted.

'Very nice curtains.'

He patted my knee. 'Off you go, then. You got the registration document?'

'Yeah.'

Just hold it up when you speak to him. That'll convince him you're not some nutter.'

'The chances of me speaking to him are very

77

slim.'

'Don't be such a pessimist. There are lights on, look.'

I got out and walked across the road, then up the garden path towards the front door. When I looked back there was Ted waving me to go on, like I was a child going into a new school. I've let him influence me too far this time, I thought. From now on any schemes I come up with I keep to myself.

I knocked on the front door, gently. No answer. I could hear music, though. I knocked again, a bit louder this time, but still no answer. I looked back at Ted with a shrug, but he opened the window and yelled, 'Go round the bleedin' back, then!'

There was a side gate, and when I tried it the thing went and opened. Then I was standing at the back door, thinking: This has got to be against the law.

I was about to knock when a dog started yapping inside. I ducked into the shadows, pressing myself against the wall. 'Shut yer trap!' came a yell. Then the back door opened and someone stepped out and dumped a bag of rubbish into the bin and went back in again. I didn't see a face, just a pair of legs wearing Japanese patterned slippers. But suddenly it didn't matter any more. I felt strangely buoyant. I slid down the wall and sat on the path with a silly smile. I had just remembered my dream from the previous night. It had featured a dog.

I hurried back to the car and jumped in. 'Let's go.'

'Well?' said Ted.

'What?'

'What happened?'

'Oh . . . he . . . he didn't want it. He says he's got

78

one.'

'One what?'

'Licence plate.'

'Well of course he's got one. The idea is he dumps the one he has and puts this one on.'

'I don't know, Ted. He just said he didn't want it. Anyway, it doesn't matter now. Let's go.'

'How much did you ask for?'

'What?'

'How much did you say it cost?'

'Two thousand.'

'And when he said he didn't want it, what did you do?'

'I said, "Thank you very much for your time," and then I left. He was busy. I could tell.'

'You didn't drop your price or anything?'

'No! I want to go.'

'Oh give it here.' And he grabbed the registration document out of my hand and got out.

'Leave it out, Ted!'

But he was already striding down the garden path and through the back gate. I sat there in my nine-year-old Fiat rewinding my dream. It was a dog, definitely, a sort of Labrador, and it was crapping on my doorstep in broad daylight, and I was trying to run towards it but my legs wouldn't move.

Ted was gone a long time. I was beginning to get concerned. Maybe the dog had got to him. Maybe Boy George had asked him in. Eventually he came striding back. He climbed in and sat with his arms folded.

'Well?'

'You're right. He doesn't want it.'

'Told you.' I started the car up.

'Nice bloke, though. You know, not big-headed or nothing.'

'No no. Very nice.'

'Did he ask you in?'

'No.'

'Nor me. Sort of spoke to me on the doorstep.'

'That's right.'

We drove back along the A41. As we got to the flat Ted said, 'Still, you gave it a bash.'

'Yeah. Thanks for . . . you know . . . your support.'

'That's all right. Don't worry, mate, your luck's going to change. I can feel it. You've got the right attitude. Things are on the up.'

You bet they were. Next day was the mid-week lottery draw. I consulted my *How to Win the Lottery* book, made a note of the numbers for dog dreams, then strode into the newsagent's and strode out clutching the winning ticket.

'The washing machine doesn't seem to have mended itself,' said Kate when I ran up the stairs.

'Don't worry about the washing machine.'

'I'm going to get someone in to fix it.'

'I'm not paying someone to fix it.'

'Well, someone has to fix it. We'll be out of clean clothes in thirty-six hours.'

'I'll fix it. Tomorrow.'

By eight o'clock the kids were in bed. At eight-fifteen Kate's period arrived and she went to bed herself, not pregnant again. 'Never mind,' I said, and turned the light out. At eight-fifty I sat in front of the telly on my own with a packet of Twiglets.

I pressed the mute button. I couldn't bear the syrupy voice-over. Outside, the sky was a dusky sort of portentous grey. I couldn't hear the traffic noise.

80

The world had stopped while the lottery balls spun. I had the feeling something truly spectacular was about to happen. I unlocked the mute as the first ball fell out

41.

16.

3.

36.

28.

11.

A buzzing filled my ears. I swallowed hard. I couldn't feel my legs. I hadn't got one number right.

The phone rang. I watched it ring four times. The only hope I had left was that the astrological wires had got crossed and it wasn't the lottery I was supposed to win at all. This was the *Reader's Digest* publicity department calling to inform me I had won sixty thousand pounds, and to ask whether I would like a champagne luncheon in the company of a popular soap star.

'Hello.'

'Will?'

'Yeah.'

'Graham.'

'Who?'

'Fucking Graham from work, you pillock.'

'Oh.'

'You still want an overnight?'

'Yeah.'

'Next Tuesday ... All right?'

'Yeah, all right.'

'Stonehenge, Salisbury and the night in Bath.'

'OK.'

'Are you all right?'

'Yeah.'
'You don't sound all right.'
'I'm all right.'
'Well, don't say thank you.'
'Thank you.'
'Jesus.'

CHAPTER FOUR

SALISBURY, STONEHENGE AND THE GEORGIAN CITY OF BATH

I was up early, as in the old days; impatient to get to work, as in the old days. Spring had arrived like a slap round the face. I'd opened the window and the smell of exotic fruit from Vinod's shop was more potent than the smell of motor exhaust. The sky was a dirty blue; the weatherwoman on breakfast telly wore a short-sleeved shirt.

I ironed my own short-sleeved shirt with gusto. I was still feeling exhilarated from my success of the previous afternoon. The shirt I was ironing was one I had washed in the washing machine, the washing machine I had repaired myself.

I had confronted it; I'd looked it in its one big eye. I wasn't paying an overalled technician fifty quid for five minutes' work. It was a washing machine. It was powered by logic. The problem was simply to do with water draining away. There must be a blockage. Logic.

I unscrewed the back and peered inside. Martin watched me, reminding me of the times I used to watch my dad repair things. He wouldn't have

82

dreamt of getting someone in. He repaired everything in our house himself. It was the only time I ever heard him use bad language; it was as if it was part of the procedure. I hadn't inherited his expertise, only his language. 'It's a bastard!' I said under my breath, and Martin nodded, as if he too knew the importance of bad language in the domestic-appliance-repair process. I poked and prodded, then had the bright idea of loosening the retaining clips that held the rubber outflow pipe in place, and suddenly we were bailing. We drained the drum successfully and when I stuck my finger in the pipe I pulled out a pencil sharpener, a pound coin and a piece of jigsaw with Waterloo Station Platform 8 on it.

I tossed the pound coin over. 'Fifty pence each,' said Martin.

'Done. We fixed it!' I called out proudly to Kate.

She didn't reply. Since Graham's telephone call Kate's mood had sunk as mine had risen. Tuesday was her late night at the library. The kids went to a childminder and I picked them up. 'If you're away it'll mean three hours extra childcare,' she'd protested. 'That will cost almost all the extra you earn. And the kids won't get to bed before nine.'

But if I did this one I could get regular overnights. I was standing at the ironing board thinking: One overnight a week, that's 120 quid a month. In six months I'd have enough for a Turbo Vac. In twenty-five years I'd have enough to buy the Climbing Rose. Think Positive.

I pulled a bag down from the top of the wardrobe as quietly as I could. I didn't want Kate to see me pack. She was jealous as well as annoyed, I knew, because the other thing about an overnight was that I would get a night away to myself. I'd stay in a hotel room with a freshly made bed, tea- and coffee-making facilities, and a TV that didn't play Disney all the time. It wasn't flying to New York Club Class or anything, but there would be clean towels, an empty wardrobe with as many coat-hangers as I wanted to use, and no laundry hanging over radiators. I'd have a nice time in my room. I'd stay in all evening, enjoy the privacy of a little corner of civilization that would be mine for twelve hours. I'd mend the hole in my trouser pocket with the mini sewing kit hotels always provided.

I packed my newest underwear, as you do.

Kate roused as I searched for my wallet. I gazed at her happy face, mouth open at the climax of her dreams, and I thought: Why don't I go and make her a cup of tea and some breakfast and bring a tray up to her in bed, like I plan to do every day in the not-too-distant future?

When she opened her eyes I sat by her and said, 'Good morning. Would you like a half-grapefruit and a freshly picked flower?'

'What?' and she farted and Stephen came in and announced, 'I'm not dead!' The door slammed shut, and the moment was lost.

I gave the kids salt and vinegar crisps for breakfast. There was no voucher inside either packet telling them they had won thirty thousand pounds. But we still had the milk bottle tops to come and our daily chance of a dream holiday. The boys watched in silence as I stood poised with my finger over the foil. 'What's it going to be? What's it going to be?'

'T. It's going to be a T,' yelled Martin.

'T,' screamed Stephen.

We only needed a letter T and an S for a holiday in Australia.

'I want an H,' I said. I still had my heart set on Hawaii.

I stuck my finger in and pulled off the top . . . M. 'A bloody M.'

'A bloody M,' said Martin.

'A bloody M,' said Stephen.

'A bloomin' M, I mean.'

'A bloomin' M, I mean,' said Martin.

'A bloomin' M, I mean,' said Stephen.

I ripped off the next one. It was a P.

'I hate Ps,' said Martin.

'I hate Ps,' said Stephen.

So did I. Not only did we have a jar full of them, not one of the dream holiday destinations had a letter P in it. Ps were pointless.

'One left,' said Martin.

'Come on, baby,' I said.

'Come on, baby,' said Martin.

'Come on, baby,' said Stephen.

'Another fucking P . . .' I glanced at them. They had mouths full of cereal. 'I mean . . .'

'We know what you mean, Dad,' said Martin.

Kate dropped me off at the Underground station. Just saying, 'See you tomorrow,' made me feel like I was escaping. I felt uplifted. On the tube I sat opposite a woman who had fish embroidered on her socks. In the paper I read the big news of the morning: you needed to eat five pieces of fruit a day to keep cancer at bay. Before I got to Welcome I bought myself a bag of Granny Smiths. My life was worth prolonging.

I walked into reception with a whistle, took my notes from Graham's desk and went out to the

85

coach bay. Roy grabbed me and said, 'You like lobster, don't you?'

'What?'

'You want to buy a lobster?'

'No.'

'They're fresh.' And he opened the plastic bag he was carrying and there was a lobster, pink and black and still moving.

'That's disgusting. Where did you get that from?'

'North Sea, I think.'

He was distracting me. I didn't see the woman sitting in the front seat of my coach until I was up the steps. Then I turned and I was looking straight at her: fresh face, shiny lips, neat teeth. As soon as I saw her I thought: Who does she remind me of?

'Hi, I'm Alice.'

I must have looked at her as if she was a gate-crasher. 'I'm the tour guide,' she explained, and I glanced down for her Blue Badge, as though I didn't believe her.

'Right . . . I'm Will.'

She was new. But they were all freelance, these guides. They had favourite companies they worked for but they came and went. I climbed into my seat. 'First time with Welcome?'

'Yes.'

What was it about her that was so familiar? The way she held her head up? The smile that crept to the corner of her mouth? I'd just assumed I'd be going away with greasy Frank or someone, but here was a woman dressed in a trim jacket who looked like an air hostess, or one of those women who work behind the cosmetic counter at Debenhams. I was looking at her in such a way now that she stopped and said: 'What?'

'Sorry. Nothing. We don't know each other . . . do we?'

'No.'

It sounded so much like a line that she gave me the kind of face that says, 'Oh, give me a break.' And then I realized that she was attractive enough to get lots of lines like that. I felt embarrassed. 'Sorry. You just remind me . . . Sorry.'

She turned her attention to her clipboard. She'd taken a dislike to me. She popped her pen and said, 'We'd better get going. First pick-up Beaumont Hotel.'

I started up and as we headed for the exit I thought, This is going to annoy me.

*   *   *

I'd made this trip before, of course, but only as a day excursion, never with luggage in the hold, and never with a guide like Alice. With a two-day trip ahead of her she took time to settle herself in, work on establishing a rapport with the clients. All the way down to Salisbury she knelt on the front seat facing them, holding the microphone like a lead singer. I'd never seen a guide work like that before. And there were few statistics or dates from her. She knew tourists were more interested in gossip and trivia. She realized you could tell them as many times as you liked that Mary Queen of Scots died in 1587 at Fotheringay Castle denying any association with Anthony Babington's plot to kill Queen Elizabeth, but the thing they wrote home in their postcards was that she was a five-foot-eleven redhead and an accomplished billiards player.

As we passed the Hogarth roundabout she made

a reference to the eighteenth-century satirical painter, but gave a more enthusiastic history of the Fuller's brewery situated nearby. As we passed over the Thames she took time to emphasize the river's importance as a line of communication since Roman times, but just as long to recount the stories of her boating holiday in 1992 during which she fell overboard and got rescued by a man who looked like Lord Lucan.

All the way down the M3 and into Wiltshire she played the clients like an audience, encouraging participation, so that by the time the spire of Salisbury Cathedral appeared in the distance between hills, everyone on board seemed to have met everyone else. 'Alice, you remind me of my daughter,' announced a Canadian woman whose husband wore a bright red beret. But Alice probably reminded everyone of their daughter, or how they would have liked their daughter to be. The Canadian woman took her picture. 'You don't mind, do you?'

'Of course not,' said Alice

'I always ask since we went to Tanzania and they thought we were stealing their souls.'

Alice led them away, these gaily dressed, strangely shaped people from faraway places. She was like a teacher taking her class on a school outing. It occurred to me she was chalking up a big score of tips for both of us.

It was later on in the afternoon though, as we were heading to Bath, that she did something I've never seen a guide, or indeed an English person, do. There was a regular stop on this excursion at a teashop on the outskirts of Bradford on Avon. It broke the journey to Bath and gave the clients the opportunity for a cream tea. Every excursion at Welcome included an opportunity for a cream tea.

But there was a hold-up south of Warminster. Roadworks caused a three-mile tailback, and we didn't pull into the teashop car park until gone five o'clock, an hour after we were due. There was a closed sign in the window, although the lights were on.

'I'll go and sort it,' I told Alice, and I went and rapped on the door-glass. A woman appeared from the kitchen. I smiled and waved, but she opened the door with a shut face.

'We're closed.'

'We're the coach party.'

'I can see who you are, but we're closed.'

'Sorry. It was those roadworks.'

'We close at five.'

'We always stop here.'

'If we do it for you we'd have to do it for everyone, wouldn't we?'

I went back to the coach. I had this image of Tom Cruise and Nicole Kidman going out for tea with their kids and being turned away because it was gone five. 'I'll pay you five thousand dollars for spaghetti and chips,' says Nicole. 'If I did it for you I'd have to do it for everyone, wouldn't I?' says the manager.

Alice was leading everyone down the coach steps by now. When I broke the news she looked at me as if I were making a joke.

'She's serious,' I said. So she marched to the café and knocked loudly on the door again.

The woman opened up. 'We're shut. I told him.'

'This tour always stops here,' replied Alice.

'You always come at four o'clock. I thought you

weren't coming.'

'But we're here now.'

'I've put everything away, sorry.'

She tried to close the door but Alice put her foot in. 'There are more than fifty people on that coach who want to come in here and spend money, probably three pound a head on food at least. They'll probably buy gifts as well, postcards, models of Wells Cathedral and the like. They're mostly American. They give big tips.'

'We can't make an exception.'

'You could make three or four hundred pounds.'

'Everyone would be wanting tea after five o'clock if we did that.'

'Really?'

'Yes.'

'Doesn't that suggest something? Doesn't that suggest that if you stayed open another hour maybe you could do a lot of business?'

The woman was confused now. 'We wouldn't get our evenings if we stayed open after five.'

'No, but you would be able to close for a month every winter and go to the Caribbean.'

The woman didn't respond. She had a glimmer of doubt in her eyes. She was imagining sipping cocktails from a coconut shell on the beach. 'Well, all right. They can come in for Coke and biscuits. But nothing hot.'

'Oh for God's sake,' said Alice. 'You know where you can stuff your Coke and biscuits.' And she turned and strode back to the coach. I hurried after her, caught her eye and grinned, but she didn't grin back. 'Some people,' she scowled, and it was that scowl that made me remember who she reminded me of: Maid Marian, as in *The Story of Robin Hood,* first published by Kingfisher 1994. ISBN 1 85697 2542. I suddenly wanted to make her like me.

Back on the coach she picked up the microphone and said, 'I'll be perfectly honest. We've had a dispute with the tea-room. She's refusing to open for us. I hope you will accept the apologies of Welcome and as we drive past feel free to make a rude sign.'

As we drove past the café window I tooted the horn to make the manager turn, and what she saw was a coach full of tourists from around the world making a variety of signs that were no doubt very uncivil in their own languages.

The rest of the drive to Bath was a cruise, through pot-bellied hills with the sunlight slicing into the valleys and the clients cooing at every thatched roof and red telephone box. As we came down into the city it looked rich and comfortable, the curves of the honey-coloured terraces open like outstretched arms. I pulled up outside the Montfort Hotel and everyone climbed down, legs asleep after the drive. I unloaded the luggage and went to park up in the overnight car park. As I locked up I felt like patting the bus on the side like a horse.

Five minutes later I was walking down corridors at the Montfort Hotel, swinging my key, trying to find room 418. I'd walked up and down so many stairs, across so many landings, through so many fire doors I wondered if I hadn't passed into an adjoining hotel, until finally at the end of a corridor was an arrow pointing up some steps, and there, next to a room marked *Do Not Block This Entrance*, was a little door with 418 on it.

It was cosy; some would have said small. There

was room for a bed and a wardrobe, basin and chair, leaving very little room for me. No bathroom, which was a disappointment, but I had a window, and it was my own space. I gazed out over the kitchen yard. 'I'm going to enjoy this room,' I said out loud.

I took my pressed shirt for the morning from my bag and hung it up. In the top compartment of the wardrobe I put my clean underpants, in the bottom I put my socks. Then I stripped off and stood in front of the mirror.

And what a friendly mirror it was, not like the one in our bedroom at home which made me pale and squat, and made my genitals look as though they belonged to someone else. This mirror made me look stretched, made my eyes shine blue and my legs appear longer and more hairy than usual. My penis looked smug. I turned to my profile. No excess there. *Stress has to surface somewhere*, I'd read in a men's health magazine at the barber's. Maybe, but it wasn't visible in this mirror.

I ate my fourth apple of the day and lay on the bed, the TV remote conveniently on the table next to me. I watched the news in the nude. The five-pieces-of-fruit-a-day story was right up there after the crisis in Sudan.

I switched the TV off, then looked in all the drawers for a sewing kit. I couldn't find one, so I rethreaded the lace on my left shoe because one side had got annoyingly longer than the other.

Then it was time for French. I sat by the window and opened my grammar book at the chapter on pluperfect verb endings: '*Les pompiers étaient arrivés.* ' The firemen had arrived.

I snapped the book shut. I had to get out of

there.

*   *   *

Gammon and pineapple with a choice of chips or baked potato, vegetables or salad and roll and butter for £5.95. That was in the Coach and Horses. Scampi in a basket with French bread and garnish for £5.80. That was the Old School House.

I strolled through town studying menus. The evening light had turned the stone pink, as though it would be warm to touch.

Cottage pie with a choice of vegetables or salad, roll and butter, £5.45 in the Green Parrot.

A couple walked past arm in arm. They stopped at a pelican crossing and he said: 'Allow me,' and then pressed the button for her. She giggled and they crossed the road, so close together they were tripping each other up. It had been ages since I'd been away on my own for an evening, and now of course I missed Kate and wanted her here to enjoy it with.

Cheese and broccoli quiche with a choice of chips or baked potato, salad or vegetable of the day with a roll and butter for £5.85 in the Old Coffee House Inn.

A tough character sat on the bench drinking from a can of Swan lager. He was wearing a black T-shirt, had tattoos and a pierced nose, and he was stomping his feet to music coming from his headphones. As I passed I could hear 'Nellie the Elephant'.

Bath seemed so unlike where I lived. In the Vaults Wine Bar you could get lasagne with chips or baked potato and a choice of salad or vegetable of the day with a roll and butter for £5.40. That sounded like the best deal in town. I looked through the window and there was Alice sitting at a table reading a magazine.

I watched her. She was nibbling something green, her eyes not looking at her plate but at the magazine folded flat on the table in front of her. She was dressed in jeans and a shirt and had lost the layer of make-up. During the day she had been so energetic and generous with herself, but here in a restaurant on her own, without her badge, she looked vulnerable. I didn't think she was really reading her magazine. It was just somewhere to put her eyes. My stare made her look up. She thought about it, but then gave me her half-smile, as if she didn't really want my company but I was better than nothing. I had to go in.

'Mind if I join you?'

'Yes,' she said.

Was she saying yes, she minded if I joined her; or yes, I could join her? She moved her magazine over to make room for me.

'I don't want to disturb you,' I said.

'I was just reading a questionnaire in *Cosmopolitan*.' She was trying to remove something stuck in her teeth with her tongue.

'What questionnaire?'

'Are you under stress?'

I ordered the lasagne with bread roll and garnish. The waiter didn't even write it down. 'Are you under stress?' I asked.

'I don't know. I've only done one question.'

I looked at the magazine. She read: *'Do you have a bright, enthusiastic view of the future?'* And then she looked at me, as if I should know the answer. I

94

said very seriously, 'Yes, I do.' Well, I did have an enthusiastic view of the future, most of the time, although it was heavily stretched at present.

'So do I,' she said after a pause, not looking up from the page. 'I'll put yes.'

She returned to her food. There was a silence, which I found awkward, although I wasn't so sure she did. I looked out of the window. There were very few people about. 'What's the next question?' I asked.

She stopped chewing and glanced at me, then suddenly looked confused.

'What?' I said.

'Are you Will Green?'

'Yeah.'

She sat back, nodded, and then smiled, a big smile. 'I know who you are now.'

'Who am I?'

'You chased that mugger?'

'Oh, that.'

'I know who you are now,' she said again. 'I didn't know I was with a celebrity.' She was suddenly happy to be with me. 'Do you do things like that?' she asked, but before I could answer she added, 'I saw your picture in the paper.'

There was another silence. She was waiting for me to say something about the incident. 'He got away with about seven hundred pounds,' I said, trying to sound modest.

'Doesn't matter. You went for him. That's great. That's brave. Well done. I don't think I've ever met a driver who would have done that.'

I shrugged. 'What's the next question in that survey?'

She grinned at my discomfort. *'Number 2. Do*

95

you become easily depressed? Can the slightest thing make you gloomy?'

'No,' I answered. The true answer to that was undoubtedly yes, but I wasn't admitting to it.

'Nor me,' she said. 'Although I do have what you would call mood swings.'

Now I wished I'd been more honest. 'Well, I have mood swings,' I said. 'We all have mood swings. But that's not depressed is it? It's just ... moody.'

'You're right. I'll put a cross. No. *Three: Is pressure at work undermining your relationship with your loved ones?'*

She lifted her head from the page and looked straight at me. I looked straight back. I was pretending to have a think about it. She said, 'These overnights don't make that sort of thing easy, do they?'

'I suppose they don't. No.'

I wondered if she was referring to my loved ones or hers? Did she or didn't she have any loved ones? I didn't want to know. It seemed to me neither of us was admitting to anything. 'Next question,' I said.

'Are you the sort who blames other people when things go wrong? No,' she said, very sure. 'I don't do that.'

'I don't either.' Well, I didn't. Except perhaps Kate and the kids. But that was what family was for, to support each other.

'Do you suffer from fatigue, disturbed sleep, indecisiveness, anxiety and irritability?'

I suffered from all those things. 'No,' I said, and almost laughed at the very idea.

'Nor me.'

96

My lasagne arrived, straight from the microwave. 'Plate's very hot,' said the waiter. 'Enjoy your meal.'

'Do you think you're good at what you do?'

'I think you're good at what you do,' I said. 'You're very good.'

'Thank you. I think you're good at what you do.'

'I don't do much.'

'That's clearly not the case, is it? As that mugger will testify. *Are you ambitious?*'

'Yes.'

'So am I. True.'

I wondered what she was ambitious for. I wanted to ask her, so that she would ask me, so that I could tell her I was currently in the process of raising money to finance an exciting new business venture. I noticed she wasn't wearing a wedding ring.

'Is your sex drive as strong as it used to be?'

I tried a mouthful of lasagne and scorched the roof my mouth. I spat it back on my fork and dived for her glass of sparkling water.

'Sorry,' I said and panted. 'Why do you think you're under stress anyway?'

She shrugged. 'There was a guide recently who took a tour to Canterbury. All the way down he behaved perfectly normally, but halfway through the tour of the cathedral he slipped into the York Minster tour. And for the rest of the day he made everything up. He had the Greeks invading instead of the Romans. He had Guy Fawkes blowing up Dover Castle. He claimed Folkestone was built of stone dragged on sledges from Wales. He resigned when he got back. He said his breakdown was the result of constant pressure from demanding tourists. He was sick to death of going to world-famous monuments and then standing with his back to them like the weatherman. He said he had grown to hate tourists—he had violent fantasies about them. He said they didn't listen to a word he said. What particularly annoyed him about that day was not one of the passengers noticed anything wrong.'

She was more at ease telling stories than answering questions. I said to her, 'Personally I like working with tourists. No other group of people are so predictable. That's important if you're trying to make a living.'

She looked at me like: give examples, and so I just launched into it. 'I used to run a sandwich shop, a good little place. It was in an unattractive area near Tottenham, loads of development everywhere. But I managed to get a loan, and we started to do very well. The builders used us. I was the only sandwich shop around. And they were a good bunch. They didn't just want egg and sausage sandwiches and stuff like that. They were willing to experiment. They were happy to try avocado and bacon bits. They liked tandoori chicken. They made you feel you were doing a worthwhile job. They used to wipe their feet when they came in. Management even started to use us. We had plans to expand—it was easier to borrow money in those days. The idea was that when they'd finished building, offices would open up and we'd turn part of the shop into a restaurant for office workers. The potential was huge. And then ... the contractors ran out of money. They were a German company; it was something to do with the performance of money markets world wide, I don't know. The building stopped. The workers got laid off. The knock-on effect killed us. We went bust very quickly.'

She nodded, chewing her food uncomfortably. I had not meant to sound emotional, but I clearly had done. I couldn't help it. It was my bloody sandwich shop!

Behind the counter a waiter sneezed over the vegetarian chilli. I said, 'I've forgotten why I told you that.'

'You were saying tourists are predictable.'

'That's right. I was just trying to make the point that that sort of situation would be less likely to happen with tourists. OK, some years are better than others, but there will always be tourists. You can't go wrong with tourists. It's going to be the big millennium earner, you know.'

She stirred some Sweet an' Low into her coffee. I blew on my lasagne and took another mouthful. It was lumpy, that was the best you could say about it.

'My sex drive is fine by the way,' I said.

'Oh, so's mine.'

She read: *Add up your scores. Eight to ten, you're well adjusted. Six to eight, you need to identify your problem areas and work towards finding solutions. Under six you are showing the symptoms of stress and depression and should seek help with counselling or drugs.'*

I didn't like the sound of this at all, but then she said, 'We both scored eight,' and she smiled contentedly and closed the magazine. 'We're both well-adjusted people.'

'Good,' and I knew we had both told each other a complete pack of lies.

*   *   *

Night had fallen by the time we left. I had that feeling of disappointment when you go to the cinema in the afternoon and emerge in the dark to find the world is still the same unresolved place. You've just seen a happy ending, and now you have to go home.

We walked back to the hotel. 'It's turned chilly,' she said and wrapped her arms around herself. I offered her my jacket. 'No no,' she insisted, but I put it round her shoulders. She felt my pocket. 'What's this?' I wondered what she might pull out, but it was my French grammar book. *Ah, parlez-vous français?'*

I laughed. *'Un petit peu.'*

'Alors, parlons français. Bath est une belle ville, oui?'

'Oui. Il est très vieux aussi.'

'Oui.'

She looked at me, waiting for me to speak next. Just when I needed it a fire engine siren wailed in the distance: *'Les pompiers étaient arrivés.'*

'Oui.' She was impressed with that.

'Parlez-vous beaucoup de . . . languages?' I asked full of confidence.

'Je parle français, and *un poco di italiano.'*

'Italiano, mon Dieu.'

She giggled. *'Tu parles français comme Victor Meldrew.'*

She used *tu* instead of *vous*. I wasn't sure if that meant I was related to her or she wanted to sleep with me.

I asked her where she lived. *'Où habites-tu?'*

'J'habite à Londres.'

She could have told me whereabouts but

presumably didn't want to. *'Avez-vous un chat noir ou un chat blanc,'* I asked.

'Je n'ai pas de chat.'

'Vous, I mean *tu n'avez pas un chat!'*

'Non.'

'Mon Dieu!'

'J'ai un lapin.'

'Qu'est-ce que c'est un lapin?'

She put her hands up to her face and put her teeth out and sniffed.

'Un hamster?'

'Non, non.' She rubbed her cheeks again, sniffed the air around her.

'Un guinea pig.'

She laughed again, and sniffed some more. I said, *'Je ne sais pas. Un* goldfish? *Mais c'est un* guess.'*

'No no, *un* rabbit!' she sighed.

'Oh, *un lapin. Bon.'*

We nearly touched then. Our shoulders almost brushed as we shared the same pelican crossing that the two lovers had earlier in the evening. Then again, in the hotel reception, I nearly put my hand on hers when the receptionist gave us our keys and Alice dropped hers and we both bent down to pick it up. I fancied there would be a spark of static when it did finally happen, a rush of energy that would cause a light bulb to explode in some far-off country.

The lift arrived with jolt. It was an antique with a grille that had to be dragged across. Inside was so cramped we had to try very hard not to be pressed together, but we managed it. I could smell her now though. The top of her head came to just under my nose. I studied the parting in her hair. I could feel a tension building, the sort of tension I'd forgotten. I closed my eyes and tasted lasagne. I had a vision of us touching once and then being all over each other. My leg began to shake. She turned and looked up at me. If ever there was a moment to kiss someone this was it. The lift shuddered to a halt, and a fifty-pence piece fell out of the hole in my trouser pocket and hit the floor.

'My floor,' I croaked. She bent and picked up the coin and handed it to me. There was nothing else to do but exit. With a hiss of hydraulics she was gone, and I was walking through the corridors heading for room 418. I noticed I had clenched fists. I was saying to myself, Well done. You resisted. I'm proud of you. You were in a tight situation and you did the right thing.

Back in my room I hunted round for the TV remote but it had disappeared. A chambermaid must have come in and hidden it. I hung my trousers up and stuffed my laundry in a plastic bag. Then I took my clothes off and looked at myself in the mirror again. The sunshine of the day had already made freckles surface on my forearms. I watched the pulse in my chest, the blink of my eye, the involuntary twitch of my groin, the silent running of my body. I removed the fluff from my belly button and flicked it across the room. I didn't want to sleep with her but I would like to have been asked.

*   *   *

The dining room in the Montfort Hotel had hunting scenes on the walls, on the chair fabric, on the place-mats and on the menu cards. Huntsmen and dogs chased foxes wherever one's gaze fell. I ate a grapefruit and made a mental note that when I moved into the Climbing Rose I would have only local watercolourists displaying their work on the walls. Customers could admire and even buy the paintings if they wished. A different painter each month would be given room to exhibit. I'd be a patron of local talent.

'I saw a recipe for cooking fox the other day,' said the Canadian woman to no one in particular. Her husband had his red beret on the table beside him, and this morning he wore glasses with sunshades clipped on to them like a visor. 'It was a kinda pot-roast, I think,' his wife said.

I sat on my own in the corner in my newly pressed shirt. Alice breezed in with good mornings for everyone, her make-up and Blue Badge back on again. 'Morning, Will.'

'Morning.'

And she strode past me as if nothing had happened between us the previous evening, which was precisely the case, of course.

And nothing happened between us for most of the rest of the day either, so that I started to think: Thank god I didn't make a pass at her last night. I mean, what was I thinking of? I could have lost my job. My family could have found out. I was putting huge investments at risk. And what was I doing thinking she found me attractive anyway?

But that afternoon, as we reached Stonehenge, I wondered if some degree of attraction between us wasn't inevitable. We were alone in the unusual world of tourists. We were drawn together because we were in a minority of two.

'Will, will you take a picture?' called the

Canadian woman. I turned to see her standing beneath a giant stone, holding her camera in one hand and Alice in the other. 'Come and stand here, Jack.' Her husband stood looking into the distance, his sunshades down like a closed shop.

I took the camera and stood with my back to the sun while they posed in the same manner they had doubtlessly posed before every monument in Europe—her with a sloppy grin, Jack with bow legs and a sneer. I focused through the viewfinder and all I could look at was Alice. I zoomed in on her; I looked at her body. 'Try and get those big stones in the background,' the woman called.

I took the picture and she was immediately moving everyone round. 'Now one with Will,' she said.

'What do you want a picture of the bus-driver for?' moaned Jack.

'Don't be so rude,' she said and pulled me between herself and her husband, then linked arms. The camera clicked. I wondered how many holiday pictures I had featured in.

'Now one of Alice and Will,' she said and Jack looked like he was going to bang his head against Stonehenge. His wife ignored him: 'Go on, put your arm round her, Will.'

And like two pieces of a puzzle my hip docked into Alice's waist, and I snaked my arm round her and she slipped hers round me. There was no hiss of steam or spark of electricity, just a sigh of cotton against polyester, but it seemed fitting that the moment should be caught on camera, and might even end up in a scrapbook in Montreal or wherever.

All the way back to London I imagined I could

smell Alice's perfume on my shoulder, and this time, as the city appeared on the horizon and the evening light stained the eastern sky ahead, I was aware that I didn't have the usual slump in my stomach, that cloud over my head. It was as if I had identified my problem area and brought about change without the need of drugs or counselling.

We dropped everyone off at their hotels and motored back to base in silence. 'That was good fun,' I said as I switched off the engine. She didn't reply; she was doing paperwork. I busied myself, not wanting the trip to end, not wanting to leave the bus.

Then when I got up to go she said, 'Hang on. Here.' I went to her and she squashed a bunch of money into my hand, coins and notes. 'Your half of the tips. Forty-six pounds and twenty pence each.'

'How much?'

'Forty-six pounds twenty p. I've never had so many.'

'Neither have I!'

'*Nous sommes une bonne équipe.*'

'What? Oh, *oui.*'

I hurried to the station and on to the tube, and flicked through my French book looking for a translation. *Nous sommes une bonne équipe.* We make a good team.

*   *   *

I had a bounce in my step as I walked down the street to the flat. I had a bagful of ice creams including a Magnum for Kate, and a bunch of tulips bought from the miserable florist at the station. I didn't get too upset at the dog turd

105

outside my door, and when I came in and found the stairway light on I didn't turn it off with an angry swipe.

The house stunk of vomit. The boys were in the bath. Kate was perched on the toilet looking dreadful, like she hadn't slept or had a moment's rest since I left her.

'What's wrong?' were the first words I said to her.

'We've all been sick. I was up all night with them. I had to wash all the sheets, and the washing machine flooded. It's gone through the floor and flooded downstairs. You'd better go and see them.'

The rubber pipe I had removed from the back had worked its way loose; I couldn't have secured it back in position properly. I went downstairs to Vinod and he led me into their first-floor living room where his grandfather was watching *University Challenge* and his mother was reading holiday brochures. It struck me how I'd never been in this house before; I'd lived above them for five years and knew nothing of their lives. The house was spotless and well decorated in bright colours, but now in the middle of the floor was a plastic tub collecting drips. The ceiling and one wall were dark and heavy with water.

'I'm sorry,' I said. Vinod's mother shook her head sadly. 'I'll fix it,' I promised. 'Don't worry. I'll let it dry out and then I'll decorate. The insurance will cover it.'

'I'd like it a different colour,' she said.

'Whatever you want.'

'Light terracotta walls. With a frosted yellow ceiling.'

'Fine. I'll do it on my next day off.'

I went back to the flat and found Kate in tears. 'What's wrong?' They were the second two words I said to her as well.

'I'm just relaxing.'

'You're relaxing by crying?'

'I've been wanting to cry for twenty-four hours but I've not allowed myself to while you've been away. Now you're back I can cry.'

She didn't answer. She just said, 'I'm exhausted. You do the kids, will you? I've had enough,' and she went to bed. I didn't offer her the Magnum. I felt guilty, and I didn't want to admit to myself why.

'Where are your pyjamas?' I asked Martin.

'I don't know.'

'In the laundry with sick on them,' said Stephen.

There were no clean pyjamas so they put on their Welcome Tours T-shirts. I gave Martin his asthma treatment. He sat there with his inhaler strapped to his face and showed me the drawing he had done at school the day before: an ocean with one island in the middle of it, and one human being on the island.

'Daddy,' said Stephen.

'Yes, my boy.'

'I prefer Mummy to you.'

It was good to be home. It was good to be home, I kept telling myself as I took a stroll to the bottle bank. It was almost full and the three bottles I chucked in made no impact. A very unrewarding visit. The man with the ponytail and the skip from Hamilton Road turned up and crammed bottles of Budweiser in. 'I wrote to the local authority and to Richard Branson about blue bottles,' he said.

'Oh yeah?'

'A woman by the name of Alison McGovern

107

from the Department of Environmental Health wrote back.'

'What did she say?'

'She said put them in green.'

'Well, there you go.'

'Unfortunately Richard Branson's Virgin Customer Service also wrote back and they said put them in brown.'

'Oh.'

'So back to square one really. I think I'll write to Friends of the Earth and Esther Rantzen next.'

As I walked back an ambulance sped past, blue light flashing, then it stopped about ten houses down from ours. There was a woman waiting on the pavement, and she stood aside as the paramedics jumped out and raced into her house. I stopped and watched from a distance. The paramedics reappeared minutes later carrying someone on a stretcher. They slid it into the back of the vehicle. The doors slammed shut. The blue light started flashing again. There was no siren, but somehow that was more unsettling. The woman was left on the pavement watching helplessly as the ambulance disappeared under the flyover. Then she went back indoors. I hadn't got a clue who lived there. It was as if this could have happened in any house in the street tonight. That one got unlucky, that was all.

I spent the evening sewing up the holes in my trouser pockets. When I thought of Bath it felt like it had happened to someone else. I was getting ready to go to bed when I saw a letter lying by the breadbin. It was a plain white envelope—not junk mail—and it was addressed to me in bold type. I felt uneasy because rarely did a letter come through the door without me knowing immediately who it was from or what was inside. When my sandwich shop was going bust a letter like this always meant bad news.

I slit the top and tried to peer in. The letterhead was a logo made up of the words 'Frame by Frame', and didn't mean a thing. So I opened it a bit more and read the first line: *Dear Mr Green . . .*

Then the second: *Thank you for the picture you sent of yourself and your son Martin . . .*

Frame by Frame were a casting agency. They had placed the advertisement for the father and son lookalikes. They said they needed a father-and-son team for a forthcoming television commercial, and they wondered whether Martin and I would like to go for an audition on Monday 11 May.

CHAPTER FIVE

LONDON'S WEST END
BY DOUBLE-DECKER

On Saturday morning I woke to see sunbeams playing on the bed. I got up and opened the thin curtains with a flourish. There was a scream of brakes on the motorway as a blue Renault went into a spin. A van from a builder's merchants in Northampton hit it broadside with a dead thud, then another car bounced off the back of the van. I saw a forehead hit a dashboard and decided that was enough. I drew the curtains closed and went to make some tea.

The rest of the day was spent redecorating

Vinod's parents' living room, perched up a ladder while life went on beneath me. Great-grandfather sat in his chair dressed in robes, speaking no English, emitting no sound at all but a gentle hum when food was handed him; Vinod's sister dropped off her children, and his mother fussed around them, following them with a sponge wiping their sticky fingerprints off surfaces; his father tried to watch the racing on the TV; his teenage brother sharpened his ice skates. I told them I could do this another time if they wanted and not be in the way, but no, they said I was no trouble. I felt invisible. I was a viewer trying to work out the plot from snatches of conversation.

In the afternoon great-grandfather was wheeled out into the yard, and he sat happily looking up at the motorway. Vinod's brother went to the ice rink and his parents took the grandchildren to the Cash and Carry. Vinod was left on his own to look after the shop.

'You want a cup of tea?' he said, holding one up to me.

I came down the ladder and sat on the bottom step. He sat at the table eating fruit. 'Is that a mango?' I asked.

'Yeah.'

'You sell many of them?'

'Yeah.'

'I've never had a mango.'

He got one from a box and threw it at me.

'I didn't mean . . .'

'Go on. Eat it.'

I had no idea how to eat it. I tried to peel it the way he had, but I made a mess down my front. He laughed at me. 'It's good?'

110

'Yeah.' And it was, even though I needed a bath afterwards, and strings of it got stuck in my teeth. 'Ever had papaya?' he grinned.

We split a papaya, then a pomegranate, and then he brought out passion fruit and figs. They were so sweet and fleshy, so fragrant and so strange. It felt odd to be having such an exotic experience so close to home.

Vinod was enjoying showing off to me. 'You have to eat five pieces of fruit a day to stop getting cancer,' he said.

'I read that.'

'So, one to go.'

For the finale he brought out a custard apple. The experience was so luxurious I felt it had to be forbidden. I felt drunk on fruit. I leant back with my belly swollen and said, 'Your business does all right, doesn't it? I mean, you keep busy.'

'We work hard.'

'What are you planning to do? Work here for ever or what?'

'This is my parents'. I want to start my own business.'

'What, a curry house or something?'

'No,' he laughed at me.

'What then?'

'A florist.'

'Round here?'

'There's money round here, you know. People like to shop local. Small businesses do well. Flowers are a good business too, and that grim bloke with the stall at the station is the only one who sells 'em. And he's just waiting for Princess Diana to die again. You have to make the effort. You have to build a reputation.'

111

Vinod had the right attitude. I said, 'I know what you mean. The general public has better taste than people think.'

'But most people in business don't give a shit,' he said with feeling. 'They think it's easy.'

'Most people in business are in the wrong business.'

He nodded. 'It takes a bit of thought. You need to think: If I went somewhere to buy a bunch of flowers how would I like it to be? I'd want to see good displays. A wide selection. Good lighting. Nice gift-wrapping, ribbons and bows. I'd want a good price. I'd want friendly service, and honest advice. It's not difficult.'

'I'll come to your florist. You come to my teashop.'

'What teashop?'

'I'm buying a teashop, the Climbing Rose. It's in the shadow of Anne Hathaway's Cottage near Stratford-upon-Avon. Nothing but homemade food, good service, children welcome, and an exciting range of arts and crafts available in the gift shop. French-speaking as well.'

'When's it going to open?'

'When I've got the money.'

'That's when my florist is going to open.'

We sat there with juice dribbling down our chins: two people who could have made the world a much better place, but were being denied the opportunity.

His parents came back and his mother set about preparing a meal. I climbed my ladder again and the room filled with rich cooking smells that rose up to me and overpowered my emulsion. An hour later an assortment of bowls was put on the table.

112

Vinod's sister returned with her husband. His young brother came back with a girlfriend. 'It's ready,' called up Vinod's mum, and I realized she had put a bowl out for me. I was still stuffed from the fruit, but I couldn't say no. I came down and sat with them and ate dal and curried vegetables, rice, a spinach dish and coconut sauce, and wonderful bread. The age range at the table was six months to ninety, and we talked about ice skating and fireworks and back axles, so that by the end of the meal I had decided that on Sunday I would get my dad round to our house and our family would have a proper Sunday lunch.

'Do you like living round here?' I asked Vinod on the pavement as I left.

'Yeah.'

'What about the motorway and everything?'

He shrugged. 'It's only a motorway.'

I called my dad that evening. He was impossible on the phone. No one I knew could get a call over so quickly. His aim, of course, was to save on the phone bill.

'Hi, Dad, how are you?'

'What do you want?'

'I wondered if you wanted to come round for lunch tomorrow?'

'No.'

'Of course you do. I'll cook a roast. You know, a Sunday dinner. Kate will come and pick you up.'

'There's no need to worry about me.'

'You're coming over. That's final!'

'All right, all right.'

He'd agree to anything rather than stay on the phone longer than thirty seconds.

Housework keeps you fit; Hoover the house and it burns off a cooked breakfast. That was what I read in the Sunday paper. So I wheeled out the old Hitachi. It moaned when I switched it on and then coughed out a cloud of dust. It was an anti-Hoover. The phone rang and it was Toby Jones.

'Mr Green? Just wondered if you'd thought any further about the Turbo Vac?'

'Yes. I'm thinking it's five hundred quid more than the other vacuum cleaners I've looked at.'

He laughed. 'But, Mr Green, the Turbo Vac is a complete homecare system. You can't compare it to high-street brands.'

'I'm also a bit worried about the Turbo Vac's ability to cope with microscopic irritants under point nought three millimetres long.'

There was a silence. Toby Jones wasn't to know it but I had become a subscriber to *Dustmite Magazine.*

'I think I'd better come round and demonstrate again,' he hedged.

'It's not too much trouble?'

'No, no, I'm local. How about Thursday evening, six p.m. ?'

'Fine by me.'

'We'll tackle the skirting boards and curtain pelmets.'

'Fine by me.'

* * *

My dad arrived and refused to take his coat off. He mumbled, 'It's almost twelve-thirty you know,' and

114

then he sat in the kitchen on the edge of a chair peering at what I was cooking, lifting saucepan lids and sticking his nose in. I liked cooking. It was time to myself. I liked to kick everyone out of the kitchen and turn the radio on and enjoy myself. This was driving me crazy.

'You want to par-boil those roast spuds,' he instructed.

'Why don't you go into the living room and have a drink? Read the paper until the meal's ready?'

'And you want to rough them up in the pan so you get crisp edges.'

'I'm cooking this meal, all right?'

'Yeah, but you won't get them crisp and brown your way.'

Learning to cook with Delia Smith had turned him into a fascist.

'I'm taking care of it, all right?'

'Do you want me to show you my carrot recipe?'

'No.'

'You just sprinkle them with brown sugar and bung them in the oven; gives them a glaze. Lovely. And don't go throwing the water from the parsnips away.'

'I'm not.'

'I'll take it home with me if you're not going to use it. It's good stock.'

'Fine, take it home with you!' I handed him the pot of water and pushed him into the living room where they were all doing the jigsaw of Waterloo Station. 'Kate, give him a sherry.'

'We haven't got any sherry!' answered Kate.

'I bought some.'

'You bought sherry?' She sounded truly astonished. 'Where is it?'

115

'In the drinks cabinet.'

'We haven't got a drinks cabinet,' she said, looking round the room.

'In the cupboard.'

'Bit posh,' muttered Dad.

'It's just sherry,' I said.

Kate poured herself and Dad a glass.

'Don't I get one?'

'Sorry,' she said, and poured me some in a half-pint tumbler.

'Is it Tesco's?' asked Dad.

'No.'

'They do a very well-priced South African at Tesco's, tastes just like Bristol Cream.'

'I'll get some crisps.' I went back into the kitchen and opened three packets of crisps in the hope I would be able to return to the living room thirty thousand pounds richer, but I wasn't.

At one o'clock I called everyone to the table and served up.

'I've got an itchy bottom,' said Martin, scratching himself like a dog.

'You need more roughage,' said Dad.

'Can we have a meal where we don't mention the word roughage?' I requested.

'What's roughage?' said Stephen.

Kate started to giggle. She had had too much sherry. She was very attractive and very annoying when she was in this state.

Martin reached out to fork a roast potato and knocked over his drink. I dived to catch it and knocked the spoon out of the gravy. Stephen tried to lick the mess off the table. I realized I was teetering on an edge. I controlled myself with a laugh: 'It wasn't like this when we were children,

116

was it, Dad?'

'It was exactly like this.'

'No it wasn't. I remember we had to brush our hair before mealtimes. We had to put our knife and fork down between mouthfuls. No elbows on the table. A glass of water with every meal.'

'You didn't?' said Kate.

'Course they didn't,' said Dad. 'He's making it up.' He took a mouthful of chicken and said, 'You should have taken the bird out and let it rest before you carved . . .'

He was only grumbling.

'That way you let all the juices seep back into the meat. Makes all the difference.'

'My bottom still itches,' complained Martin, reaching underneath himself with his fork.

'Can having an itchy bottom kill you?' asked Stephen.

Only an hour earlier I was wondering why we didn't have these family meals more often. The answer always became clear the moment we sat down to eat them.

My dad said to Kate, 'How's your Heritage Walk coming on?'

'Fine, thanks,' said Kate.

'What Heritage Walk?' I'd never heard anything about a Heritage Walk.

'The Heritage Walk I've been researching for the last three weeks.'

'You never told me about this.'

'I told you about it just the other day.' She looked at Dad and threw her eyes up. 'He's not really interested in my work.'

Why did they always gang up on me whenever we got together? I said, 'How can you have a

117

Heritage Walk round here anyway?'

'A lot of interesting people have lived round here,' said Kate.

'No they haven't. Who?'

But I never got an answer. Stephen somehow managed to tip his whole plate over himself. Peas and potatoes and gravy littered his lap. I yelled at him. Dad said, 'I've always admired the way the Chinese eat in their vests. That way you can get good and messy.' Kate couldn't stop laughing and then she started to choke. I smacked her on the back too hard, then suddenly remembered the apple pie in the oven. I dashed to the kitchen but it was burnt.

I wished Ted would turn up and take me down to the pub.

'I don't mind it burnt,' said Dad when I brought in the pie. 'Anything but waste it.'

It wasn't too bad if you smothered it in custard. I sat down again and wondered if we could salvage a family conversation from the wreckage of the meal. I said, 'Has Martin told you, Dad? He's going to be in a TV advert.'

'No he isn't,' said Kate. 'He's going to be in an audition.'

'We've been invited to an audition. Which we're going to win, aren't we, Martin?' And Martin leant back in his chair until it toppled, and he fell over backwards and banged his head on the radiator. I yelled at him.

'Can you kill yourself banging your head on a radiator?' asked Stephen and I yelled at him for a second time.

'It's one-thirty,' said my dad.

'Fuck off, Grandpa,' said Stephen.

118

We all fell silent. Martin picked his nose and ate it.

'Fuck off yourself,' said Grandpa, and took the newspaper to the toilet.

Kate giggled, and poured herself another sherry. 'Richard Todd,' she said.

'What?'

'The seventeenth-century actor, dramatist and songwriter. He was born on Argyle Road. He's on the Heritage Walk.'

I covered my face with my hands. That was when the children started to throw bread pellets, and my dad called out from the toilet: 'Oh look, Gary Rhodes is on tonight, eight-thirty, BBC2.' I sat there in my own little darkness and wondered, if right now I was suddenly to find myself in one of those impossible situations where I had to sacrifice my life for a member of my family—if, say, Stephen and I were in a plummeting, engineless plane with just one parachute between us, or if the only way to save Martin's life was by leaping in the path of a sniper's fire—whether I would do it. Would I give my own life to save theirs? And the answer was an overwhelming, and utterly incomprehensible, yes, of course I would.

*   *   *

On the morning of Monday 11 May Martin and I dressed for our audition in matching outfits: red checked shirts, black jeans, white trainers. I brushed his hair back, the way I brushed mine, bringing attention to our ears. I wanted them to see our ears. Our ears were very similar. Our ears were going to win this for us.

'My trainers are still too tight,' said Martin.

'Are you sure about this?' Kate frowned at me from the door; she was finally taking an interest.

'Where's the harm?'

'He's missing a morning of school.'

'For heaven's sake, it's an experience.'

'Selling your child?'

'Oh shut up.'

'Have you got his puffer?' she called after us.

Of course I had his puffer.

We boarded a double-decker to the West End. Martin ran upstairs and sat over the driver. I remembered how the idea of driving a bus was such a thrill as a kid.

I pulled a thread off his shirt. I wasn't selling him; I was doing this for him. Just say we did win, there'd be money in it. I didn't know how much, but he'd be able to buy new trainers for himself. Maybe I'd be able to buy us a new car, or at least get the old one fixed. Maybe I could buy a string of teashops. I had no idea. I flicked his hair back into place. A couple of women opposite beamed at us. We looked so much like a father and son. I beamed back. We needed to beam a lot today; we needed to project.

The address we'd been given was down an alley in Soho. We stopped outside and I gave Martin a last checkover. He already had a stain on his shirt. I put some spit on my hand and rubbed it and just made it bigger. 'We would have given you the job, Mr Green, but we didn't go much for the smudge on your son's shirt. So sorry.'

'What are we going to do in there?' asked Martin.

'I don't really know. Just hold your head up and

speak clearly, OK? They'll be looking for a father and son who can hold their heads up.'

I'd imagined a scene in which we were greeted by a pretty receptionist, given coffee and up-market biscuits, and then called into a smart white office with big windows. They'd ask us to read from a script, get to know us, maybe give us lunch, take a few pictures, exchange banter, and then say, 'You're both perfect. We'll be shooting next week. Will five thousand pounds up front be enough?'

But, of course, it was nothing like that. We took the lift to the third floor and there was a piece of paper Sellotaped to the white wall, felt-tipped with the words *Frame by Frame Casting* and an arrow pointing down the corridor. We followed more signs to two large swing doors, and pushed them open to find ourselves in a large cold room with about fifty fathers and their lookalike sons.

Every one of them looked like they'd just stepped out of an advertisement. And of course no father had made the mistake of dressing up in the same outfit as his boy. The idea was to dress down—the kids had basin haircuts, the dads had stubble. Martin and I had beginners written all over us.

'Would you just like to give me your names?' I turned to see a woman wearing her hair up like a carrot top and a shirt the shape of a tent.

'Will and Martin Green.'

She checked us on a list, gave us a professional smile, told us her name was Vanessa and that it might be a wait. 'Don't worry. Drinks are on their way.'

'What do we actually have to do?' I asked, sounding more like the child than the father.

121

'Oh, they'll tell you once you get in there.'

'In where?'

But her phone rang and she was gone. We found some seats next to a man doing a newspaper crossword and his son playing with a computer game. I said good morning to him and he replied with a sound that wasn't a recognizable word. He glanced at me as if I'd come to do the drains or something.

Many of the fathers seemed to know each other. Each new arrival was met by some other hopeful with open arms and big hand shakes. The children snarled. They had names like Casper and Jason, and they spoke with London accents, while their fathers sounded as though they'd just come off the grouse moor. Martin sat on his hands and looked round the room. He muttered, 'I don't know any of them.'

'Any of who?'

'The other children.'

I knew what he meant.

The man next to me with the newspaper spoke: 'Where was Picasso born?'

It took me a moment to realize he was speaking to me, asking me for help with his crossword.

'Picasso?'

'Yes.'

'Picasso. Don't know. Sorry.' Prat. Honestly.

'Do you know any mountain range in Romania—other than the Carpathians?'

'Nope.'

He looked at me now, sitting there with my arms folded. 'You should have brought something to read. I couldn't sit there like that and do nothing.'

Every so often a man in shorts and clutching a

clipboard came in and called out two names, and a father-and-son team would jump up and go with him. But there seemed to be little order. I said to my neighbour, 'What we need is numbered tickets like you get at delicatessen counters in supermarkets, huh?'

He yawned and said nothing.

Martin leant heavily against me. 'I'm bored.'

'It'll be our turn soon.'

'Not for some time,' said our neighbour. 'You should have brought something with you.' He turned to his son: 'Harvey, lend this boy something to play with.'

Harvey didn't like the idea of that at all, but his dad insisted.

'He can play with this,' said Harvey. 'The batteries are going flat.'

It was another computer game, a Gameboy. Harvey handed it to Martin. Martin didn't know what to do with it. 'He doesn't know how to work it,' sighed Harvey.

'Yes I do,' said Martin.

'Well, show him,' said Harvey's dad.

Harvey sat next to Martin. Martin sat back with contempt in his eyes as Harvey showed him round the Gameboy and said things like, 'Don't you even know how this works?'

Harvey's dad said to me, 'I don't mind them playing with the computer as long as they learn something from it.'

'I know what you mean.' We had a computer at home, one of those old Amstrads with the green screen. You needed to bang the top of it every time you switched it on. The only thing you learnt from it was how to be patient.

'He's got this Playstation at home with a football game on it. You can have any country in the world play any other country. It's actually very good for their grasp of geography. Before I let Harvey play on it I make him find out the home team's capital city, language, longest river and main export.'

I didn't know what the hell he was talking about.

'He goes and looks it up on the main computer upstairs—we've got a children's encyclopaedia CD. Or he even looks it up on the Internet.'

I had an urge to headbutt this man. He was underlining the secret fear I had that by not giving my children a computer they had already been left far far behind.

'Computers aren't everything,' I said, the chant of a person whose life is so undynamic he doesn't even have a password.

Harvey's dad shrugged. 'You're probably right.' Another condescending smile, and he went back to his crossword.

But something had occurred to me concerning Harvey and his dad: they didn't look very much alike. In fact, a glance around the room showed me that not many of these father-and-son teams did. The ones with the red hair stood out, but otherwise it seemed to me Martin and I were in with a good chance. My confidence resurfaced. I said to Harvey's dad, 'You've done this sort of thing before, have you?'

'Oh, many times.'

'Is this a lot of people?'

'Yes. It's annoying, to be honest. The agencies are normally more selective. They don't really know what they want, you see.'

'It's our first time.'

124

'Have you got an agent?'

'No.'

'You need an agent. Bryan Harper at CTP is all right. I'm with him.'

I made a note of the name. Bryan Harper was the one man I didn't want as my agent.

Harvey snatched the Gameboy back from Martin. 'You'll break it like that! He'll break it.' Martin looked at me like: I'd rather be at school than here. I winked at him.

I said to Harvey's dad, 'You get a lot of work, do you?'

'Fair amount. Not much telly any more. That's why this place is so crowded, everyone wants to do telly, pays much better. I get mostly catalogue and brochure work. I've been doing it a long time. I was in the Milky Bar adverts back in the seventies.'

Never. 'You mean, "The Milky Bar Kid is big and strong?"'

'"The Milky Bar Kid just can't go wrong." That's right. That was me. I was the Milky Bar Kid for three years.' He folded his arms and looked smug.

He was lying. He looked nothing like the Milky Bar Kid. I said, 'What happened to the glasses, then?'

'Oh, I never wore glasses; they gave me a clear pair to wear for the filming. None of us wore glasses.'

'You mean there was more than one of you?'

'Oh yes. As one got too old they just drafted in another.'

'What, like Lassie?'

'Exactly. The Milky Bar Kid campaign lasted about ten years. The first boy was fifteen by the

125

time I came along.'

'I never knew that.'

'We have reunions now and then—all the Milky Bar Kids. The original lad was called Terry Brooks. He's a grandfather now. He drives a truck, I believe.'

Vanessa finally came round with a trolley of drinks. By the time she got to Martin and Harvey there were just two bottles left, a cherry cola and an orangeade. They both went for the cherry; they both had their hands on it. If this had been Stephen and Martin I knew how nasty it could get.

'Let him have it, Martin,' I told him.

'No,' said Martin.

Harvey's dad didn't say anything, no doubt trying to foster a competitive spirit in his kid. This was the kind of situation the boy would have to face in future life. I just didn't want Martin to get over-excited and start coughing. 'Let him have it, Martin. We'll have an ice cream afterwards.'

Martin let him have it, but he hated me for it. He kicked me. I smiled at Harvey's dad. He had turned to the business section of his paper.

I wanted to know what Harvey's dad did for a living, but that was a question I never asked people these days because then they felt obliged to ask me what I did. He'd only say he worked in computers anyway.

But then he folded up his paper, gave another yawn and asked, 'So what do you do?'

'Me? I have a restaurant.' It just came out. I didn't dare look at Martin.

'That's nice. Whereabouts?'

'Near Stratford-upon-Avon.'

'Very nice. What's it called?'

'The Climbing Rose. It's a restaurant and gift shop. I'm in the process of doing it up. It's a good little business. What do you do?' I needed to change the subject before he tried to book a table.

'I'm unemployed at the moment.'

I felt a surge of glee that was difficult to suppress. 'Oh, well. Something will turn up. Always does.'

'It's no bother. My wife has a software business. It's nice to spend some time at home with Harvey in fact.'

I was trying to think of the last time I had hit someone. It was at school when I was about thirteen, and I was provoked far less than this.

Another hour passed. The man in the shorts came in and asked for Harvey and his dad. 'Good luck,' I called after them, happy to know I'd never see them again. I played scissors, paper, rock, with Martin. He won fifty-eight to forty-five. Vanessa tried to get the kids involved in a singing game, until a lad with a bubble-cut fainted and was carried out and never seen again. I wanted to go home after that. When our names were finally called I really didn't care any more.

The young man in shorts led us into a much smaller, much warmer room where we were introduced to a casting director, a photographic director and a director director. To one side was a white screen the size of the wall and trained on it was a range of lights and a video camera on a tripod. We were asked very nicely if we wouldn't mind standing against the screen, Martin in front of me. We did as we were told. Martin said, 'Are we on TV now?'

No one cracked a smile. They were either taking

us very seriously, or not seriously at all.

'It's our first time,' I said.

'You're doing fine,' said the photographic director as he focused his camera on us. The casting director wrote something down. The director director said to us, 'OK, just tell us your name, how old you are, and the name of your agent? When you're ready.'

A light came on on the camera. I looked into it, gave a big smile and said too loudly, 'Will Green. Aged thirty-seven and a half. My agent is Clarissa at Broomfield and Whitton. Your go, Martin.'

'My name is Martin Green, I'm eight and half. My shoes are too tight.'

'Great,' laughed the director. 'Now. Can you drink this for us?'

We were brought a bottle of Robinson's Lemon Barley Water and two full glasses on a tray. We drank them happily. They filmed us drinking happily. We put the glasses down and licked our lips and the casting director said, 'That's great. Thanks very much. We'll let you know.'

That was it? 'That's it?' I said.

'Yep. Thanks for coming.'

'So . . . that's it?'

'Yeah.'

Three minutes later we were outside, blinking in the sunshine, not knowing what to do next. We bought ice creams and found a little park to sit in. Someone had left chewing gum on the bench and it stuck to Martin's trouser leg. He didn't care, and I didn't either. He said to me, 'Dad?'

'What?'

'Can we go to Disneyland one day?'

'One day.'

*   *   *

When we got home Kate was hanging laundry over the back of the television. It was the only space in the house left. I flopped into a chair. Martin went to the jigsaw. Kate looked at me: 'Well?'

'Well what?'

'How did it go?'

'Fine. He's a natural talent. So am I. They've given us a hundred grand and we're going to be on the Royal Variety Performance.'

The corner of her mouth looked like it might just curl into a told-you-so smile.

'Don't laugh at me,' I warned her.

'I'm not laughing.' She hung a pair of pyjamas from the doorhandle. 'But I mean, what did you expect?'

I just wanted to say something that would hurt her. 'You know, for someone who is so good at giving money away you are very, very uninterested in doing anything about earning it!'

She stopped, clutching a sock. 'What's that supposed to mean? I bring in money. I do my bit.'

'A bit isn't enough.'

'It's the best I can do.'

'It's not enough!'

I got up and left the room. I wanted to blame her for not owning a software company that could see us through this period. She called after me, 'Don't walk away from me!'

I grabbed my costume and a towel. 'I'm not arguing with someone who hasn't the slightest idea what I'm talking about.'

The pool was the best place to be. The sharp

taste of chlorine always soothed me. I did lap after lap, paying no attention to anyone else in the water. I wanted to drain myself of all energy. Swimming was the panacea. Fuck the Milky Bar Kid, and the director director, and fat Vanessa. Fuck Kate too. I imagined them all on a zebra crossing. I was driving my Welcome coach; I had them in my sights and I mowed them all down. All except Kate to whom I gave another chance, as long as she promised to come up with three original money-spinning ideas by morning.

My legs collided with someone, but instead of pulling away I kicked out. 'Well really!' The voice fell away as my head went under and I exhaled. I didn't look back. I was swimming away from a sinking ship, saving myself.

Kate called from the kitchen when I came in: 'Graham from work phoned. He wants you to do another overnight.'

'What night?'

'Thursday.'

I didn't say anything. I picked up the newspaper. *Ten dead in American Midwest heat wave.*

'Did you hear me?'

'Yes.'

She came into the sitting room and stood at the door. 'You know Martin has an asthma clinic appointment on Friday morning. You said you'd take him.'

'I'll take him next week. They don't mind.'

'And you know I'm chairing a meeting that night, Thursday.'

'No, I didn't know that.'

Ten-year-old fails in Channel swim bid.

'It's been on the calendar for three weeks. Can't

130

you go away another night?'

'Ask Graham, not me.'

'If it was anything else I'd do my best to get out of it, but I can't get out of this.'

I looked up from the paper. 'What meeting?'

'It doesn't matter what meeting.'

'What meeting?'

'The Continuing Struggle in East Timor.'

There was no answer to that.

She spoke very calmly. 'If you go on this trip it's going to mean paying for five hours' babysitting.'

'If you don't go to your meeting not only will we save five hours' babysitting, we'll be thirty pounds plus tips in profit.'

The door closed quietly. I heard her slippers pad into the bedroom, then that door closed quietly too.

I went downstairs to Vinod's and bought a mango and a roll of dental floss.

CHAPTER SIX

YORK AND A TOUR OF BRONTË COUNTRY

Roy came to speak to me as I settled myself into the driver's seat.

'I don't want to buy anything,' I said.

'Blimey, I was just going to ask you if you were all right.'

'I'm all right. Why?'

' 'Cos you don't look all right.'

'I'm all right. Why do people keep asking me if

131

I'm all right?'

'You'd better be all right,' and he winked at me.

'What?' And then I saw Alice walking across the tarmac from the waiting room.

Roy leered: 'Graham says she asked for you special.'

She stopped to speak to a couple who looked lost. She waved at another guide. She was heading my way. I thought: Just as I'm about to give up, there she is again, walking towards me.

'Are you sure you're all right?' grinned Roy.

'Next person who asks me if I'm all right gets a smack in the mouth. All right?'

'All right, all right.'

*   *   *

I didn't know what to do so I decided to ignore her. I ignored her all the way up the M11 to Cambridge. I told myself the whole idea was ridiculous. Maybe she had asked Graham for me as her driver, but only because of the tips we had earned the last time. That was all it was—a professional and a perfectly understandable request. And anyway, she was probably in a relationship. And what did it matter if she wasn't? I was. She may not have had a ring but I did. I made no attempt to hide that. I made sure it was in full display as I sat with my hands grasping the steering wheel. I mean, I was beyond this sort of thing. Kate and I had got affairs out of our system in our long period of non-commitment before we settled together. We knew how these situations were destined to be disasters, how they ended with a bad taste in the mouth and a wish you'd gone home when you had the chance.

132

Affairs were for the immature, for people stuck in dodgy marriages.

I continued to ignore her in Cambridge. While she took the punters off on a tour of the university colleges I went to Millet's and bought a new shirt: a pale blue cotton number for £2.99. I could have bought two for £4.99 but decided against it.

We motored a few miles out of town, then stopped for a 'traditional pub lunch' in one of those chain-inns, a huge roadside affair called the Wheatsheaf that may once have been a local inn, but was now eighty per cent car park and had bars on three levels. All the clients became confused because they had to order their drinks from one counter and food from another. The woman behind the bar lost her patience with a couple from Holland because they used words she didn't understand—not Dutch words, English. She yelled at them the way I did at my children. Finally one of our party managed to order a pork pie without annoying the management, so everyone one else did the same. They sat there munching cold crusts and drinking ginger beer. Alice sat trapped among them. She looked at me once and smiled hopelessly, but there was nothing I could do. I bought a packet of crisps and went back to sit on my own in the coach. There I studied auxiliary verbs for half an hour. *Je ne l'ai pas vu*—I have not seen him. Up on the luggage shelf I saw her overnight bag and I was tempted to have a look inside, but I resisted and made do with reading the address-tag: *14a Tremayne Rd, London N4*. I imagined her in a one-bedroomed flat with wooden floors and thick curtains, shoes off, feet up on the couch, supper on a tray, watching telly on her own.

I ignored her throughout the afternoon as well, as we headed up the A1 and she told stories of Dick Turpin and Black Bess. 'No one is to worry though,' she joked, 'a Welcome coach hasn't been held up by a highwayman for, ooh . . . weeks now.' The clients all laughed and then she glanced at me and added: 'It doesn't matter anyway. We've got Will as our driver. He could deal with a highwayman, couldn't you, Will?' I blushed, but didn't look at her. I kept my eyes on the road ahead, the Great North Road to York.

I managed to keep this up until five o'clock in the afternoon when we rolled up outside our hotel and everyone filed off the bus. She and I were the last and as she reached to get her bag her waist-length jacket rode up and pulled her blouse with it so that I could see flesh above her skirt, a smooth and curved marble-shaded band of back. I looked away, but this glimpse of her had burnt a trail across my eyes. I could think of nothing other than sliding my hand up inside her clothing. Suddenly I realized she was talking to me.

'You know that couple from Mexico?'

'Yes.'

She moved closer to me, almost whispering. 'They think we're on the James Herriot Tour. I can't convince them.'

She giggled and clutched my arm, and I realized that trying to ignore her just wasn't going to work.

*　　　*　　　*

My hotel room in York was notable because it achieved with ease what I had thought was impossible: it was smaller than the one in Bath.

134

Everything in it seemed miniature: the half-size wardrobe; the nine-inch TV, the skylight window. Even the bible was a pocket version.

I lay on the bed with my feet sticking over the end and reminded myself I was here to do a job, not to be pampered. I was here to earn money for my wife and family. I was only in this room to sleep. I was going out now to find a chip shop, then back to watch *The X Files* and an early night.

I strode silently through the thickly carpeted, heavily double-glazed corridor to the lift. I pressed the button and the machinery ground away above me. I whistled softly. I counted my teeth with my tongue. I peered through an ajar bedroom door where a cleaning trolley stood against a wall, and there I noticed a flash of red and grey. I moved closer and took a second look. It was the unmistakable outline of a Brock XL.

The Brock was the American vacuum cleaner favoured by hotels and commercial premises world wide—apparently they had one in the White House. It was the executive vacuum cleaner. Not only did it have a unique bristle action which vibrated grit and grease off the carpet to a depth of five millimetres, it also had a vacuum pump actually isolated in the unit's handle which gave an enhanced air-filtration process. Brocks were expensive, but they were the cleaners' cleaner.

I couldn't resist it. No one with an interest in vacuum cleaners could have. There were no chambermaids about so I decided to give it a whirl.

To begin with I found it very impressive. I thought: Here is an intelligent vacuum cleaner. You just pointed it and it was off, sniffing out dust, as if on auto-pilot. It was like dancing with someone who knew all the steps. But as I moved out of the bedroom and gave it a go on the straight, it seemed to me to be sluggish, overweight, and the dual motor made it the noisiest model I had tested so far. As I passed the lift the doors opened and I wondered if I should take it downstairs and give it a proper workout in one of the reception areas, then I glanced up and saw Alice looking out at me.

I clicked off the machine; it exhaled and fell silent. I grinned at her. She was out of her work suit again, dressed in a black skirt and a baggy pullover.

'It's a Brock,' I said.

'A what?'

'A Brock XL. Supposed to be one of the best vacuum cleaners on the market. They claim to remove ninety-nine point eight per cent of allergens, and that's an impressive performance, believe me. Unfortunately it handles on the heavy side, feels like a bit of a dinosaur. Parts are expensive as well—and hard to get hold of in this country.'

She nodded keenly. She was trying to be kind.

'Going down?' I asked.

'Yes.'

'Good,' and I stepped into the lift with her.

*   *   *

If there were a newspaper column entitled *My Perfect Evening*, that night in York would have to be my entry. Alice and I left the hotel together and walked round the damp town looking for somewhere to eat. A town crier was performing in a square and we joined the small crowd. 'Hear ye, hear ye, hear ye. A lorry jack-knifed this morning

136

on the road to Leeds.' He was a big man with big feet and a big beard. He had presence the way television newscasters didn't. 'Local doctor flies to Sudan as the crisis grows worse,' he bellowed as I led Alice away.

We walked nowhere in particular. We wandered like tourists, following any alley or street that took our fancy. We climbed some steps and emerged on the old town walls. She said, 'I'm always a bit frightened coming to York. I'm afraid I'm going to bump into my ex-husband.' She had a way of personalizing everywhere. Places were always backdrops for events in her life.

'He came from here?' I asked, trying not to be bothered.

'Still does, I think.'

Now I was worried we were going to bump into him. They'd stop and have to talk and they'd suddenly realize they'd made a big mistake. They'd make up and walk off together and my evening would be ruined.

'How long were you married for?'

'Just a year. I think I only married him because a number of other women wanted to. I had three rivals. He used to play us off against each other. We should have just ganged up on him, but instead we competed for him. He was into outdoor activities, walking and climbing, that sort of stuff, and he decided to give this party. All he put on the invite was *come to my party at . . .* and he wrote a map reference, and *please bring a bottle.* I checked it on a map, and it was in the middle of the Yorkshire Moors. I phoned him to see if he was joking, but there was no answer, and so I thought, well I'm not letting the other two beat me. So I bought a train ticket to some tiny, Godforsaken place in the middle of nowhere, and stayed the night in a bed and breakfast where I found someone's sock in my bed. Then in the morning I hiked five hours to this pile of rocks on a moor somewhere.'

'And he was there?'

'Yes. He was drunk. He'd carried three bottles of nice wine in his rucksack and drunk the lot. All he said to me was: "You're late."'

'Did the others turn up?'

'Of course they didn't. They never left home. They weren't so stupid. I climbed in his sleeping bag and he said to me, "I'm yours. You've won me." And then he proposed. I was so pleased with myself for beating the other two I accepted. We had our honeymoon on the Pennine Way.' She started to laugh and I couldn't help laughing with her.

'Never again,' she said.

Was she saying she would never marry again, or go on the Pennine Way again, or be so devoted to a man again? As before I decided I didn't want to know. I liked the way we gave each other only what information was necessary. I got the feeling our time together was limited; we were like strangers meeting on holiday. These overnights took place in a world far away from the one we had both left behind at the bottom of the motorway. There was no thought of family or mortgages here. There were no issues to confront. I was happy to be sheltered in this walled city for the night where no one from outside could reach us. If this was to be a holiday romance then we could be whosoever we wanted to be; there was no need to start worrying

138

about real lives.

I said to her, 'Describe your fridge to me.'

'It's oblong and white.'

'I mean what's inside it.'

'Why do you want to know that?'

'A person's fridge defines them.'

She shrugged: 'Left-over vegetables. A half-tin of tuna fish. Some cream past its best-before—'

I interrupted her: 'You mean there's not a bottle of Australian white wine and some crème fraîche?'

She grinned and thought again. 'Well yes ... there is some Australian white wine and fromage frais actually. And there're free-range eggs and ... olives and Jarlsberg cheese, that's my favourite, I like to spend lots of money on good cheese. There are mushrooms, bacon, exotic jams ...'

'You keep your jam in the fridge?'

'Yes.'

'See.'

'See what?'

'I told you a person's fridge defines them.'

'Keeping jam in my fridge doesn't define me!'

'What else?'

'Er ... fresh orange juice, fresh pasta, and there's a giant bar of Toblerone for emergencies.'

'What emergencies can a giant bar of Toblerone help with?'

'The emergency that occurs when the bar in the top cupboard is finished.'

Eventually we found a chip shop and had cod and chips and mushy peas, and we ate them in the orange glow of the floodlit Minster, sitting on a bench in memory of Mrs Margaret Barnes-Patterson. We told each other more stories. We seemed most comfortable communicating in that way. She told me about the time she watched television for twenty-four hours non-stop to raise money for a kidney machine, and how she once went three days without knowing the clocks had gone forward. I told her about the time I entered a Buddy Holly impersonation contest and came third, and the time when the fire engine sped past and I said a prayer, and it turned out to be our own house that was on fire.

When we did swop personal information it was trivia. After describing our *Fridge File* to each other we went on to swop our *My Hols* and *Break of Day*.

'What's *Break of Day*?' she asked.

'It's a new one. I think it's in the *Express*. People describe how they like to start their day. The one I read had Sebastian Coe. I can't remember anything he said except he doesn't start his day with a run.'

'I like to start the day with croissants and a cup of coffee on a tray with some nice letters propped up in a toast rack.'

'What do you mean, nice letters?'

'No brown envelopes. Airmail letters, or at least letters with handwriting on the front. And a poem, that would be nice. I'd like whoever brought me the breakfast to read a little poem to start the day.'

'What poet?'

'Wordsworth.'

She looked up at the Minster and I looked at her neck. I didn't think she had a lover. I had the feeling instead that she was a sad soul who had been unlucky in love, always gone for the wrong sort—like her first husband—and she had given up trying.

A mist drifted into the city. We walked back to the hotel with our footsteps echoing on the

140

cobbles. The Minster glowed like something industrial. 'Do you think the town crier sleeps with his bell by the side of his bed?' said Alice.

Then we were back in the hotel waiting in silence by the lift doors again. We stepped in and as the doors closed I inhaled her perfume. My pulse thumped. I wet my lips and felt my face pale. I think I had stopped blinking.

'Are you all right?' she said, and I couldn't smack her in the mouth so I took hold of her and kissed her on the mouth for three floors. The lift came to a stop making the same noise our lips did as they parted. I swallowed heavily and said, 'Come back to my room.'

'No.'

'Good. Well done. Well resisted.'

'Your room sounds awful. Come back to mine.'

Her room was roughly five times as big as mine. I stood by the door picking up brochures and pretending to find them interesting. I watched her as she went to the window and pulled the curtains shut on her view of the Minster. I saw her skirt ride up her legs as she bent over the writing table and turned off a lamp. These illicit peeks of her body excited me beyond belief. I wanted to bury my face in her.

She went round the room turning off all the lights except one, so that the bed was back-lit with an arc of shade slung across it. I had decided not to say anything more—I didn't trust myself. I would just be physical from now on; I would act instinctively. As she passed within my grasp I reached out for her and pulled her towards me. Her arms hooked around my neck. Our lips hit so hard our teeth collided. I steered her towards the

141

bed, carefully avoiding pieces of furniture.

The smell and the taste of her body was irresistible now. I was running my hands over her and fumbling for fasteners. A button popped off her shirt and I watched it roll across the floor in slow motion and eventually settle under the luggage rack. 'Calm down,' I said to myself, and I tried to think of some film in which I might have admired the way the hero seduced the heroine, so I could think myself into the part. I dismissed Batman and all the Disney characters that immediately came to mind, until there alone stood Harrison Ford in that film about the Amish, *Witness*. There he was gripping Kelly McGillis with such passion there was a pool of frustration left on the floor. I had this scene running behind my eyelids as I held Alice's face and kissed her with what seemed to me like a huge longing.

Our clothing peeled away. There was a jangle of coins and car keys as my trousers hit the floor, and then there we were with nothing else to do but look at and touch each other's nakedness. I puffed my chest out, held my stomach firm and ran my hand down her thigh. It was time to say something.

'I knew as soon as we met we'd make love.'

Which was a bit corny and was also untrue, but she smiled so sexily in the half-light, with wisps of hair falling across her face, that I think I got away with it. 'So did I,' she replied. That was a lie as well.

She lowered her head and kissed my chest and a foreplay checklist popped up in my mind, the one I was so used to ticking off before I made love to Kate. I was with a different woman in a strange room, but I had to start somewhere familiar.

And it all seemed to work wonderfully well, at

142

least as well as can be expected for the first time. She looked so happy to be with me. She gasped and smiled just when I needed her to, and I loved the way her eyes grew glassy, and her shoulders arched with excitement. I became breathless with desire. I couldn't remember how I got here. I was driving a coach up the A1 and everything went blank. I just didn't want it to be over—I knew how bad I was going to feel afterwards. Then somewhere outside a clock struck out for midnight. I tried to count the chimes but by the third I was lost.

I lay with my face buried in the pillow, trying to turn my back on the tide of melancholy that began to creep over me even before the last waves of pleasure had died away. I felt sad because my life was normally so different from this. My life didn't take me to these parts of the world, into bedrooms this size with luxury bathrooms. This was an existence inhabited by other people, the sort I ferried around and was sometimes lucky enough to get a tip from.

Then I was awash with guilt. I thought of Kate and remembered that Toby Jones had said he would come round to our house last night to redemonstrate the Turbo Vac. Kate would have had to deal with him. They could have gone to bed together and I wouldn't be able to object.

I looked at Alice's shoulder, knowing that something was gone for ever. I was full of sighs. The best thing was to go to sleep.

That same clock woke me as it struck four o'clock. I sat upright, very sober, very alert, knowing exactly where I was. I lifted back the curtain an inch and saw the grey dawn render the Minster shapeless. Then I turned very slowly to see

Alice sleeping on her side, just the thin sheet pulled over her. With the light of the dawn lying across her she looked like a sculpture under wraps. I picked up my clothes and tiptoed to the bathroom to get dressed. Alice used Colgate toothpaste and wore contact lenses.

The bedroom floor creaked as I crept for the door. As I turned the key I saw the button that had sprung from her clothing on the floor under the luggage rack. I got down on my knees and picked it up, and put it on the table by the bed. I made so much noise I must have woken her. By the way she lay so still I could tell she was pretending to be asleep. She knew I was sneaking out, and she didn't want to stop me and ask why.

Stepping out into the corridor was like jumping off a moving train. I felt something carry on without me. With my feet on the ground again I walked quickly down the corridor and up the stairs to my room. There I tucked myself up in my own bed; the kitchen staff were already working in the yard outside my window. I lay under the covers for a moment, reminded of being in my bedroom as a child. This was where I felt comfortable, but I sensed that this was where I could not stay much longer.

*   *   *

And then I was back to ignoring her. But she seemed to accept this behaviour, encourage it even. She cared about her job; she wore her Blue Badge with pride and didn't want to appear unprofessional, whereas I didn't give a toss.

From York we drove to Haworth, the village at

the heart of Brontë Country. 'I think she wrote Jane Austen,' said a South African voice as Alice led them away. She took them on a walking tour of the village, and then to the parsonage where the Brontë family once lived. I found a gift shop and bought a box of fudge with a photo of some Swaledale sheep on the front for Kate, and a *101 Dalmatians* multi-pen each for the kids.

As I drove back to London the waves of remorse came riding in from the west and settled in the form of a low-grade pain across my chest. I found my lips moving as I struggled to conjure some defence. It was *Confessions of a Coach-driver*, that was all, I told myself. Ask any driver and they'd say it had happened to them at one time or another. I'd just imagined that if and when it did happen to me it would have been with someone called Betty from Ohio and we'd have done it on the back seat of the bus in the corner of the coach park while everyone else was on a tour of Blenheim Palace.

As we came into London on the Finchley Road we hit heavy traffic. But I was glad of the time to think. I knew that before I parked this bus I had to find a way to salvage something positive from this trip, or I might go home and do something stupid—like tell Kate exactly what had happened.

Then I found my excuse as we passed the cricket ground. On a billboard high above the roundabout I saw an advert for a film starring Harrison Ford. There he was, looking out over the traffic, firm but purposeful, assured that whatever he had to do, whomsoever he had to kill or sleep with, he was doing it for the greater good, in an effort to reach a happy ending. And that, it seemed to me, was how I should be behaving, only with a little less bluster.

Last night I had been given a taste of what my life could be like. I had been shown there was a fixture for me over on the other side. It didn't matter who had done the showing. Alice was the fantasy—I knew that. Kate was reality—I knew that as well. It was up to me now to find a way to get my family as well as myself up and over that gap.

Back at Welcome I jumped down on to the tarmac, stretched and looked at Alice with a broad grin.

'What are you looking so happy about?' she said uncertainly, glancing round to see if anyone was watching.

I said, 'You've given me an appetite.'

'I'm glad to hear it.'

And we split the tips again—sixty quid between us.

*   *   *

I composed myself outside my front door, held my head up, took a deep breath, made a hearty face and strode indoors.

'It's me,' I called from halfway up the stairs, and only then remembered that I had left under a cloud.

'Hi,' called a voice from the kitchen, an unfamiliar voice, because it was bright and jolly, and ended on a definite great-you're-home-from-work kind of beat. And there was Kate, sticking her head round the door. 'How was York?'

'York. Fine. Well, all right. You know, it was work.' I kissed her, a darting kiss, so that she wouldn't smell my clothes. But she pulled me towards her and gave me a hug.

'Haven't put my arms around you in ages.'

'No.' I knew I was standing there like a piece of wood, so I rubbed her back once or twice, put my weight on one leg. I could hear the sound of *Star Wars* and smell food.

'You're cooking,' I said, wriggling away.

'Be ready in ten minutes.'

'How's it been here?'

'Oh, fine. Normal. I mean we've missed you.'

'I've missed you.'

'But we've coped.'

'Of course you have.'

Why was she being so pleasant, so understanding? Why wasn't she giving me unreasonable looks? 'Where are the kids?' I said and went into the living room.

'I'm home!' I boomed, and they jumped all over me, although Martin remembered to hit the pause button on the video first. 'And I've got presents!'

'Presents!' screamed Stephen. They leapt about like puppy dogs. I held the bag with their multi-pens above them until Martin climbed on the arm of the couch behind me and grabbed them.

'Presents,' he shrieked and they ripped the paper off them with such excitement that they were bound to be disappointed.

Stephen looked at his pen. 'I didn't want a pen.'

'Course you do.'

'I didn't want a pen,' he said and started to cry. Martin was already back watching *Star Wars*.

We all sat down to macaroni cheese. I gave Kate her present.

'Fudge.'

'Yeah.'

'Thanks. Lovely. So what's York like?'

147

I could feel myself blushing. I looked down at my plate. 'Fine. This is nice. What is it?'

'Macaroni.'

'Is it?'

'We eat it three times a week, most weeks.'

'It's different tonight. You've done something to it.'

She was looking at me oddly. I hadn't talked about York long enough. 'Yes, York was lovely. Nice hotel too. Although my room was tiny. We should all go some time—a family trip. I got loads of tips too.' And I took the wad of notes from my pocket. 'Where's the Amnesty tin?'

'There's no need to do that,' said Kate.

I took the collection tin from the counter top and stuffed some notes in. 'There you go. Thirty quid. Fifteen for us, fifteen for the whales.'

'That's Greenpeace.'

'Of course it is. I meant, fifteen for the wrongly imprisoned and tortured and . . . See, boys. Charity starts at home.'

'I didn't want a pen,' said Stephen in his little voice.

'Thirty quid is a lot of tips,' said Kate.

'The guide I was with is very good.' I didn't know why I said that. I was staring at my plate again. 'This is lovely macaroni.'

'What makes the guide so good?'

'Oh, I don't know. It's hard to say. She's lively and quite attractive—I suppose.' I couldn't believe what was coming out of my mouth. 'I mean, I don't do anything really. I just sit there and drive, but I still get half the tips. Stephen, don't wipe your mouth on your sleeve.'

'We don't have table manners when you're

148

away,' said Martin.

'Will?' said Kate, in the way she did when something serious was going to follow.

'Yes.'

'I want to have a talk about something later.'

Oh my God. 'About what?' I smiled insanely.

'Later.'

'What are you going to talk about?' shouted Martin. 'I want to know.'

'So do I,' yelled Stephen.

So did I. Jesus. I felt a bar of heat pressing against my back. I wondered if I was going to spontaneously combust at my own kitchen table in front of my whole family.

'Did the Turbo Vac salesman come round?' I asked.

'Yes,' said Kate, clearing the plates. 'He's quite cute actually. I wanted to buy one.'

I put the kids to bed, taking longer than usual, hoping Kate would be asleep by the time I was done. But no, she was watching a programme presented by John Pilger, the man she would really like to have married. She said, 'I'm going to make a cup of tea. Do you want one?'

'No.'

She went to the kitchen. I sat there and gazed at film of Burmese activists. She couldn't know. She couldn't possibly know. Who could have told her: Roy, Graham?

'Has anyone from work phoned?' I called.

'No. Why?'

Just wondered.'

Maybe someone off the tour, someone who knew we had slept together. That Dutch couple: they had guessed the driver was sleeping with the guide and decided to reveal all. No, that was being paranoid.

She came back in and sat next to me with a mug of steaming tea. 'Are you watching this?'

'Yes,' I said, and the credits started to roll.

She switched the set off. I couldn't swallow. 'Yes, York is very nice.'

'Now, Will . . .'

'Maybe I will have a cup.'

I jumped up and went to the kitchen. If we had had a back door I might have run away from home. Relax; she couldn't possibly know. I focused on an empty bottle of squash by the bin.

'Will, what are you doing?'

'I'm just going down the bottle bank.'

'Will you come in here and sit down? I want to talk to you.'

I went back in and sat down. 'What?'

'I don't know how you're going to react to this.'

'What?'

She looked at me and bit her lip, then said, 'I want to adopt a granny.'

The world stopped. I noticed a little ornament on the mantelpiece that I'd never seen before, a china hippo. I said, 'Pardon?'

'I want to adopt a granny . . . You know, it's a scheme run by Help the Aged.'

'This is what you want to talk to me about?'

'Yes.'

My head rose, taking my shoulders with it, as if I'd just taken some heavy object off my back. I breathed deeply. She said, 'Well, don't look like that. Let's discuss it.'

'No need to discuss it. It's fine by me.'

'Really?'

150

'Really.'

She looked at me and smiled, then put her arm round me and pulled me towards her.

That night she put on the satin nightshirt she got from Marks & Spencer's when she took back the slippers I bought her for Christmas. I didn't want to make love; I wanted to hide in a corner of the bed, but she was insistent. I was like a machine, a bedroom appliance, but that, if I thought about it, was what she wanted—something to impregnate her. She wanted efficiency before pleasure.

'Make it count, Will,' she said urgently.

I was determined not to think of Alice, but I couldn't help comparing the two bodies, Kate's more angular, more brittle, Alice's more smooth and more pink. I thought of the Cotswolds when I thought of Alice. Kate had sharp edges reminiscent of the Cornish coast. I had a notion it was impossible to impregnate someone when you were thinking of someone else.

'I love you,' she said, which she never normally did during sex. It was as if we'd agreed sex wasn't the time to say I love you. It was too easy. It wasn't brave, the way it was when you said it over the dishes or when you looked at each other across a supermarket aisle.

'And I love you,' I whispered and never meant it more. 'No matter what happens I will always love you. I won't be able to stop.' I sounded desperate.

She buried her head in my neck. 'You're sure about this granny?' she said firmly.

'Yeah. Where's she from?'

'I don't know.'

'What's her name?'

'I haven't got that far yet. You sign up and pay a

151

direct debit, and the money goes to an elderly person in India or South America or somewhere. They chose who.'

Direct debit. How I hated those two words. 'How much?'

'Twelve pounds a month. It's not much. The kids will love it. We can write to her and she'll write back. We can afford it. If you keep doing these overnights and getting these tips we can anyway. And, besides, you might even get that advertisement thing. They'll pay you quite a bit for that, won't they?'

'What advertisement thing?'

'Didn't I tell you?'

What advertisement thing?'

'Those people from the audition phoned. They want you to go back for a second look. Sorry.'

*   *   *

Frame by Frame held the second audition three days later at the same address as the first, but on a different floor. Martin and I turned up well prepared this time. I didn't shave; he chewed gum. We both had reading and writing material.

'Hello, Will. Hello, Martin,' chirped Vanessa when she met us at the lift. She was dressed in a brighter-coloured tent, and was much more friendly. She led us past rows of offices as she said, 'Trevor, the director, thought you were both very natural. So many of the kids we get offered are too well trained. They've lost all their spontaneity.'

This was more like it. This was how I imagined it would be. On this floor young professionals sat busy at computers or on telephones. There were prize-winning advertisements in frames on the walls; there was trendy furniture. I was happy here, so was Martin. Then Vanessa opened the door to a room with a television and a coffee trolley in it, and three other father-and-son teams. We walked in and she quickly closed the door behind us.

The Milky Bar Kid looked up from his crossword and nodded. I acknowledged his nod with a nod. Martin and Harvey ignored each other. I should have known there would be a shortlist. The situation suddenly became even more competitive than the time before.

I opened my newspaper and read and reread the first paragraph of an article concerning the International Monetary Fund's forecast for the Millennium. Martin read his Disney comic. Pair by pair we were called out as before. No one spoke. It was like the waiting room of a dental surgery. Our turn came and Vanessa led us into another room to meet the casting director, the camera director and Trevor the director director again. Now, though, there was another director, the Managing Director, the only one in a suit.

'Will and Martin Green,' announced Vanessa.

'Will and Martin! How are you?' said Trevor. 'It's good to see you again. Have a seat. This is Marvin White, the client.'

Marvin White looked like he was happy to have a day out of the office. 'Like peas in a pod,' he said and laughed. I held Martin's hand for comfort. It dawned on me I didn't even know what product I was supposed to be advertising.

'Right,' said Trevor. 'You two are fine. The thing is . . . Will and Martin, can you play tennis?'

'Yes,' said Martin.

153

'Yes,' I said.

'Good,' said Trevor. And Vanessa gave us each a tennis racket, and we all trooped out of the office and up a flight of stairs back to the empty barn of a room where we had waited with all the other hopefuls at the first audition. A limp beach tennis net was now strung across the middle of the floor.

'Right,' said Trevor. 'Off you go.'

'What?' I said.

'Play tennis.'

'What, here?'

'Yeah.'

And so Martin and I stepped out into the middle of the room and hit some soft balls to each other, just the way we did in the park. Martin was good; my tuition had given him style. I wasn't so bad myself.

After a couple of minutes Trevor said, 'Can you jump over the net, Will?'

So I jumped over the net.

'Now Martin.'

And Martin jumped over the net.

'And back again.'

And so we both jumped over again.

The directors stood in a huddle. Marvin White looked at his watch. Trevor said to me, 'Tell you what, why don't you go and get some lunch?'

Two of the other father-and-son teams never made it to the afternoon session. They presumably failed the tennis test. The only pairs to reappear after lunch were ourselves and the Milky Bar Kid and Harvey.

We sat in silence in the little room with the TV which neither of us dared turn on. Finally the Milky Bar Kid said, 'Nervous?'

154

'Bit.'

'Don't worry if you don't get it. I'm surprised you got this far, to be honest.'

'Why's that?' I said. I might have snarled.

'I don't know. You don't look like the tennis sort.'

I felt I should go into the other room and warn Trevor the director and his client that I, for one, would never buy anything that this man and his boy advertised.

'How's the Climbing Rose?' he asked.

'Fine. You found a job yet?'

'What sort of food is it you do exactly?'

'Traditional English.'

'What, roast beef and Yorkshire, that sort of thing?' He chuckled into his crossword. Next to him Harvey had picked up the free gift from Martin's Disney comic—some sort of plane. Martin saw him and grabbed it back. So Harvey grabbed it back again. The Milky Bar Kid maintained his non-interventionist policy as before, and this time I did the same. Martin looked at me and I gave him a do-whatever-you-want expression. He tried to grab the gift back from Harvey. Harvey held on. Martin held on. One could only be impressed at the resistance of a toy that was free.

But Martin was able to draw on experience gained from many similar fights with a younger brother. He waited until Harvey had committed all his strength into pulling in one direction and then he let go. Harvey went flying backwards with force. He crashed into the television table behind him and suddenly there was blood everywhere.

I had never heard a child scream quite like Harvey, and I had never seen a lip swell up quite as quickly as Harvey's did. The Milky Bar Kid nose-dived into a panic: 'What happened, Harvey? What did he do to you? Your boy hit my boy!'

'I didn't do anything,' protested Martin.

'He says he didn't do anything.'

'Look at the blood.' The Milky Bar Kid laid Harvey on the floor. 'Calm down, Harvey. You're all right. Jesus, look at his lip!'

At that point Vanessa entered with Trevor. Whether Trevor had made up his mind to give the contract to me and Martin or to the Milky Bar Kid and Harvey I don't know, but there before him was one father-and-son team sitting happily reading, and the other with the son splattered in blood and crying hysterically and the father propping him up like a dummy and threatening him if he didn't pull himself together. 'He'll be all right really,' pleaded the Milky Bar Kid. 'It's just a nick!' But Trevor did what I would have done in his position and chose us.

We were taken back to the office where Marvin White, the client, sat looking sleepy. We were put in front of more bright lights, told to stand this way and that, look happy, look sad, look cross, look mischievous, hold this glass of Robinson's Lemon Barley Water. That was when it dawned on me what product we were advertising.

I couldn't see anything in the light, only hear low voices. Then out of the glare boomed Trevor, 'The camera likes you, Will, and Martin. We'll need you for about three days, in two weeks' time. Will that be all right?'

'Yes,' I said. 'That's fine.' And I wondered if now was the time to ask about money.

'You'll need to get a note from Martin's school, will that be all right?'

156

'Yes, fine.'

'And you'll need to come in for a costume fit. Nothing complicated, a tracksuit and some tennis clothes. We're going to film it in Wimbledon. That all right for you?'

'Fine.'

'We don't have a script yet, but basically the idea is you're playing tennis with your son and you're beating him now, but you know soon he's going to beat you. And it's a young person's world, and everything's changing, and the younger generation has no respect for the older one, but there are some things that remain the same no matter what happens, i.e. Robinson's Lemon Barley Water. That's the idea. You don't have any lines to worry about. It's all voice-over. Is that all right?'

'Yeah. Fine.'

'Great. Any questions?'

Just one burning question. 'No. Fine.' I realized I was shaking as I spoke.

'Great. See you in a couple of weeks. Vanessa will give you all the details.'

Vanessa didn't give us the details. I followed her through the offices, expecting her to launch into discussions about money, but she just led us to the lifts and said, 'Well done. I'll be in contact. I've got your numbers, haven't I?'

As the lift door opened I stammered, 'Just one thing.'

'Yes.'

'How much are we being paid for this?'

She looked stumped. 'I don't know. Your agent will sort that out. They'll contact him.'

'Yes, actually, I've just changed agents. I'm no longer with Broomfield and Whitton. I'm with . . .

157

Bryan Harper.'

'At CTP?'

'That's right.'

'We'll speak to him, then.'

I phoned CTP from a phone outside. As Bryan Harper spoke to me I got the feeling he was watching me from a window nearby.

'And you want me to represent you?' He spoke softly and quickly.

'Yes please.'

'Leave it with me.'

'How much . . . sort of . . . roughly . . . will we earn? You know.'

'Hard to say. Give me your number and I'll be in touch.'

We took the train home. I read the International Monetary Fund article over and over again. I found it hard to understand how I could have behaved so badly and yet been rewarded so well. Martin had to nudge me when we got to our stop. I left my jacket on the seat and he ran back for it. When I got home the phone was ringing. 'Will. It's Bryan Harper.'

'Hello, Bryan.'

'They've offered twenty-six for the two of you, for a series of three ads.'

'Twenty-six . . . what?'

'Twenty-six thousand.'

'Pounds?'

'Yes. I'm going for thirty.'

'Good idea.'

'They should meet us halfway.'

'You reckon?'

'Yes.'

And he was right; they did.

158

CHAPTER SEVEN

A MAGICAL MYSTERY TOUR

Paul my Business Banking Manager had developed a skin complaint since my last visit. An angry rash burned beneath his shaving shadow. It made him look worried. It made me wonder if he'd had bad overnight news from Tokyo or New York or maybe both.

I tried not to let it distract me. I was putting on a good performance. I had the confidence of a man who knew he had put together a good business plan and cashflow forecast, a man whom the camera liked, a man on the brink of success.

I spoke with conviction. 'My agent, Bryan Harper at CTP, is drawing up a contract which, after his deductions, will bring me twenty-five thousand pounds for this Robinson's Lemon Barley Water deal alone. That's net, Paul. Then there are the residuals. And who knows how much work will come our way once we're on the air. Bryan Harper says we'll be inundated. One of his clients did a fishfinger commercial last year and he's got a holiday home in the Dordogne now. Trouble is he's too busy to ever go there.' I laughed. Paul smiled. The words 'holiday home in the Dordogne' made him stroke his face self-consciously.

'Have you had a look at my revised business plan for the Climbing Rose?' I asked.

He nodded slowly. 'I have done, yes. I'm rather concerned about the performance of the business over the last two years.'

'It's not good, is it? But, as the vendors' agents have admitted, their clients have lost interest since their rather acrimonious split. That's why they're selling. There's another tea-room on the other side of the village and that does fine business. Anne Hathaway's Cottage isn't going to go away, Paul. The demand is there; my figures illustrate that. With the right person at the helm, the potential is good.'

His skin rasped as he drew his hand across his chin. He looked like a man who had run out of reasons to say no. He said slowly, 'Of course we'd want to cover ourselves with an h.p. arrangement from a finance company.'

'That seems reasonable to me.' I didn't care how the deal was done.

'And rather than a business loan for twenty thousand pounds you might like to rework these figures using an overdraft. If you're able to buy the freehold as quickly as you think, it might work out cheaper.'

That sounded like good advice. 'That sounds like good advice, Paul.'

He bit his fingernail. He wasn't in good shape. 'I'll run it past my manager,' he said. 'See what we can do. I'd say the chances are good.'

I slapped my knees and got up. Out of the window the railways lines and multi-storey car parks merged with endless housing estates, but I was seeing the pleasant green fields of the Heart of England. I said, 'You know, I've always thought advertising is something this country is good at.'

'Definitely,' agreed Paul. He had never expected me to come to him with a serious proposition. Me of all people. He said, 'My favourite ads are those ones with Papa and Nicole.'

'Renault.'

'Citroën.'

'I think you'll find it's Renault.'

'Listen, I should know. I went and bought a Citroën on the strength of them.'

Best not to argue with him. The man was an idiot. I smiled and shook his hand. 'One more thing, Paul. Could I have an interim overdraft facility of two thousand pounds? I'm going to have all sorts of expenses.'

'I should think we can agree to that . . .' he said quietly, as if he didn't want anyone else to hear, then added the magic word to the sentence that made me realize I had cracked it. He said, I should think we can agree to that . . . 'Will.' And I strode out of that bank with my chin up and arms swinging. My BBM was a pillock, but that didn't matter, we were on first-name terms.

When I got outside I listened to my voice-mail on the mobile phone Frame by Frame had given me. 'We need to be able to reach you at all times,' Vanessa had said. She had called to say Martin and I were needed for a wardrobe fitting on Friday, and to tell me I needed to fill out insurance and consent forms.

Bryan Harper also had rung. When I called him back he said, 'I'm going to recommend you two for the Bird's Custard campaign, Will. It's time to start getting excited!'

'Maybe I should pack up work.'

'No, don't do that yet.'

I was excited. I'd had my lucky break; the camera liked me. I slept well. I woke each morning full of energy. During the day I kept my head up. I

161

laughed out loud in public. I didn't mind attracting attention. When I went to work I'd sit in my coach knowing that my days at Welcome were numbered. I'd say to myself: It's been a good job; it's kept me ticking over. I've been to places people pay huge amounts of money to go to. It's taught me a lot. I recommend coach-driving to anyone who needs to get through a sticky patch.

One night I had a dream in which I was striding through our flat with a Turbo Vac sucking up those bastard dustmites. They were retreating. They were cowering in corners, but they couldn't hide. I woke still feeling the thrill of victory. I called Broomfield and Whitton estate agent's and spoke to Clarissa. 'Has the Climbing Rose accepted my offer yet?' I asked.

'We haven't heard,' said Clarissa. 'You know what she's like; a bit disorganized.'

I found this so annoying. I wanted everyone to be as keen as I was. 'I'd like to pay another visit if I may . . .' I said.

'Of course,' said Clarissa. 'I'll tell her you're coming.'

' . . . with my family.'

*　　　*　　　*

I wanted a celebratory outing, a family outing with Kate and the boys, with Dad, with Ted and Rita. I wanted to be a successful man taking his extended family out for the day. So I hired one of those people carriers, a VW Caravelle, and went to Marks & Spencer's to buy a picnic.

I filled a trolley with all the things Alice had said she kept in her fridge. I don't think it was done consciously, but when I got to the check-out I noticed the Jarlsberg and fromage frais. I'd even bought a bar of Toblerone. I didn't care. And I didn't look at the price of anything. I was going to buy what I wanted today.

Kate wasn't sure about the idea of a mystery outing—which was how I'd billed the excursion. 'But where's it to?' she said to me, perplexed.

'It's a mystery; that's the idea.' I put my arm around her. She'd been very subdued over Martin's and my success. She'd seemed unsettled. She'd just given a little grunt of satisfaction when I told her we would get paid twenty-five thousand pounds, and that was just the start. 'We'll be able to adopt a grandpa as well,' I told her, and that seemed to keep her happy. She never asked what we were really going to spend the money on, and so I never told her. My plans were still secret. This was what the outing was for. I wanted to surprise her, see her put her hands to her face in disbelief.

When I opened the door of the Caravelle for her, though, her unease showed. She sat in the front with her legs together and arms folded, and a face that said, 'How much was this?'

'Stretch out,' I said. 'Relax. Enjoy yourself.' I was speaking to her the way I spoke to the tourists at Welcome.

'Is this our new car?' said Martin.

'Just for today, my boy. But we're going to get a new one soon. Don't worry.'

'I didn't want a pen,' said Stephen, and he slammed his door shut.

Ted and Rita arrived. Rita wore stiletto heels and a big hat with matching earrings. She climbed in the Caravelle and said, 'Don't kiss me, I've got

163

conjunctivitis.'

As I put their bags in the back, I whispered to Ted, 'We're going to have a look at it.'

'At what?'

'My café.'

'I couldn't give a shit.'

He was in an odd mood. He sat with his chin in his neck and let Rita do the talking. 'I wouldn't mind you coming round to our place in this,' she said, running her hands along the Caravelle's grey upholstery. She wouldn't normally let me park outside their house in Totteridge, not in the Fiat. 'The car a man drives is all a woman needs to know about him,' she once said to me.

We motored up to my dad's and I tooted the horn outside his house. He opened the door and called out, 'I'll be with you a minute.'

'He's not on the toilet, is he?' moaned Ted.

I didn't want to wait. I wanted to get going, find a nice picnic spot, get to the Climbing Rose in good time. I wanted the day to run smoothly. I went inside and found him steaming the stamp off a used envelope.

'What the hell are you doing?'

'There's not a mark on it,' he said. 'I can use it again.'

I pushed him out to the van. 'He was only steaming the stamp off a bloomin' envelope,' I said with a laugh.

'So?' said Kate.

'Just 'cos you've come into a bit of money,' said Ted.

'Steam is very good for the face,' said Rita.

'I'll send a card to someone with it,' said Dad. 'Make someone happy.'

They were doing it again—ganging up on me.

We motored round the M25 and on to the M40. It was a lovely summer's day; I was surrounded by my family and we had a picnic in the back. Life was good, and I drove away from London imagining I was being interviewed for the *Relative Values* column. *Father and son Will and Martin Green, who appear in the Robinson's Lemon Barley Water commercial, talk about their relationship: 'I enjoy doing the adverts because it gives us a chance to spend time together,'* I would say. *'I suffer from asthma but Dad always encouraged me to be a normal kid,'* Martin would say. *'It's a lot easier now, of course, that we've moved away from the city...'* we would both agree.

'Good business to get into, advertising is,' said Ted to Martin.

'Don't say that.' Kate told him off. 'It's not a business for him.'

'I'm only allowed to do it if it's fun,' said Martin.

'Course it'll be fun,' said Ted. 'You'll earn a stack of money.'

Kate glared at him.

'What?' protested Ted.

'Can we sleep in this car?' asked Stephen.

'I always wanted to be a model in adverts,' said Rita, shuffling in her dress.

'It's something the British are good at,' said Ted.

'Why does everyone say that?' sneered Kate. 'How can you be good at something that's worthless?'

'Advertising is very important,' I chipped in.

'No it isn't,' said Kate. I glanced at her, and almost pleaded with her not to draw some link between the amount of packaging we use in the

165

Western World and the crisis in Sudan, because I knew she could easily do so, and Ted would be unable to resist provoking her, and the next hour would be an argument.

'I'm not tall enough, though,' said Rita. 'Not to be a model. That's what they said.'

'My favourite adverts were the Oxo series,' said Dad. 'With Katie Boyle.'

'It wasn't Katie Boyle,' Ted told him. 'It was just Katie.'

'Tell you what, Martin,' said Rita, 'can I have your autograph? Now you're going to be rich and famous?'

'He's not going to be rich and famous,' I told her, trying to support Kate who had gone quiet again and was looking out of the window.

'Yes I am. You said I am,' said Martin.

'I said people might, now and again, recognize you in the street. And you were going to get enough money for a few extras. You can buy yourself a computer and some football boots.'

'And what's he going to do with the rest of it?' asked Ted. 'Or is this not an equal partnership? I can give you financial advice if you want, Martin. That's what uncles are for.'

'Friend of mine's a model and she goes out with a footballer,' said Rita. 'She says he's always covered in bruises.'

After an hour I came off the motorway and started to look for a picnic spot. I followed a B road through lovely lanes. I was so used to driving everywhere on motorways I'd forgotten what real countryside was like. It was brimming.

'There's a spot,' cried Kate, pointing to a track off the road. But I wasn't going to stop just

166

anywhere. I wanted a perfect spot on such a perfect day. I wanted a field of bluebells by a river with a castle in the background and an information board handy.

'I've got a car behind me,' I said and drove on.

We motored down narrow lanes and over crossroads with old black and white signposts. Gliders looped in the sky. There was a heat haze rising off the earth. I was trying to keep our bearings but the hedges were so thick and high I was easily lost.

The children were growing restless. Stephen was asking Martin if he wanted to look at his bum. 'There's a good spot,' said Kate. 'There's a stream as well.'

'I want somewhere special,' I said.

'A stream is special.'

'Let's just go on a bit.'

Martin moaned, 'I feel sick.'

'No you don't,' said Ted.

'I can't stand people being sick.' Rita cringed. 'It's revolting.'

'I'll have to go to the toilet in one hour twenty minutes,' Dad informed everyone. 'Just thought I'd give you good warning.'

We passed a sign for a windmill. 'There!' said Kate.

'Let's just get past this wood . . .'

'There's a windmill, for God's sake, it's perfect.'

'I want a view.'

'This is a view. A view of a windmill! Stop the car here.'

I gave in, and turned off by a National Trust sign into a small car park with an honesty box. 'Quick! Out of the car,' said Dad, grabbing the picnic hamper. 'If anyone asks we never saw the sign.'

The windmill stood starkly up a track in the middle of an open field, casting a fat, cool shadow. 'You're turning your nose up,' said Kate in disbelief.

'I'm not.'

'Why are you turning your nose up?'

'Well . . . there could be somewhere nicer further down the road.'

'This is a lovely picnic site. I'm very happy with it. Everyone is happy with it.'

She was right. So I decided to be happy too. I even put fifty pence in the honesty box. We had the money. The National Trust needed to be supported.

We walked up the track carting the food in bags and boxes. Successful man taking his extended family on a picnic by a windmill.

We set chairs and a table out, and greased the kids with sunblock. Dad put his cardigan on and pulled his hat down. Rita laid out, pulled her dress up over her thighs and pointed her nose at the sun. 'You'll get skin cancer,' Martin told her.

'Oh, I don't bother about things like that,' said Rita.

'She'll get skin cancer, Mum, look.'

Ted opened a can of lager and lit a Hamlet. He immediately looked happier. He even smiled affectionately at the kids. 'You know what?' he sighed. 'I've always thought children and alcohol go well together.'

Dad said to Stephen, 'Do you know what the windmill does?' and when Stephen said no, Dad took him off on a tour. I listened as he explained about wheat and bread, and the miller, and

168

watched him making grand gestures. I felt so proud of them. I felt so proud of myself.

We laid the picnic out, and sat round in the shade of the windmill's arms. Everyone tucked in, but when I looked at the food I didn't feel hungry. I felt nervous. I just ate fruit.

'You can get that Stilton a lot cheaper at Safeway,' said Dad.

I could see Kate frowning as she unpacked the salad vegetables. 'These are from Guatemala,' she said, holding up a packet of baby corn.

'I've got some lovely English strawberries,' I said, trying to sideline the sweetcorn issue. I knew that whenever Guatemala was mentioned in our family things started to go downhill.

'We're getting a granny,' announced Martin.

'A what!' laughed Ted.

Kate explained the Adopt-a-Granny scheme. Ted listened quietly while the idea sunk in, then he began to ask the questions I'd wanted to ask.

'So let me get this straight . . .' he smirked, wanting to annoy his sister as much as I wanted to relax her. 'You pay a direct debit to an agency and you get to support a granny in India or Honduras or somewhere?'

'That's right,' said Kate.

'I wouldn't want someone else's granny living with me,' said Rita. 'I'm bad enough tripping over the cat.'

'She doesn't come and live with us,' I told her.

'That's a shame for Grandpa, isn't it?' said Ted.

'So who chooses the grandmother?' asked Rita.

'That was my next question,' said Ted, cracking another lager.

'They choose the person in most need,' I told

169

him, trying to take Kate's side, trying to make this sound reasonable.

'They don't come in a brochure, then?' asked Rita. 'Like Men Of Alaska.'

Ted spluttered into his can. I laughed too, in the hope Kate would. But she shook her head. 'You're really not interested, are you?' She was ignoring Rita and talking to Ted. 'With just a little effort, a little money, you could easily change someone's life. Give them a happier, more healthy old age, but you can't be bothered.'

'That's what I say to him,' said Rita.

'Listen,' said Ted. Just 'cos someone lives in a poor country it doesn't mean to say they're unhappy or unhealthy.'

'I never said that.'

'Yes, you did. It's bloody condescending, if you ask me. You never get people adopting a Western businessman, do you? And they suffer too, you know.'

'It's not the same and you know it.'

'We businessmen suffer from stress. I'm suffering from stress right now,' and he swigged from his can. 'The stress of having to be as successful as my neighbour, the stress of having to compete. It's Western stress, that's all, and it's a huge pressure. People think just 'cos someone earns a nice little salary they should be healthy and happy, but it isn't the case. I bet you I'm no happier or more healthy than most people my age in Honduras.'

'You should eat more fruit,' I told him.

'He's right,' said Rita.

'These people in Honduras don't have enough to eat,' said Kate.

'But what I'm saying,' argued Ted, 'is that that isn't such a big deal if your next-door neighbour doesn't have enough to eat either. It's like living in Totteridge and only having one car. It makes you unhappy, and being unhappy makes you unhealthy. It's all relative.'

'He's got a point,' Rita said. 'It's all relative.'

'How can you be so . . .' Kate came so close to saying stupid that Rita started to redden. 'These people need money just to survive, not to build extensions to their kitchens.'

'All right,' said Ted, looking round for a bar to lean against. 'So we're better off than the impoverished in Honduras, but the Hondurans are better off than some people in Africa, aren't they? But do you think the people from Honduras adopt grannies from Africa? I don't think so. It's all a bit suspicious, if you ask me.'

'What is?' retorted Kate, getting annoyed with him now.

'Well, it sounds to me like there's some fat cat sitting on a beach somewhere doing a nice trade in grannies over his mobile phone. The grannies are being abused. It ought to be stopped.'

I left them to it. It would just end in tears. Dad had wandered off round the windmill again and I went to join him. He seemed impressed by its giant features. He said, 'It was very windy the night you were born, did you know that?'

'No.'

'There was a storm. Telephone lines blown down, that sort of thing. The night Colin was born, on the other hand, was a lovely sunny evening, middle of summer.'

'I thought it might be.'

171

'Big red sunset out of the hospital window. It's funny how you remember the weather.'

Emotional leaks like this were very unusual for him. 'You're feeling all right these days, aren't you?' I asked.

'Fine, thanks.' He stuck his tongue into his cheek. 'Did we ever tell you we named you after William Shakespeare?'

'What?'

'It's true.'

'You didn't?'

'We did.'

'Why?'

'Your mother hoped you might become a famous playwright, known throughout the ages, that sort of thing. She had high hopes for her children.'

'I hope I haven't been a disappointment,' I said, and gave a nervous laugh, but he didn't answer me. He looked into the distance, squinting at the horizon. In this light I could see the veins on his face fanning out into a delta. I said, 'We need to get you to the toilet, don't we?'

* * *

My plan was to get back on the motorway and find a service station for Dad to go to, but everyone had different ideas of where the motorway was.

'Who's map-reading?' I asked.

Rita had the map on her lap, but Ted said, 'Give it here.'

'Why?'

'Because.'

'Because what?'

'Because, and I don't want this to sound sexist,

172

but I have come to the opinion over the years that women are lousy navigators.'

'You're just appalling,' hissed Kate.

'Well, what conclusion would you draw if all the women you've been in a car with who have taken charge of the navigation had failed to get you to your destination, and the opposite has been true of the men? It's to do with spatial awareness, nothing to be ashamed of. Men are instinctively better map-readers, while women are better at folding sheets. I read about it in a book.'

And that was the big trouble everyone had with Ted. His opinions were outrageous. They went against everything you knew to be just and true. And that made it really unsettling when you found yourself agreeing with him.

'OK, you want to go left at the next crossroads,' he announced with confidence, 'and that takes us straight to the M40.'

'Better had,' said Dad.

But I turned left at the next crossroads and there was no sign of the motorway. Instead, after a couple of miles, we came to a little town, the name of which had been obscured by a ring of flowers and a cardboard sign that read *Garland Day*. 'This isn't on the map,' complained Ted.

'That's 'cos you're lost,' said Rita.

'Only because you got us lost first.'

'I'm not lost,' said Stephen.

We drove slowly into the town centre. Bunting was strung from lampposts and houses. On the green was a maypole, and there was a game of skittles being played outside the pub. A small crowd browsed among craft stalls. By the church was a public convenience, but there was a queue of

173

what looked like folk dancers outside. I double-parked opposite.

'They're morris dancers,' said Dad. 'They'll be ages.'

'I don't think they're morris dancers,' said Kate. 'I've never seen dancers dressed like them before.' She was right. They had animals' heads on. They looked fierce.

'I'll take him to a pub,' I said. 'Everyone stay here.'

'I hate morris dancers,' said Ted. 'I'll come with you.'

'They're not morris dancers,' insisted Kate.

The Dragon Hotel was decked out in flowers and flags. Inside was a smoky rabble. 'Nice place,' remarked Ted. I asked a lad clearing tables, 'Where's the toilet?' And he replied, 'I don't know, I'm new.'

I looked round and there was Dad emptying someone's drink.

'What the hell do you think you're doing?'

'No point in wasting it.'

I dragged him into the hotel reception and found the toilet. 'Just go in there. I'll wait for you outside.'

He scurried off, only stopping to ask the receptionist if she had a newspaper he could read. She handed him the *Daily Mail.* 'Is there a Recipe of the Day in here?' he inquired ever so politely.

'Just get in there.' I pushed him into the toilet.

Back in the pub Ted was sitting at a table with two pints. 'Just having a quick one,' he said.

I walked right past him and went outside. I didn't want to stop here. I wanted to keep to our schedule and get to the Climbing Rose. But then I

174

could see them all climbing out of the Caravelle. Rita sat on a bench and browned her legs. The kids went to buy ice cream. 'What a nice little town,' declared Kate, eyeing a cobbler's stall, and I knew it would mean half an hour wasted and ten quid frittered away. Not that the money mattered, of course.

'Maybe we should get back in the car,' I suggested to her.

'But it's lovely here. What's wrong with here?'

'Nothing's wrong with it.'

'Well, why not stay here a while? We're enjoying this. Your dad's on the toilet. Ted's drinking and smoking. Rita's lying in the sun. The kids are having ice cream. Why can't you just enjoy yourself?'

'Because . . . we're not meant to be here, that's why.'

She shook her head and went and inspected the selection of homemade shoes.

I leant against the Caravelle. I didn't like this place; I hadn't from the moment we stumbled into it. It was unusual, but not in an attractive way. There was a sweet sickly smell to it, an animal smell. There was strange music in the background, and—something really odd—there were no tourists apart from ourselves. Everyone else looked local, and they were ugly and badly dressed. There should have been tour buses in a place like this, and souvenir shops, but there were none. I found that suspicious.

Ted joined me with a pint in one hand and a pamphlet in the other. 'This is Floral Day,' he said.

'There's the Green Man.' Kate pointed, and over on the far edge of the green was a figure

175

completely covered in leaves, his legs swathed, his arms almost rigid with foliage. Children were creeping up and trying to touch him, then running away with screams of fear and laughter. But he didn't appear amused. There was something dark about him. He was spinning angrily, launching himself at spectators. They backed off in giggles, but he reminded me of some squat Frankenstein creation the way he lurched at them. A little boy kicked his arse and he turned in rage and chased all the screaming children down an alley.

Ted read: '*The Green Man is a tree god who goes back to pagan times, a symbol of the Christian and pagan threaded together. He keeps the devil away from the crops. He is also a fertility symbol.* Rita, you keep well away from him, all right?'

I couldn't help glance at Kate and see her sad smile.

'Do my legs look funny in these shoes?' inquired Rita.

Martin appeared with two ice creams. One he was licking, the other was dribbling pink down his hand. Kate licked his fingers for him. Martin said, 'Where's Stephen?'

'He was with you,' I told him.

'No he wasn't.'

'He went with you to get an ice cream,' said Kate.

'I haven't seen him,' said Martin, licking Stephen's ice cream now. 'You'll get lung cancer,' he told Ted who was puffing on a Hamlet.

I spun round but there was no sign of Stephen. We were suddenly all scanning the scene around us, looking for a six-year-old in red T-shirt and blue shorts.

'Rita, stay here with Martin,' I told her firmly.

He wasn't at the ice-cream stall. The ice-cream man said, 'Don't panic now.' But just him saying 'don't panic' made me feel more worried. I was suddenly frightened of this peculiar place.

I ran back to Kate, my mind already racing ahead to the evening, and we still hadn't found him, and the police were questioning us and everyone else in the town. *Has he done this before? Was he upset by anything?* My heart was revving. Thirty minutes ago I was having one of the happiest moments of my life, watching my dad explain windmills to his grandson. Now our family had been torn apart by a child molester. 'I told you we should've left,' I said to Kate.

'He can't have gone far. Look on the other side of the green.'

I hurried by the church, past the maypole and the demonstration of wood carving, to where the dancers with the animal headgear were gathered. I burst into their ranks. 'Have you seen a small boy, red shirt, blue shorts?'

They shook their bizarre heads, but then one of them, a bear, said in a muffled voice, 'He was with the Green Man.'

'What!'

'The Green Man got him.'

I caught a flash of green, and there was the Green Man running through the churchyard like a robot, chasing a group of screaming children. They taunted him, hooting with excitement, but no one could see the Green Man's face, and I became convinced that if I ripped that mask off, underneath I would find a slobbering village idiot sucking on a bone.

I vaulted over the wall and ran after them. I sprinted round the church, leaping over graves, just catching glimpses of him, shouting at him to wait. But then I realized he was on the other side of some railings. I ran the length of them trying to find a way through, but they became a hedge. I tried bursting through that, but it was much too dense. Thorns scratched me until blood dripped from my hands and arms. So I ran round the graveyard again, and out of the gate down an alley. I could hear the children's pup-like yelps, but they were always just around a corner, always just out of sight.

Then when I caught a glimpse of him through the houses, he was going in the opposite direction to me. This was like being in a maze. In desperation I jumped over someone's gate and ran through their garden, down the side of their house and out of the back yard, only to catch sight of him disappearing down another alley. I hated this town so much. I wanted to turn back the clock and never to have come here. I wanted to be back on the motorway. I didn't want there to be an outcome to this situation; I wanted it never to have happened.

I was losing energy, staggering with a tightness in my chest. Then suddenly I came across the children, playing quietly in a garden, pulling the petals off flowers, the Green Man nowhere to be seen. I hardly had the breath to speak 'Have you seen a boy in red shirt, blue shorts?'

They looked at me as if they shouldn't speak to strangers. Then one of them glanced down the alley, and there was a green back just disappearing.

I ran down that alley like a dog, turned the corner and saw the Green Man sauntering across a

178

little square. I thought of the mugger that night on the Jack the Ripper tour, but this character wasn't going to escape. I could see nothing but fury as I ran up behind him, leapt and jumped on his back, arms round his neck, easily forcing him to the ground. I straddled him, my knees pinning him. He struggled as he turned to face me, but I had him by the throat. 'Where's my child?' I yelled at the green head. 'What have you done with my child?' And I ripped off his head-dress to reveal the terrified face of a young woman.

She had striking blue eyes. I stared at her, appalled at the way I was thinking: She's quite attractive.

I released my grip on her neck. She choked and I jumped off her, helped her up. 'I'm sorry. I've lost my small boy. I thought . . .'

'What does he look like?' she gasped.

I described Stephen, and she led me down another alley and suddenly we were back on the main street again, not that far from the Caravelle. In a little garden of remembrance a Punch and Judy show was in full swing with a group of kids watching, and there in the front row sat Stephen, cross-legged. I left the Green Woman without a thank you, waded into the kids and took Stephen by the arm. I was shaking with anger as well as fear now. 'We're leaving,' I told him as calmly as I could.

But Stephen had other ideas. 'No!' he protested as I picked him up, and he started to kick.

'We're leaving!' I was trying to be firm, but not to cause a scene.

'No no. Let me go!'

'I've got an ice cream for you.'

179

'I don't want an ice cream.'

'I said we're going!'

He was kicking and yelling so much I had to grip him tightly and drag him away. 'Don't be silly now. You're coming with me.'

But he screamed and struggled: 'Mummy, Mummy!'

So I just swept him off the ground, and that's when I saw my way was blocked by a tightening ring of adults, reasonable people every one of them, dressed in summer clothes, shorts and sandals, and all looking at me very gravely indeed. None of them would have dared to call me an abductor, but all of them were ready to stop me leaving with this protesting child. Now I was the monster.

'Mummy,' squealed Stephen as he saw Kate across the square. I loosened my grip so he could wriggle out and run off. He jumped into Kate's arms and she made a big fuss of him while I was left staring at the mob.

'Kids, eh,' I chuckled. 'What can you do with them?' and I edged away out of the ring and didn't look back.

We all clambered on board the Caravelle. My dad came back from the toilet looking much happier. 'You know what the Recipe of the Day was in the *Mail*? Tuna fish bake.'

'Can't stand fish,' said Rita.

Ted climbed in smelling of cigars.

'Come on, hurry up,' I said. 'Let's get out of this place!'

'Still don't know where the motorway is,' said Ted.

'I do,' said Stephen.

'Where?'

180

'Don't shout at him,' said Kate.

'Turn down by that pink house,' said Stephen.

We turned down by the pink house. Five minutes later we were cruising along the middle lane of the M40, safe again, the town—whatever it was called—as distant as last night's bad dream.

*   *   *

It was only three-quarters of an hour to the Stratford-upon-Avon exit. Dad listened to the afternoon play. Rita told Kate what it was like to have a skin peel. Ted read the Northumberland page of the map. The kids sat in the back seat and amused themselves by pretending to be orphans called Rick and Peter. As I steered up the off ramp and came down through the gears I tried to revitalize the day. I said, 'Who can guess where the mystery destination is?'

'Margate,' said Rita.

'I hate Margate,' said Dad. 'I prefer Broadstairs.'

I motored round the ring road and took the signs for Anne Hathaway's Cottage. The tourist buses were lined up outside decanting their visitors, but this time I headed for the car rather than the coach park.

'Who was Anne Hathaway?' asked Ted. 'Remind me.'

'She was married to William Shakespeare,' Martin told him.

'Oh yeah,' said Ted, rubbing his eyes. 'Anne Hathaway, of course.'

Everyone was looking to me for instructions. 'We can take a tour of the house to start with, and then I've got a surprise.'

'Do we have to have a tour of the house?' asked Rita.

'Please can we have the surprise first?' pleaded Martin.

'I don't like old people's houses,' said Rita.

'They've been cooped up in the car too long,' said Kate.

'Fine. We'll abandon the tour of the house. It's time for the surprise!'

I led them through the car park and past the gardens adjacent to the Cottage, until the Climbing Rose became visible set back among the trees. The vegetation along the path had become even more dense since I was last there. Rita stung herself on nettles and started to cry.

'Here's a dock leaf,' said Dad, and he bent down and rubbed her leg so hard she screamed.

'Leave her alone,' said Ted. 'It's only a stinging nettle.'

'I'm allergic,' she wailed.

'Shall we buy her an ice cream?' suggested Martin.

'Ice cream!' said Stephen.

The building was as pretty as I remembered it. And as neglected. Some slates were missing from the roof—that would have to be looked at.

'What is this place?' asked Kate.

I wasn't surprised by her reaction. It was natural. Only I could see the woodwork freshly painted, the new curtains in the windows, the shrubs trimmed and blooming, coloured bulbs strung in the trees. I held the door open for everyone. Ted gave me a face: 'Is this it?'

'Yeah.'

'You should knock it down and open a Pizza

Hut.'

Inside, the same overworked waitress was running round throwing cream teas at bewildered tourists.

'Where shall we sit?' I asked her.

'Anywhere you bleedin' want,' she answered.

'What did she say?' said Kate.

'She's a bit overworked.'

'Why have you brought us here?'

'You'll see. Sit down.'

We all sat down and I ordered toasted teacakes all round.

'I don't want mine cooked,' said Stephen.

'One plain one. Please.'

'You can't have it not cooked,' said the waitress.

'Why not?'

' 'Cos it'll be frozen, that's why.'

'I want mine frozen if he's having his frozen,' said Martin.

'You can't have a frozen teacake,' I said.

'Well you have to have it cooked then,' said the waitress, and she walked off. End of discussion.

'She needs a good slap round the legs,' said Dad.

'So what do you think?' I said to Kate. 'What do you think of this place?'

'Why?'

'I wanted you to see it. What do you think of it?'

She looked around. 'It's . . . lifeless.'

'It is, isn't it? Lifeless teapots, lifeless plastic chairs, lifeless decor.'

'It's a dump,' said Rita.

'You're right. You're saying all the right things. And yet the place is busy.'

'That's 'cos there's only one waitress,' said Ted.

I leant forward. 'I want you all to think what it

could be like—with a little work. If the menus were hand-written; if the scones were warm; if there were homemade cakes; if there were milk shakes; if there was a freezer with a glass lid so you could choose from a range of locally made ice creams. And think of the extra business we'd do if we stayed open as long as Anne Hathaway's cottage. Think what we could do with this place.'

My extended family were looking at me as if I needed urgent medical help.

'We?' inquired Kate.

'Come with me,' I said, and took her by the hand.

We left Rita and Ted and Dad with the kids and strict instructions. Then I asked the waitress if the owner was around. 'Just go through,' she flapped. 'I'm not bothered.'

I led Kate through the kitchen: 'It's a good size,' I pointed out. 'Plenty of storage space. You've got to think of the potential.'

Her arms were folded around her body as if she was trying to protect herself. 'Will?'

I called up the stairs: 'Anyone in?'

'Who is it?' a gravelly voice responded. I could hear Australian accents on a TV.

'What are we doing here, Will?'

'You'll see.'

I led Kate up the stairs. I called, 'The estate agent sent me round.'

'What estate agent?' said Kate.

Upstairs was a jumble of old newspapers and empty coffee cups. I peered into the living room and there was the woman with the blotchy legs I had seen before in the garden. She was sunk into a settee watching the afternoon soaps through a cloud of cigarette smoke. She tried to turn her head to see who I was, but her neck was in a whiplash collar.

'I'm Will Green. I believe the estate agent phoned and told you I was coming. I don't think they actually gave me your name?'

With effort she moved herself round to look at me, and now I could see a glass in her hand and a gin bottle on the floor by her side. I moved into her view and she tried to focus on me. 'Didn't the estate agent call?' I asked.

'I don't know what you're talking about,' she muttered and tried to flick ash in a saucer on the floor but missed. She saw Kate: 'Who are you?'

'Maybe we could have a look round?' I asked politely.

Kate pulled me back. 'Come on, Will. I don't think now is the time.'

'You don't mind if we look round do you, Mrs . . . ?'

'Sod off.'

'Come on, Will. I want to get back to the children.'

'We've come all this bloody way, the least she can do is let us look round.'

'I said sod off!' She was becoming irritated now.

'She's very drunk,' whispered Kate.

'I can see that.'

'Did you hear me?' She was trying to get to her feet.

'Yes, all right. We'll just have a look in the bedroom. Have a look in here, Kate.'

'Will!'

'See, it's another good-sized room, and the other bedroom is just as big. The kitchen is small, but I

185

mean I'd only plan living over the place for a while. In time we'd get a house in—'

'I'll call the bleeding police if you don't get out of here.'

I was angry with her now. 'How can you let this place get into such a state anyhow?'

'I want to go, Will.'

'There's even room in the garden for an annexe, if Dad ever wanted to—'

'I'm calling the police!' the woman yelled and she reached for the phone but it was too far from her.

'Yes, we're going,' said Kate. 'Are you all right?'

The woman threw a book at us. It bounced off the wall and down the stairs. Kate hurried back down and through the kitchen. As we burst through the swing doors into the café she grabbed the waitress: 'If you want us to pay, give us the bill now because we're going.'

'I don't care,' she said.

I appealed to Kate: 'You're not trying to like it.'

Kate turned and gave me the look that eighteen years has taught me precedes a yell: 'I want to get out of this place right now!!'

The room went quiet. The waitress started to tremble, and then dropped her tray and buckled in a silent spasm of weeping. A couple with young children got up and left.

Now Kate couldn't resist the waitress. 'Are you all right, dear?' she asked and put her arm round her.

The waitress sobbed uncontrollably: 'This is the worst job I've ever had.'

'Give her five pounds, Will.'

'Five pounds!'

186

'She deserves a tip. Give it to her.'

I offered the waitress a five-pound note. It was like waving smelling salts under her nose. She stuffed it in her pocket. 'I quit,' she said, and took her apron off.

'Good for you,' said Kate. 'Can we give you a lift somewhere?'

*   *   *

We dropped the waitress in Stratford. She and Kate were so friendly by this time I thought they were going to swap addresses and keep in touch.

'Where to now?' I asked everyone, trying to pretend that the day hadn't taken an irreversible dive.

'Home,' chorused the whole Caravelle.

No one spoke all the way to Oxford. Kate sat next to me looking out of her window. The kids fell asleep, so did Dad. Rita looked out at the hard shoulder. 'I'm thinking,' she replied, when Ted asked her what she was doing.

A storm blew up from the south. The sky grew so dark it became the colour of the road. I switched my lights on and the dash lit up like a cockpit. I felt like a captain at the controls, heading into turbulence that just might swallow us. I turned to Kate: 'So, really, what do you think?'

She glanced at me and shook her head in disbelief.

'What?'

'I don't want to talk about it.'

'I reckon it's a good bet. The gift shop's a little gold mine.'

'I don't want to talk about it.'

187

'We'll talk when we get home.'

We got caught in a tailback on the M25. I sat in the gloom looking down on the wet cars. I'd been wrong to surprise her. I should have known by now she doesn't like surprises. I should have broken the idea to her gently. I just wanted to give it to her ready wrapped, a present she could hold in her hands and say to me, 'How did you know? It's just what I wanted.' I didn't want her to have to do any of the work.

We came back in along the M1, past our flat. I could peer into the living room and practically see the television. She couldn't want to stay living there. She wouldn't take much talking round.

Ted and Rita offered to take Dad home. They gave hurried goodbyes and thank yous. Rita yawned. 'I need my beauty sleep.'

It was a awkward end to the day. Kate and I carried the kids in and put them straight to bed. Then she kicked her shoes off and said, 'I'm going to bed myself.'

I brought her a cup of tea and sat with her, making small talk about Stephen running off, about Dad and the windmill, somehow managing to make the day sound less fun than it was. She knew what I was working towards. I took her empty cup from her and said, 'So, come on, tell me what you think?'

'About what?' She was looking for her place in *Middlemarch.*

'You know about what? The Climbing Rose Tea-rooms and Gift Shop.'

'I can't think what you have in mind.'

'I think we should buy the leasehold. Forty thousand, they want. I've been to see the bank. With the money from the advert as a down

188

payment we should be able to borrow the rest on a business loan, or even overdraft.'

She looked up but didn't say anything, then back to the book again. I kept going. 'I've worked it all out. Within two years we can buy the freehold, and still have enough to—'

She slammed her book shut and said very firmly, 'I don't want to move to Stratford-upon-Avon. I don't even want to discuss it. I can't think of anything more ridiculous.'

'Stratford's a lovely place. And it's a good business. Don't worry about first impressions, that's why it's a good price. We can turn it around, make it our own.'

'You're doing it again. You're not listening to me. I'm not moving to Stratford, all right? I've got better things to do.'

'Like what?'

'The things I do now. The things I do are very important to me. I know you can't understand that, but it's true.'

A car horn blared. I waited for a crash but none came. 'This is the opportunity we've been working towards.'

'You may have been. I haven't.'

'What does that mean?'

'It means I've never had plans to move to a café in Stratford.'

What was she talking about?

'We've always talked about moving out, about buying a business.'

'No we haven't! You have. You've never stopped to ask me what I thought.'

'Well, why didn't you tell me what you thought? You've seen me working on business plans; you've

189

answered phone calls from estate agents.'

'I thought this was just another one of your wild schemes.'

'So you were just humouring me all this time?'

She looked away. It was true. She said, 'I never thought you'd manage anything like this. I didn't think it would ever be an issue.'

I rubbed my eyes with my palms. I didn't want to get angry. I wanted to get working. 'Listen. You'll be all right. You'll get used to it. You'll find things you like to do.'

'Oh shut up! Don't patronize me! You've no idea what I like to do. Or what I need to function. You don't have any interest in what I do!'

She turned away. She knew, like I knew, that this argument was going in the same direction as all our arguments: nowhere.

'What do you want, Will? What do you really want?'

'I want to live happily with my family.'

'Well, that's good, because that's just what I want. And I would be very unhappy living in some tourist-board version of England. I like my job. I like my friends. You don't bother with friends, but I do. I'm happy here.'

'I don't believe you're happy here!'

'I am. And so are the boys.'

'Well, I'm not.'

She looked at me and I knew she wanted to say, 'That's your problem.' Instead she settled for: 'Running away to Stratford isn't going to change that.'

'I'm not running away! And I don't believe you're happy here.'

'Oh all right, I don't want to look over the

motorway for ever. I'd like a bit bigger house. I'd like a garden. But I'm not doing something I would hate to get it.'

'Think about the kids. The schools out there are better than here.'

'How do you know that?'

'They're bound to be. And the air quality. It would do Martin's asthma the world of good.'

'Air quality? Anne Hathaway's coach park is just round the bloody corner!'

I cursed, and went to the window and watched the headlights. She sighed and came over to me. 'Will, you're looking at what you don't have rather than what you do. Why can't you just look around you instead of looking . . . miles into the distance? You say you're only trying to make us happy, but you're trying too hard. You're a good man who loves his family. You're a good father. Your family love you. Why can't you be happy with that?'

She was going to say there are so many people worse off than you.

'There are so many people worse off—'

'Don't say that, OK! I hate it when you say that!'

There was a child at the door. It was Martin standing in the shadows. 'Are you shouting?'

'No, we're not shouting.' I went and put my arm round him. 'We were discussing. What would you rather do, Martin? Stay here in this flat with all these houses around and the traffic, or go and live in the country above that teashop we saw today?'

'Stay here.'

'You're just saying that. You haven't thought it through. Back to bed.'

Later, I walked the day's bottles down to the bottle bank. The satellite dishes high on the houses glowed in the moonlight, tuned into a beam I planned to receive myself one day soon.

A freshly mashed cat glistened on the tarmac.

My friend with the ponytail and the skip from Hamilton Road was there with a bag of bottles.

'You ever hear back from Friends of the Earth?' I asked.

'No,' he said.

I threw my green bottles in. They made a contemplative chink as they hit the pile halfway up.

She'd come round to my thinking in the end. She had to. I'd keep things going, but I'd take it easy. Be more subtle. I'd make her see sense.

'How about Esther Rantzen?'

'No.'

Then the clear bottle. It hit the bottom of the bin with a splash and reached all four corners.

I mean, she couldn't be happy here. She couldn't be. She was just frightened of change, that was all. I wasn't running away anywhere, either. And I did have friends. This guy was my friend. I just didn't know his name, that's all. I smiled at him and he glanced at me uneasily. I said—just being chatty: 'So how's your house coming on?'

He looked startled. He said quietly, 'Maybe you can help me there.'

'Not with doing up houses, not me.'

But he took something out of his pocket, a bone, the size of a turkey leg, and he held it out to me: 'What do you reckon that is?'

I fingered it. It was just a bone. 'I don't know. Why?'

'I found a bunch of them under the floor when I dug up the kitchen.'

CHAPTER EIGHT

A TOUR OF THE LAKES WITH
A TUDOR BANQUET

Toby Jones probed the corners of our living room with his Turbo Vac, one arm placed languidly on his hip, his double-breasted suit flapping in his wake. He whistled while he worked.

'Ah, a bookshelf,' he said as his gaze fell on our Book Club collection of classics. 'The Turbo Vac has a specially designed adapter for reaching the dusty tops of books on bookshelves.' He changed the nozzle with a flourish and shoved the probe in between *Mansfield Park* and *Northanger Abbey*, books we had never opened. I wondered how they had escaped the boot sale all these years.

'So are you any nearer making a decision, Mr Green?' he asked. It seemed to me he was desperate for a sale. He'd been to demonstrate three times now and the house was cleaner than it had ever been. I was beginning to wonder what the point in buying a new vacuum cleaner was. I'd just get Toby Jones to come once a week.

'Yes and no, Toby.' I was trying to look simultaneously enthusiastic and cautious.

His eyelids drooped. He looked tired. 'Maybe I should speak to Mrs Green again.'

This was his problem. He was uncomfortable trying to sell to someone who wasn't a woman. He hadn't put on that aftershave so freely or ironed that shirt so precisely to impress someone like me. He wanted to sell to someone who noticed his

193

cufflinks and the sparkle in his blue eyes. He wanted to compliment me on the interior design of my house, and tell me how young I looked.

'Toby, how many times do I have to tell you? Mrs Green couldn't care less. I'm the one you have to impress.'

He looked at me timidly. He reassessed the situation; he thought back to his training days. He decided to try to sell his vacuum cleaner the way he would have done a Ferrari. 'You see, Will, the great thing about this Dustsearcher model of the Turbo Vac range is it actually has two motors. And when the turbo kicks in . . .'

But I wasn't listening to bullshit any more. I'd read more brochures, more test results, more bulletins from the Asthma and Bronchial Disease Council than any salesman on the road. I stood too closely to him and said, 'A turbo is all very well, Toby, but I understand this is a permabag model.'

'That's right.'

'And that incorporates a bacteria-killing screen, I assume?'

'Yes. That's right.'

'So answer me this: What happens when the permabag gets clogged up with dirt which, inevitably, over a period of time, it will?'

'I . . .'

'I'll tell you what will happen. Your bacteria-killing screen will be rendered non-functional. Worse, it will propel the collected bacteria back into the room just vacuumed.'

'Yes.'

'You see, I'm surprised that a machine as sophisticated as you say yours is hasn't gone for the bagless option.'

194

He stalled. 'There's only one vacuum cleaner on the market that is bagless.'

'And we all know which one that is, don't we?'

'Yes.'

'Not the Turbo Vac, is it?'

'No.'

He packed away his equipment, then stared at the floor. Poor man. I began to feel sorry for him. 'Are you happy in your work, Toby?'

'I've been having a hard time recently to be honest, Mr Green. I've been wondering if I'm really . . . if I'm . . .' He swallowed his words. His hands were shaking as he fumbled with his attachments.

'If you're really what?'

'Nothing . . . Sorry.' And he zipped up his bag and left. I felt bad, because in fact I'd been talking complete bollocks about bagless systems. I was baffling him with his own science. The truth was I thought his Turbo Vac was wonderful. My extensive research had shown it to be the best model of them all and I coveted it. I even dreamt about it. But at seven hundred quid a go it would have to wait until my first pay cheque from Robinson's Lemon Barley Water, like all sorts of things.

The day of the advert grew nearer. I arranged for time off from Welcome. 'Bleedin' TV personalities,' was all Graham said.

Vanessa took us for a wardrobe appointment. A young woman called Sandy kitted us out in tracksuits and expensive Nike trainers. 'You can keep these after the shoot,' she said to Martin, as she laced them up for him. Martin looked at me with wonder; he wanted confirmation this was really true. It was finally sinking in what we had achieved. He looked like he might cry with joy.

When I told Vanessa I had to go away for a few days, she didn't look happy. 'We don't want you injuring yourself.'

'Don't worry.'

'Is it work?'

'That's right.'

'You're very busy, aren't you?'

'I am.'

'We were lucky to get you, I suppose.'

That's what I liked to think—they were lucky to get me.

*   *   *

I was off to the Lakes, a three-day, two-night tour incorporating visits to the Wedgwood factory in Stoke and to Chester. There was of course, as Kate pointed out, no need for me to take these overnights any more. Not that she made a fuss this time; I don't think she cared any more. We weren't saying much to each other. We looked after ourselves.

But I wanted to go away one more time. I needed to talk to Alice, and the sort of conversation I wanted just wouldn't have felt right in the Welcome waiting room or out on the street. We only existed on our trips away, and I wanted to sit with her in a teashop overlooking water with hills in the background and explain myself.

I sat in my driver's seat waiting for her, rehearsing, reminding myself I was about to start work in the world of advertising where reputation was everything. My face would be seen in living rooms and on billboards up and down the country. My image was of a family man, a father, and image in this business was everything. The press might take an interest in my private life. I couldn't afford scandal to bring about my downfall. I had too much at stake. I had to end this affair before it really started. I had to be sensible.

And then there she was striding across the tarmac. As if in slow motion her blonde hair swung round her shoulders and bounced off her collar. She'd had some sun since I last saw her; she had no tights on over her smooth brown legs. She climbed the steps and we smiled at each other in our official capacities. I looked away and saw myself sitting in a café in Windermere, putting my hand over hers, on top of the table rather than underneath it, and saying, 'Don't be sad; we'll always have York,' and I felt a pain, not in my heart exactly, but in that region.

This tour of the north-west was most popular among Japanese visitors. They went to Stratford and Bath and York like everyone else, but I often thought those excursions were just warm-ups for the real thing. This tour of the Lakes was the real reason they had flown across nine time zones. They had come to visit Beatrix Potter country.

A number had booked on our trip. They were waiting outside their hotels in colourful raingear, and as the coach stopped they moved forward in well-ordered groups. They were generally the best mannered of all tourists and the least trouble. They were also well informed. Few people on the Brontë or Shakespeare trips had bothered with any of the books, but on this tour the Japanese clutched the complete works. 'Peter Rabbit is very popular in

Japan,' said one gentleman to me when we stopped in a café for tea and scones on the journey north. 'More popular than Princess Diana. More popular even than Thomas the Tank Engine.' He handed me his card: *Taro Kimura. Development Consultant.* Then he asked me to sign his *Guide to Lakeland.*

The Japanese made the other nationalities on board look conspicuous, although the McCardles from Iowa would have stood out in any crowd. They quickly introduced themselves to me as George and Cal. He said, 'We went to France, Will, we didn't like it. The crap in the streets is appalling. Don't know if it was the dogs or the French.' And he guffawed.

They seemed to resent being surrounded by Japanese. They made a point of sitting as far away from them as possible. They took refuge in the Norwegian couple and the family from Germany. I overheard George as he chatted to the Norwegian man in the café. He leant forward and said, 'I was in shipping. I did business with those people. You can't trust them.'

His wife stood outside and filmed the coach with a sweep of her video camera. 'We've been tracing our roots,' she said to me. 'Both our families came from Scotland. We've got a tartan. George will wear it one night.'

We motored through the rain and the roadworks up the M6 to Stoke. I was driving too fast, I knew, but I wanted to get to the Lakes; I wanted to get to our hotel and spend time with Alice telling her how I couldn't spend time with her any more. 'How long have we got here?' she asked me when we reached the Wedgwood factory.

'Forty-five minutes,' I lied. 'We're behind

198

schedule.'

It was long enough. Stoke was nowhere to bring tourists. They had little interest in the factory and its history. All they wanted to do was buy a blue and white pot to take home. They hurried off keenly, the Japanese contingent leading the way, but most of them were back within half an hour, clutching their plastic bag with the Wedgwood logo.

Chester was a similar sort of stop. The black and white buildings had been seen on posters from Tokyo to Turin, and if there was a chance to tick them off no self-respecting tourist would refuse it. Few were keen to go on Alice's guided walk round the Roman walls, though. Any suggestion that involved walking was rarely greeted with enthusiasm. And under a bleak sky most wanted to get their picture of the famous black and white Rows and get out of town. The youngsters in the Japanese party went to McDonald's and then to a record shop. They bought music by the kilo and hurried back through the rain to the coach. One lad waved his CDs shyly at me; I was happy to play them over the system. 'Louder,' yelled one of the girls and I turned up the volume, so that when Alice arrived back with her small, bedraggled party the bus was a disco. I thought the older ones would object, but one of the kids produced a Beatles collection and the whole bus sang along and stamped their feet. Only the McCardles looked unhappy. They sat looking out of the steamy window at the wet pavements, trying to spot dog shit to write home about. The rest of us cruised north, into Cumbria, swinging along to 'Polythene Pam'.

*   *   *

Our hotel was a large slate building on the shores of Lake Windermere. From every room but mine you could see fells rolling down to dip their feet in the icy water, and in the distance mountains rose in a display of ruggedness that didn't really belong in England. From my window I could see nothing but the wall of the next building, but I was getting used to this. I listened to the staff fill the dustbins in the yard, and the howl of cats fighting over scraps, and I thought: A few more weeks and this will all be over.

I lay on my narrow bed and tried to study my French grammar, although it struck me I was making little headway with this language. Six months I'd been at it and I knew that if I went to France I would still be stumbling about waving my arms. I grew bored and stood in front of the mirror and made French faces. I posed for the cameras. It was a shame I had no dialogue in this commercial. I could do dialogue.

'I bet he drinks Carling Black Label,' I said with a laddish chuckle.

'The Lion goes from strength to strength.' A sort of solid sexiness needed for that one.

I curled my lip. What was the French for lip? Didn't know. I raised an eyebrow. What was the French for eyebrow? Hadn't a clue. 'Ours was always going to be a brief affair,' I whispered into the glass, and imagined a look of helplessness in her eyes.

I turned sideways on. 'I'll never forget you. You made me think differently about myself.'

Or I could just tell her the truth. 'I have a wife

200

and two children. I don't want to deceive them, or you. I can't behave like this.'

I breathed in and held my chest. French for chest? No idea. Hopeless.

I tried to look honest. 'You kept me going when I was about to give up. You inspired me. I owe you everything. I want to say thank you.' I had tears in my own eyes now.

There was a knock at the door. I smoothed my hair and tucked my shirt in. I knew who it would be.

There she stood in a thick-knit pullover and a baseball hat. Although it didn't matter what she wore, a wave of her perfume was enough to make me reconsider everything. She said, 'It's a lovely evening. Let's hire a boat and go out on the lake,' and, well, it would have been rude to say no.

*   *   *

The sun was still high in the sky at six o'clock, the evening a washed-out pink and blue. The town bathed in a rare light that made the lake look safe and easy to handle. There were no other hire boats out. Apart from some sails in the distance feeling for the breeze, we had the lake to ourselves. I rowed for the middle and watched the shore open out. The traffic noise of the town was dim so that all we could hear was the scuffing of the rowlocks. Then when I stopped and rested there was just the sound of a ripple against the bow, and the lazy drip of water from the oars. The rest was silence.

She dipped her fingers in. 'This is my favourite part of England. I'd like to move here one day.'

'And do what?'

'Open a guest house,' she said dreamily.

'I thought you'd say that.'

'It's not very original.'

'It's a good idea,' and I had this ridiculous urge to add: 'It's perfect! We could open a teashop and guest house. I could look after the ground floor and you could do the top. I could sell homemade lemon drizzle cake and you could kit the bedrooms out with designs from those country magazines.'

I had to take a deep breath and remind myself this was all going to stop.

She took the oars and rowed out further. I asked her: 'Have you got the money for this guest house venture?'

'No.'

'What are you going to do to make it happen?' I felt protective towards her, as someone who had been in her position and found a solution.

She shrugged and leant over the oars. 'Well, I've thought about it long and hard, and weighed up the different possibilities, and decided there is really only one route open to me.'

'What's that?'

'Crime.'

'I see. Any particular sort of crime?'

'Something to do with drugs, I thought.'

I nodded. 'That should do the trick.'

'I've always thought that if you have a dream you should chase it.'

She shivered and tucked her chin inside her pullover. I looked at her and she became self-conscious. 'What?'

'Nothing.'

'Let's get back; I'm cold.'

An hour later we were lying end to end in her

bath with drinks from the mini-bar balanced on the rim, soap suds climbing over us, the welcoming fruit bowl wedged between the taps. I fed her a grape and she said, 'Did you know you should eat five bits of fruit a day?'

'I did know that, yes.'

'I just wonder if a grape counts as one piece, the same as an apple, or do you have to eat five bunches?'

I soaped her back and she purred. 'I want you to know I've never had a bath with one of my drivers before.'

'I've never had a bath with one of my guides.' I tried to make it a joke, but I was glad we'd said this. I wanted what was between us to be special, as if we couldn't possibly behave like this with anyone else.

She turned over and water lapped over the side. 'Shall we ask for the Paris trip?' she said with a wink.

'You mean a panoramic motorcoach tour including the Champs-Elysées, Notre Dame, the Eiffel Tower and a guided tour along the River Seine?'

'We could go to a lingerie shop and you could buy me some sexy French underwear.'

'There's no chapter in my grammar book called: "At the Lingerie Shop".'

'You'll have to get by with your hands.'

We got out and lay on the thick carpet and massaged each other with the free bottle of kiwi-and-orange-scented oil (ingredients: essence of kiwi, essence of orange, oil) made in Welwyn Garden City. I ran my lips all over her and she tasted nothing like kiwi or orange. She tasted and smelt of sex, and I thought, having done all the hard work in York, it would be a shame to end this right now, tonight, with her lying naked on the floor here just waiting for me to make love to her. Best to enjoy these last few days away, and then draw a definite, absolutely final line underneath everything after that.

Yes. That was the best idea.

So we made love with the curtains open on the lake, and the sun going down beyond the mountains, and it occurred to me: This is better than the adverts. She made love playfully, pushing me away and then pulling me back; biting me and whispering French in my ear which I didn't understand and never wanted to. We slipped off the bed on to the floor. 'What are you doing to me?' she said, as if I were taking the lead when all along I assumed she was. I wondered: Is that the sign of a good lover? Someone who makes you feel you're an even better lover? Or maybe I was taking the lead. I rolled across the floor with her in my arms. She groaned with what I first thought was pleasure, but was probably my weight forcing all the air out of her. It was so much fun to make love in a big room, with enough floorspace at the bottom of the bed to tumble on to, with a high ceiling and large mirrors in strategic places. This was sex without reins. Even when I knew what she was going to do it always surprised me when she did it. She asked me to touch her here and kiss her there, so I felt free to ask her the same, and there was never any question of stopping before we were both so full of each of other we could do nothing else but roll apart.

I let my arms flop and lay for a while with my

head next to her stomach. I could hear her intestines chatter. I opened my eyes and the first thing I saw was one of those tasteless paintings of dead pheasants hanging off a tin plate with goblets of wine. 'You know what?'

'What?'

'I'm really, really, really . . .'

'Horny?'

'Hungry.'

*   *   *

We found an Italian restaurant in town. 'My treat,' I said and held the door open for her.

The waiter had baggy eyes and chest hair sticking out of his collar. He led us to a table in a corner beneath a faded picture of Venice. There he lit a candle and announced sadly, 'It is my mother's birthday, have a drink on the house.'

'What's your mother's name?' Alice asked him as he poured glasses of wine.

'Mimi. She died two year ago. The best mother in the world.'

'To Mimi,' we toasted his mother. The wine hit my stomach with a crash.

The waiter said, 'So many things I wanted to say to her, but I never did it. I have looked for a woman like her but I cannot find. Is not possible.' He sighed and looked at his shoes. We rearranged our cutlery. Then he said, 'I recommend the grilled peppers and the swordfish.'

We had grilled peppers dripping with olive oil and a bottle of red wine, then swordfish kebabs with wild mushrooms and a bottle of white wine. I ate and ate. 'I can't remember feeling this hungry,'

205

I said.

The waiter looked alarmed. He said to Alice, 'You want to watch him.'

A man with a basket of roses came round. 'Would you like to buy the lady a rose, sir?' he asked me. He had a Welsh accent and terrible teeth. He'd done his best to dress himself up but he smelt bad.

'Yes I would. How much?'

'Just three pounds, sir.'

I didn't care what it cost. I gave him a note and took the flower.

'Have an evening to remember, sir.' He bowed and shuffled off to the next table where the diners waved him away without a glance.

Alice looked reflective. 'Are you enjoying yourself?' I asked. I wanted this evening to be even more perfect than the one in York.

'Yes.'

'You're sure about that?'

'Positive.'

She smelt her rose and said, 'Maybe we should forget France and go on the Welsh Whirl.'

'The Pembrokeshire Coast, Carmarthen Castle. Breathtaking Snowdonia. Four nights; six meals.'

'Or the Scottish interlude.'

'Edinburgh Castle, Loch Lomond and the Dales of Dumfries. Single room forty-five pounds extra.'

We laughed, and yet I wondered if this was a joke. I'd started the evening wanting to take her hand and tell her we couldn't go on, and now I wanted to take her hand and tell her I loved her. I leant forward so I could feel the heat from the candle on my face: 'Do you believe in the pursuit of complete and utter happiness?'

She swallowed and said thoughtfully, 'To a point.'

'No no. You can't believe in complete and utter happiness to a point. It's all or nothing.'

'Do you?'

I paused. 'Yes.'

'But you had to think about it.'

'It's a big decision.'

The night was clear and cold. On the way home we passed a bakery and the warmth of the ovens made us loiter. I pressed her against the slate wall and kissed her neck. She looked up at the starry sky and giggled. I kissed her again, but a shout disturbed us, and then a slammed door and more shouts. The pubs had closed; the dregs were spilling out on to the street. There was the sound of glass breaking and a scream; noises of violence. 'Let's go another way,' she said, so we cut down to the waterfront and walked quickly back. A siren passed nearby as we reached the hotel. 'I always tell my passengers to be in bed before the pubs shut,' she said.

There was no space between us that night, no difference. Our skin was the same shade, our limbs a knot. She breathed in the air I breathed out. Afterwards, as we lay still, I said, 'The thing is, tourists like violence. True, they like to view it from inside their coaches, or from their hotel windows, or from a theatre seat—they like to see it from within their bubbles—but they like it all the same. Do you know what Graham told me? The most popular trip of all at Welcome is the London Dungeon. It's true. You can forget all your palaces, all your castles, all your pub lunches. What they want more than anything is torture and horror, thumb screws and racks and wax models of Dr Crippen. They like violence. It makes them think they're in the real world.'

She didn't respond. She was asleep. I looked at her in the light from the bathroom. I propped myself up on one elbow and examined her, searching her body for imperfections, a blemish that didn't belong, a sign of stress, but she was flawless. She reminded me of a perfect piece of fruit. But then lots of things were reminding me of fruit those days.

I slept with her the whole night, and when I woke I no longer felt uncomfortable being next to her. I wanted to make love again, but it was still early and I had an idea. I left her sleeping and went out to find the bakery we had passed the previous evening.

They were clearing up, their work done for the night, but I was able to buy a bag of croissants, and on the way back I leant over a garden fence and picked a yellow flower that wasn't a daffodil. Back at the hotel I went into the kitchen and persuaded a chef to give me a grapefruit. Up in the room I cut it in two with my Swiss Army knife, and then slit one half around the rim and into segments. I made some coffee with the tea-and-coffee-making facilities and put the lot on a tray with the flower in a vase.

I pulled open the curtains just enough so she could wake with a view of the lake. All was ready. I gently touched her shoulder. She stirred, and I sat on the bed and placed the tray next to her, then opened the collection of Wordsworth's poems I'd brought from the hotel lounge:

'She dwelt among the untrodden ways
Beside the springs of Dove,
A Maid whom there were none to praise
And very few to love:

A violet by a mossy stone
Half hidden from the eye!
Fair as a star, when only one
Is shining in the sky.'

She lay there in silence, watching me, just her eyes and nose above the sheets. No one could ever have done such a thing for her before. I had never done this for anyone before. And it was so easy.

*　　　*　　　*

I shouldn't have been driving a coach that morning. I felt sluggish from the wine and the late night. A dull ache spread across my forehead as I followed the waymarked scenic routes that ringed the lake shorelines. Once I clipped the kerb and a Wedgwood bag fell down from the luggage rack.

The weather didn't help. A hail storm swept in over the hills and pelted the bus making a racket like rocks hitting the roof. Clouds swung in low and filled the valleys, and then rose to clear the liver-coloured peaks. Then the sun blasted through and lit up the water like some special effect. It was frightening, non-stop weather, but the bus was warm, and everyone was sleepy, lulled into thinking they were watching some audio-visual display, the sort of fifteen-minute feature which summed up an attraction so that you didn't need to go and bother with the real thing. George McCardle sat wearing a cardigan, chinos and sneakers. He looked out over Grasmere and said, 'You'd only last a few minutes in there, boys.' Then he fiddled with the air-conditioning vents.

Taro Kimura and his family concentrated hard on the scenery. They consulted their texts, looking to spot Peter Rabbit's fir tree or Mr McGregor in his garden. They sat near the front of the coach and photographed everything they saw. When we reached Beatrix Potter's house at Hill Top, the first thing they did was file into the shop to buy more film.

I never saw anyone work so hard at their tourism as the Kimuras. They read every leaflet they were given. The kids watched every information film, and they never tired. At Hawkshead we visited the Beatrix Potter Gallery and they were first off the bus to view the collection of original drawings from the books. Left alone I put my head back and felt myself falling asleep, but then sat up with a jolt as the McCardles climbed back on board. 'Don't worry about us, Will,' Cal insisted. 'You may as well get some sleep, the Japs will be hours. They're buying up the whole damn gift shop.'

I wondered if they were this offensive all the time, or just when they were away because they knew they would never see the people they met on holiday again. I doubted they had ever kept in touch with anyone they had met on their travels.

'Anyway, if you ask me the Potter woman was overrated,' moaned George.

'She wouldn't sell that kind of stuff today,' agreed Cal.

'Rabbits and ducks,' George muttered. 'Was it her who beat her children, or that other woman?'

I longed for the day to be over, but there was a visit to a model village to get through yet. I drove to it with my window open, feeling the breeze on my face. When we got there I felt so sleepy I thought I'd better take a walk.

I tagged on the end of the group as it strolled round the model castles, windmills and railway stations. The tour came here because the site was thought to be in keeping with the Beatrix Potter theme of miniatures, and it really was the sort of place that charmed tourists immediately. Everyone photographed everyone else until their batteries ran out. They posed along the pathways and the little humpback bridges, scenes that reminded me of the jigsaws we had at home. I found a lawn to sit on, and when the sun came out I couldn't stop myself nodding off again. I dreamed fitfully about Robinson's Lemon Barley Water, and about Toby Jones coming round to my door with a collection tin for Christian Aid. I was woken with a gentle shake on the shoulder from one of the attendants. 'Sorry, you can't lie down here,' he said quietly, not wanting to cause a fuss. 'You're in the exhibit, see.'

I sat up and realized I was actually lying in one of the fields that made up the miniature municipal playing field. Had I rolled over I would have crushed an entire cricket team.

I managed to hold it together to the end of the afternoon without plunging the coach into a lake. I even managed to find the remote stately home where we were to spend the night. There was to be a Tudor banquet that evening and expectations among the clients were high. As I pulled up outside the moderately grand house, out on to the steps came Lord and Lady Whoever-they-were, looking as if their worst nightmares had come true. They had done something terrible in their lives and their penance was to shake hands with tourists and then, God forbid, welcome them into their home.

The Japanese stood back now and let the Americans assume control. 'You own this place, lord?' quizzed George McCardle.

'I like your mullions,' said Cal.

The lord gave a wooden smile and extended his arm towards the door in a manner that said: 'Please, don't expect me to speak to you.'

My room was in the staff quarters. Most of the space was taken up with boxes of cleaning materials. It was clearly a storeroom on other days; they'd just wheeled a bed in, but I didn't care, I knew I wouldn't be sleeping here. I lay down for a while, but now of course I couldn't get to sleep. I changed my shirt and went off to find Alice.

'Come in.' I heard her call as I knocked on her door, and I strode in to find her sitting at a dressing table wearing just her pants.

'I could have been anyone,' I said, but I didn't really hear my own words. All I could think of was how arousing she looked sitting there brushing her hair, her breasts reflected in the mirror.

I walked over to her and put my arms round her and buried my head into her neck. She laughed and wriggled. 'Goosebumps,' I said. 'I find goosebumps sexy,' and I tried to steer her over to the bed.

'No,' she whispered. 'Come with me.'

She stepped into a dress and shoes and took my hand.

'Where are we going?'

'I want to show you something.'

She led me down a long hallway, through door

after door, along walls lined with dark wooden panelling, under grim oil paintings of ancestors. We passed tapestries with frayed edges, rusty crossed swords and dented, dull suits of armour. And all the time, through each door we passed, the voices grew louder and louder, until we emerged on to a gallery overlooking a grand dining room and the Tudor banquet.

At a long table all the Welcome passengers sat dressed in Tudor costume, goblets in one hand, legs of meat in the other. The Japanese contingent were getting the hang of the place now. They stabbed their food and wiped their chins on their tunics. The Americans and Europeans were already at the throwing-bones-over-their-shoulders stage.

Minstrels wandered behind them, keeping safely out of arms' reach. Serving wenches dumped plates of roast potatoes in front of them. I saw George and could make out the lurid colours of the McCardle tartan over his legs.

A Japanese kid threw a bread roll at the German kid. It missed him and landed at the head of the table where the lord and lady sat dressed like Henry VIII and Anne Boleyn, trying to be part of it all, a look of tension and utter misery on their faces. They ate the soup and nothing else. I saw him glance at her, and it seemed only a matter of time before they would make their excuses and go upstairs, where they would hug each other briefly and drink poison.

Alice and I stood above it all leaning over a railing. I was thinking how content all the tourists looked for once. All day they'd wanted to be part of the proceedings, to walk the fells with Beatrix

Potter or Wordsworth. This was the nearest they would ever get to joining in, and they seemed happy with that.

'Come on,' said Alice. 'This isn't what I've brought you to see.' And she led me off again, along more corridors, past more pictures, down more creaking steps, until we came to a room marked the Jedburgh Suite.

She was trying to be quiet now, as she tried the door and slowly pushed it open. In the darkness I could see little except an outline of a big piece of furniture. Then she found a light switch. The room was suddenly floodlit, and there before us was an old and very grand four-poster bed, wrapped in purple and gold curtains. On the wall by the side was a polished plaque with the words: *Mary Queen of Scots slept here on her journey north to Jedburgh in 1561*.

Alice put her arms round me and said, 'Whenever I see a bed Mary Queen of Scots slept in I want to have sex in it,' and she rubbed her lips across mine like some temptress. I closed my eyes and saw Mary Queen of Scots' carriage coming up the A69 through Brampton and then taking the A68 north exit at the roundabout past Hexham.

She pulled open the curtains and tied them round the gnarled posts. The bed looked much too small for an adult. 'I thought Mary Queen of Scots was five foot eleven,' I said.

We lay down carefully. The whole structure creaked like a ship. The mattress was like lying on a bag of crisps. I yelped as the edge of something dug into my back. 'Sssh,' she said, and rolled over so her hair fell on my face.

We removed what clothing was necessary, and

214

then she straddled me and I was immediately comfortable. The bed was like a cloud, and looking up at her I caught a glimpse of her as the future, as reality, and it seemed to me that this was where I belonged, in a four-poster bed where Mary Queen of Scots had slept on her way north to Jedburgh in 1561.

CHAPTER NINE

WIMBLEDON

My mobile phone was my link to the real world. It never left my side. I charged it up by my bed as I slept. When my voice-mail rang me it was always good news.

Clarissa from the estate agent's called to say the vendors of the Climbing Rose had accepted my offer. Paul my BBM told me my business plan had been approved. Vanessa from the Lemon Barley Water production office left a message informing me a car would pick us up at seven-thirty a.m. on Wednesday and take us to Wimbledon. Bryan Harper's secretary Zoë called to say the contracts were drawn up and to ask if I was on e-mail. I hated having to say no. I wanted everything now. I didn't want to wait for lawyers to communicate with each other. I slammed a door in impatience. Stephen opened it and slammed it shut again in sympathy.

I contacted a local estate agent and arranged for a valuer to come round and look at our flat one morning when Kate was out. The valuer was about eighteen years old and he stood on the doorstep and flashed his ID like a private detective. 'Simon Fuller. Account negotiator for Grays, Coward and Rothenberg.' Then he looked over his shoulder and stepped inside.

'You've not got a ghost or anything, have you?' he asked as I showed him round. He chewed on a toothpick and seemed to be looking for something.

'No.'

'Blue plaque?'

'No.'

'And you're not on this new Heritage Walk they're putting together? No one famous was born here?'

'No.'

'Just looking for an angle, you know.' He clicked his tongue then went into the bedroom and saw the motorway. 'That's the M1, isn't it?'

'Yeah,' I admitted. 'We've got double-glazing, though.'

'No, it's good. The M1 is good. It was the first motorway in the country, did you know that?'

'No.'

'It's listed.'

'What?'

'It's bound to be. You can put three grand on the asking price for that.'

He wanted the dimensions of the rooms but had forgotten his tape measure, so he lay down on the floor and then made me lie down so that my feet touched his head.

'I'm five foot eight,' he announced proudly. 'How tall are you?'

'Five eleven.'

'Is your head touching the skirting?'

'About nine inches off.'

'We'll call it twelve and a half feet.'

We did this in all the rooms. He wrote the measurements down on the back of a petrol receipt. He looked at a picture of Kate on a shelf and asked, 'Is that Julia Roberts?'

'No. It's my wife.'

'She looks like Julia Roberts.'

'No she doesn't.'

'Yes she does.'

He was the strangest estate agent I'd ever met, but I had the feeling that if anyone could sell my flat for a price above what it was worth, it was him.

The evening before the shoot was warm and windless. Martin and I sat drinking Robinson's Lemon Barley Water. I wanted to spend time with him. I was worried I'd not explained everything fully. 'You're all right with all this, aren't you?' I asked him.

'Yeah.'

'You don't look all right.'

'I'm all right.'

I took him out to the tennis court. The laces on his trainers flapped loose. I'd tried to buy him new ones but he'd said no. He made a scene about it in the shoe shop in fact. He said he wanted to wait for the pair of Nikes. I let him have his way. 'This time tomorrow those will be in the bin,' I laughed.

He said nothing. He seemed to be taking things very seriously.

We knocked balls to each other. He was improving each time we came here, timing his shots, hitting the ball deep. I had to raise my own standard each time we played. The day would come soon when I would have to play my best to beat him, and soon after that our levels would wave to each other as they passed on the scale. Then he'd have to take it easy whenever he played me. In fact there'd be no point in playing me other than to humour me. It would be his way of amusing me, instead of the other way round.

The park keeper leant against the fence. 'He's coming on, isn't he?'

'Guess what? He's going to be playing at Wimbledon.'

'Getaway!'

'It's true. He's going to be on the telly.'

'This lad?'

'Yes. And it's all thanks to you. All because you let him play without a booking.'

'I don't know what to say. I . . . feel quite proud.'

'So you should be.'

We went home and I put Martin to bed. He said, 'When I get my new trainers will they give me the box they come in?'

'I expect so.'

'Good. I want to keep them in the box.'

I kissed him goodnight. Stephen woke up and saw me: 'Daddy?'

'Yep.'

'Where do you live?'

Before I could get close to thinking of a suitable response to that question, he added, 'There's someone at the door,' and a second later there was a knock. I backed out of the room. Maybe it was time we took Stephen to see someone.

'There's someone at the door,' I called to Kate.

'I know,' she replied and I saw her sigh. She knew it would be Ted and Rita.

They came in and sat in the living room. Kate

said nothing. I said nothing. Ted said nothing. Rita said, 'I'm sick to death of these people on the radio who moan and moan just because they were abused as children.'

'Might as well leave the girls to talk, eh?' said Ted.

'I want an early night to be honest, Ted.'

'Oh for God's sake,' and he pushed me out.

He kicked a can down the street. He seemed to be in the same rotten mood he'd been in on the day of our outing to Stratford.

'Are you all right?' I asked him.

'Yeah,' he grumbled.

'You sure?'

'Yeah.'

'Your shirt buttons are done up in the wrong holes, you know.'

For some reason the pub wasn't so busy that night, and the drinkers looked subdued, meditative even, a word you wouldn't normally use to describe the clientele at the George. None of them was playing darts or shouting at each other. The landlord was shaking his head and huddling with his favourites. The barmaid who looked like Kevin Keegan saw to us. I paid for the drinks as I had always done since I'd got the Robinson's job. I didn't mind.

Ted stood staring into his beer, not saying anything.

'You're not all right, are you?' I said.

'I'm all right.'

'You've brought me down the pub and now you're not going to say anything.'

'All right. You really want to know what's wrong?'

219

'Yeah.'

'I'm pissed off. With you.'

'Me? Why?'

'For suddenly being successful.'

'What's that supposed to mean?'

'It's not right. You getting a cushy job and being paid a bunch of money. It doesn't suit you. I mean, how am I suppose to feel?'

'How about, pleased for me?'

'That's asking an awful lot, Will. Have you any idea what it's like when a mate—worse, a brother-in-law—suddenly gets successful? I mean, our relationship is based on you being a failure.'

'Why should I be the failure all the time?'

' 'Cos . . . you're good at it. It's you; the you we know and love. You can't get successful and expect people to treat you the same. You've done the worst thing you could possibly do: you've changed your status.'

He took a great swig of his beer. I said, 'Well, thanks for being so honest.'

'I don't know how you can do it, to be frank—how you can be financially dependent on your eight-year-old kid.'

'Well, I did worry about that for a while, but I got over it thanks to the support of my friends and family.'

He sneered. 'You just don't think of others, that's your trouble. Where's my cigar? You didn't buy me a cigar, see.'

I tried to get the landlord's attention. He saw me and came over and then did a very strange thing indeed. He spoke to us in a chatty, sort of landlordy way. He said, 'So what about Mickey?'

'Who's Mickey?' I asked.

220

'You know Mickey. The bloke with the skip on Hamilton Road?'

'The bloke with the ponytail?'

'What about him?' said Ted.

'They found another body.'

'What?'

'They found another body in his house.'

'What do you mean, *another* one?' I said.

'He found the first one cemented into the floor in the kitchen. So the police went in and now they've found another one in the wall in the hall. That makes two.'

'Fuck,' said Ted.

'They're going to dig up the patio tomorrow.'

We walked home via Hamilton Road, and there were the police cars and vans parked and double-parked. The skip was gone, and all the windows in the house had been blocked up with black screens. They were framed with intense light.

'How many bodies did he say?' asked Ted.

'Two.'

'Bet there's more. There's always more than two.'

We stood and watched for a minute. An officer stood guard outside the house, but he didn't look the sort to answer questions. In the houses opposite faces looked out from the corners of curtains.

'I used to meet him at the bottle bank,' I said quietly. 'On a regular basis.'

'I'll tell you what,' said Ted. 'I bet it puts the price of his house up. That sort of thing always does. You can't plan for it, of course. You can't second-guess the property market. That's the beauty of it.'

The alarm went at six the next morning. I sat up and looked at Kate lying there in her T-shirt from Glastonbury 1983. It was faded and dotted with little moth-holes. I thought of Mary Queen of Scots and got an erection.

I let Stephen sleep while Martin and I had breakfast. He said, 'I'm going to open the milk bottles, Dad, are you ready?'

Now that it didn't matter if we won a free holiday I really expected to win each time we took the cap off a bottle.

'It's a Y.'

'We've already got three Ys.'

But we never did win.

We dressed in the new clothes I'd bought for the day, cords and Gap T-shirts.

'My new trousers are too short,' complained Martin.

'They can't be too short for you.'

'They are.'

'They fitted you on Saturday.'

'I've grown.'

'You can't grow in two days.'

But he had. He saw me shake my head, and he looked apologetic, as if he'd done wrong. He was feeling nervous so I hugged him. I didn't want him to think I was cross with him for growing. We brushed our teeth, and waited for the car.

Kate stumbled in with Stephen. He said, 'I've just had a dream and it was so good I'm not going to tell you what it was about.'

'That's not fair,' said Martin.

'It's my dream,' said Stephen.

Kate yawned and smartened Martin up, tucked things in that I wouldn't have tucked in, did his shoes in double knots, smeared sunscreen all over him.

'Good luck,' she said and hugged him.

'I want to know what his dream was,' demanded Martin. All these hugs were making him more nervous. There was a knock at the door and we all jumped.

A big man in a dark suit and sunglasses led us away to a big blue Peugeot. He opened the back door and Martin climbed inside. But I wasn't going to be one of those media people who thought he was above talking to the driver, no way. I opened the front door to get in the passenger seat.

'What do you think you're doing?' the driver snapped at me.

'I want to sit in the front with you.'

'Bollocks! Get in the back like everyone else. Who d'you think you are?'

We headed towards the North Circular. 'Which way are you going exactly?' I asked, but he didn't answer. 'It's just 'cos you could have gone up to the M25 and gone round. Everyone thinks the M25 is bad but I reckon it's always quickest. I drive a coach, see ...' I thought this might endear me to him, but he just grunted. ' ... when I'm not acting, that is, you know, in adverts. I'm Will, by the way. This is Martin.'

'We'll listen to the radio, shall we?' he suggested, and at the press of a button a voice from a cosy studio said, 'People on reduced incomes are much more prone to heart disease, mental illness and teenage pregnancies.'

Not a cloud in the sky, just an orange wisp of smog gathering to the east. Summer weather, tennis weather, filming weather. The multi-coloured metal roofs of the traffic simmered in the dips and curves ahead. As we inched along in the fast lane I took notice of the adverts on the billboards. The men all had gleaming teeth, beautiful wives and impressive kitchens. They had pedigree pets and big lawns for them to roll about on. They went on holiday to paradise islands. They received financial advice from good-looking financial advisors. I studied the way the models posed, their nonchalant grins, the way they made their eyebrows work in their favour. I practised my smug face and my determined face. I tried to look paternal. I tried to look firm. I decided I was more cut out to sell lawnmowers than aftershave. 'Let's have a look at your nails,' I said to Martin. He held out his hand; his nails were chewed and full of muck. 'You had a bath last night. How can you get your nails that dirty already?'

He looked up at me with big eyes. I put my arm round him. 'Can we have a new computer, Dad?'

'You can have what you want, son,' I said. He looked out of the window happily, and I could see myself looking out of the window of my dad's Austin A40 and asking for a new bike or something and my dad saying, 'Bikes don't grow on trees, you know.'

*   *   *

I couldn't remember ever having been to Wimbledon before, and, absurdly, I imagined it to be the tennis courts and nothing else. I'd pictured a

224

purple and green, ivy-clad mothership rising out of open country, but as we passed the Welcome to Wimbledon sign we were still stuck in traffic, and there were shopping centres and blocks of flats around us, and familiar graffiti on all the railway bridges. Our driver looked for a shortcut out of the jam and took turnings behind breaker's yards and dog tracks. Only when we finally approached the gates of the All England Lawn Tennis & Croquet Club did I get the feeling of privilege with which you always associated the district.

But then we drove straight past. I didn't say anything at first, maybe he was taking us to another entrance. But after we'd gone on for another mile or two, I leant forward and said, 'I thought we were going to Wimbledon.'

'He likes to say he lives in Wimbledon. It's more Merton Park.'

'Who does?'

'Trevor Fallon, the director. Have you met him?'

'Yeah.'

'Wanker, isn't he?'

Then we were driving down an avenue of nice big houses until we came to one with a line of vehicles and trailers parked outside. Our car stopped in the road.

'Out you get,' ordered the driver.

Martin and I stood on the pavement as the Peugeot drove off. It was nine-fifteen a.m. and I already felt cheated. I wondered if I should phone my agent and complain, but then there was Vanessa striding towards us, with various communication devices clipped to her waist.

'Will! Hi.'

'Hi.'

'Hello, Martin,' and she patted him on the head. We both looked disappointed. 'Are you all right?' she asked.

'Fine.'

Martin said nothing.

'Are you sure?'

'Fine.'

She led us into the house, introducing us to various members of the crew as they passed, wiry young people with nice skin, wearing clothes that looked too big for them. I shook hands with an Yvonne, a Hanna, a Darren and a Fred. They all made a quick fuss of Martin, asked him what team he supported, then hurried on.

I still wasn't sure what was happening. I felt disoriented. I'd imagined myself on Centre Court, and here I was in someone's tastefully decorated suburban home. I didn't like to ask anything for fear of appearing stupid. But then Vanessa led us into the back garden, and there at the bottom of the lawn was a grass tennis court. In the middle stood Trevor Fallon dressed in shorts and baseball hat, waving his arms in the air as if he were directing traffic. Vanessa took us straight to him, and he looked at us as if he'd never set eyes on us before. Finally it registered, and he held out his arms and got as far as pronouncing the first syllable of Martin's name before someone thrust a phone in his face, and that was the last we saw of him all morning.

'How about a doughnut?' suggested Vanessa.

Trevor Fallon had thrown open his house for the crew. The kitchen table was laid out with snack food and drinks. I had a banana and an apple in quick succession. Fruit calmed me, I had

226

discovered; it was crisis food; it was a fix.

Martin wasn't so easily relaxed. He picked at a doughnut. Vanessa patted him on the head again. I wondered if I should tell her there was nothing kids hated more than being patted on the head.

'There's a TV upstairs,' she said. 'Lots of videos, and a table football table.'

I decided to save the story of how I thought we were going to be playing on Centre Court for when I was the established face of Lemon Barley Water, for when I was having lunch with the directors. Vanessa's phone rang. 'You bitch!' she said and hung up.

She took us upstairs to a bedroom where family snaps stood on a dressing table and there was an exercise bike by the side of the bed. 'This will be your dressing room,' she said.

A woman smelling of cigarettes and mints joined us. 'This is Lesley,' said Vanessa. I shook hands with Lesley. 'She's going to cut your hair.'

We were being treated like celebrities, but this just made us both feel strange and awkward. 'Where are you from?' I asked Lesley, looking at her in the mirror, trying to be friendly, but she didn't answer. 'Vanessa will be back in a minute,' was all she said.

Lesley cut our hair very nicely and very quickly, and then Vanessa returned with Sandy from the costume department who had kitted us out the previous week. It was good to see a familiar face. 'Hello, Sandy,' I said cheerfully.

'Hello . . .' she replied. She'd obviously forgotten our names.

She handed us our tennis shirts, shorts and socks and tracksuits, and then left. Martin looked uneasy:

'She hasn't given us our trainers.'

'Don't worry,' I said, and almost patted his head.

She was the last contact we had for an hour. I looked out of the window and saw a man on a sit-on motormower shave the court one last time. The day was so still and clammy half the crew worked with their shirts off: Trevor Fallon was still on the phone. I couldn't believe it took this number of people to make a soft-drink commercial.

There were some magazines on a table. I threw Martin an old copy of *Motor*. 'Pick a new car for us,' I told him. He fumbled it and dropped it. We were both as nervous as each other. I wanted something to do, something to rehearse—a required look, that particular sort of shrug they were after. I needed to know what my character was. I needed work. I heard someone shout at the bottom of the stairs: 'Well, you can tell him to go screw himself!' and I wondered if the only way to get what you wanted in this business was to have a tantrum.

I flicked through a woman's magazine and read the problem page: *I am eighteen years old and live with the burden of my abortion*—Maddie from Margate; *it has been two years since a guy kissed me*—Sarah from Bristol; *I am twenty-five and feel like I am falling into a bottomless pit of despair and depression*—Joanna from Dumbarton; *I am thirty-seven years old and I'm so desperate to open a gift shop and tea-rooms in the shadow of Anne Hathaway's Cottage that I have a feeling I might be putting everything else in my life into jeopardy*—Will from North London.

I threw the magazine back on the table and said, 'Martin. It seems to me, more and more, that life is a question of getting one's priorities right.'

'This is the sort of car I want,' he said, holding up an advert for a four-wheel drive, a photograph of a chunky vehicle being driven up a mountain pass by a chunky guy. I wondered if he got to keep it after the shoot. We'd need a four-wheel drive if we moved to the country, for sure. One of those big bull-nosed jobs with a fridge in the back.

Vanessa came back in. 'Why aren't you having lunch?'

'We need shoes,' I told her.

'But lunch is on the table.' She spoke as though lunch was the only reason we were there.

A range of sandwiches had been laid out in the kitchen, proper sandwiches that bulged and were made with good breads, the sort I used to make in my sandwich shop. I sat down next to Mick the sound man and Pete the electrician.

'I can't stand pickle,' said Pete.

'You're weird,' said Mick.

We talked sandwiches. Mick told me about the time he had been sound man on a Sean Connery movie, and how Mr Connery liked to have a fried egg and bacon bap every morning at ten o'clock or he was moody for the rest of the day. I said, 'I can understand that.'

Trevor Fallon came in and I said to Pete and Mick, 'I bet he chooses a cream cheese, chives and pineapple.' We all watched him, and sure enough, cream cheese, chives and pineapple it was. They both laughed. Trevor Fallon looked self-conscious. 'What's funny?' he said and checked his flies. I felt my confidence rise. I was more at ease talking to these two.

Outside a man was painstakingly repainting the

white lines on the court. We'd been there five hours and done little but eat. Martin was becoming restless, but then Sandy arrived with two boxes with the Nike logo on the side. 'Our trainers are here!' he yelped as if it was Christmas. He pulled open the box and threw the tissue paper aside. Sandy helped him on with them like a shoe-shop assistant, then he ran to Trevor Fallon's full-length hallway mirror and looked at his feet from every angle. He was completely satisfied, and he carefully pulled the shoes off and put them back in the box.

'What are you doing?' asked Sandy.

'I don't want to get them dirty,' he explained, and tucked the box under his arm.

'You've got to wear them,' I told him.

'I don't want to. I'll wear my old ones.'

'Martin!'

He ran away from me, just as Vanessa came rushing in. 'Come on,' she ordered. 'They're waiting for you.'

Martin ran up the stairs and into the bedroom and blockaded the door. I had to push my way in. 'For God's sake, Martin. Come on!' I took his arm but he dug his heels in.

'What's wrong?' called up Vanessa.

'Nothing. Nothing's wrong.'

I gave him a menacing look, and gripped his arm. 'What are you doing!' I hissed.

'They're waiting,' yelled Vanessa.

'Get your shoes back on, for God's sake! What's the matter with you?' And he gave in, but I'd never seen him behave like this.

Vanessa led us back to the court, stepping over cables and round spotlights, to where Trevor consulted with his cameraman. I hadn't realized how hot it had become. We'd been inside and not noticed that the clear sky had been coated with a compost of smog. Trevor had huge sweat rings under his arms.

He spun to greet us. 'Martin! Will!' He shook my hand, then put his arm round Martin. He couldn't think of any small talk so he said, 'Right. Listen. We'll do this in stages. Today we'll shoot some casual hitting the ball back and forth, nice and easy. Then we'll move on to close-ups later if we have time, but probably tomorrow.'

'Fine.'

'All right, Martin?' Martin was looking at the ground. Trevor peered at him. 'Is he all right?'

'Yeah.' I bent down to him. 'Come on, lad.' He wouldn't look at me. I put my arm round him. 'Let's play.'

I hoped finally getting on the court would relax us both. We hit a few balls and I felt myself loosen up, but the opposite seemed to be happening to Martin. At first I thought he was sulking over the shoes, so I hit shots to his forehand in an attempt to get his confidence going, but his face screwed up as he attempted to go for them; he was beginning to look over-heated. He went to chase a ball but had to stop, he couldn't run. I stopped playing and went to the net. 'Are you all right?'

He nodded and muttered, but then he looked at me and I could see he was struggling. His breath was a rasp; his mouth was wide open, his eyes watering and bloodshot. He was starting to splutter. The freshly mown grass, the pollen, the still day, the general excitement and stress of the occasion. I realized with horror that he was surrounded by the triggers of an asthma attack. He didn't stand a chance.

'What's the matter?' asked Trevor, as I led Martin off the court to a chair.

'He needs a drink, that's all.' I was speaking calmly, but I was thinking: Please God, not now. 'It's just the standing around, and the heat.'

What I needed was his Ventolin inhaler, and I'd left it in my trouser pocket. 'I just need to get something from the bedroom.'

'What?' moaned Vanessa.

I said to Martin, 'I'll get your puffer. I won't be a minute.'

He didn't respond, but I feared this was because he couldn't; he didn't have the air in his lungs to talk. I sprinted back into the house, up the stairs to the room. The door was locked. I ran back to find Vanessa. I was starting to panic. 'I need to get into the room!'

'Sandy has the key,' she sighed.

Sandy was on the toilet. 'Just a minute,' she called when I banged on the door.

'I need the key to the dressing room. Now!'

'All right, all right, no need to get hostile!'

She passed it under the door. I sprinted up the stairs, shoving a technician out of the way. I grabbed the puffer and ran out again.

The crew had gathered round Martin now. He looked at me with despair as I put the puffer in his mouth and gave him a shot.

'Is he going to be all right?' asked Trevor.

'It's just the cut grass,' I said.

'He doesn't look all right.' The cameraman was peering over him now.

Martin started to cough; his chest was pumping. 'Give him some space, will you?' I gave him

232

another shot. When I put my arm round him he just curved into my body like a baby. 'You've got to sit up straight,' I said gently.

'Shall we call the doctor?' asked someone.

'He'll be all right,' I insisted. 'Just a little reaction. Sort of hay fever.'

'He's not choking, is he?' said Vanessa.

'Looks like an asthma attack to me,' said the cameraman.

'You never said he had asthma,' moaned Vanessa. 'Does he suffer from asthma?'

'A bit. I'll take him inside. Get him out of the heat; he'll be all right in five minutes.' I looked up at the day. The air was stale and full of insects. He was drowning in it.

I carried him back to the house; I don't think he could have walked. Vanessa and the cameraman came with me. Trevor Fallon took a phone call. 'You never said he had asthma,' Vanessa kept whining.

I sat Martin up on a sofa and stroked his brow. 'Take it easy, boy.' But he couldn't take it easy. There was a huge struggle going on inside his chest. I gave him another hit of Ventolin, but the drugs weren't working, and now I noticed his lips were starting to change colour.

'*That* is an asthma attack,' said the cameraman firmly. 'He needs to be treated!'

'I know,' I said, and I put my hands to my head as I knew what I had to do. Nothing else mattered now. 'He needs to go to hospital,' I told Vanessa.

'Hospital!' she screamed. 'Oh Jesus!'

Just shut up and get me a car, will you?'

Trevor came in. 'He's got to go to hospital,' cried Vanessa as she ran out.

233

No one said anything else to me. I phoned St George's to tell them we were coming, then carried Martin to the back seat of the Peugeot we'd arrived in. The big driver in the black suit drove us away. 'Shall I put the radio on?' he asked.

'Just drive!'

*   *   *

Fifteen minutes later we were in a cubicle in Casualty, a nebulizer churning away by Martin's side, a mask strapped to his face, a drug-soaked mist teasing open his airways.

The effect was immediate and life-saving. I sat by him and watched the swell of his chest fall like an easing sea. Within minutes he was asleep. The doctor put oxygen tubes up his nose and said, 'He'll be all right. Let him rest.' We were moved to a children's ward and left alone.

I pulled the curtain round us and sat there and watched him breathe. I wanted to weep, but I had too much to do. I phoned Kate at work and left a message, then I rang Vanessa's mobile.

'How is he?' she asked.

'He's going to be all right. But we'll not be able to come back today. They want him to stay here under observation.'

'You had us all scared.'

'We'll be all right tomorrow.'

She paused for a moment. 'The thing is, Will, we've had to bring in an understudy father-and-son team. We had to.'

Well, what did I think would happen? The whole crew would hang around eating doughnuts until Martin got better?

234

'What are you saying?'

She was embarrassed. 'We've started with them now. We'll have to continue with them.'

'With who?'

'We always have someone on standby in case something goes wrong. You can never tell with kids, you see. You met them at the audition. He used to be the Milky Bar Kid.'

A rush of adrenaline burst into my stomach. 'You can't do this!'

'We had to, Will. Don't worry, there'll be other jobs. You're very good.'

'But you've got us under contract.'

'These things happen.'

'He was overcome by the heat, for God's sake. It could have happened to anyone.'

I was trying to keep my voice down and trying to get angry at the same time.

'Sorry, Will.'

'I'll sue!' Now I was panicking.

'Oh don't be stupid. When you signed the contract you confirmed that neither you nor Martin suffered from any medical condition. You lied. Martin suffers from asthma . . .' She waited for me to deny it. 'The result is we lost the best part of an afternoon's filming. You're lucky we don't sue you!'

Martin slept until early evening. I spent the time reading labels, on anything, on my pullover: *70% cotton 30% polyester, made in Mauritius*; on the bed frame: *Bedwell Medical Equipment, Ware, Hertfordshire. Ring 0345 98 48 79 for service.* I was trying to find something to concentrate on, something that would distract me from the reality that was cornering me like a rising flood. I kept repeating to myself. This isn't true; this sort of luck happens to other people; this much effort can't go to waste; any minute now my trusty mobile will ring and it'll be Trevor Fallon saying the Milky Bar Kid is a disaster and can we go back in the morning. I remained composed, but that was because a children's ward is no place to lose control. I could feel a swelling inside of me. I was teetering on that edge again, and this time slipping. My phone rang, but it was Kate. I told her what had happened and she wanted to speak to Martin not me.

'He's sleeping.'

'Bring him home as soon as you can.' And she hung up.

The hospital discharged us at seven-thirty and we took a taxi back. I watched the meter click up to forty-five pounds. It was going to be an expensive day, although we had come away with two pairs of good-quality trainers and some nice tenniswear.

As we turned off the North Circular I heard a sniff and saw that Martin was crying. 'Hey, what's the matter?' I said softly.

'We're not going to be on the TV now, are we?'

'No. Doesn't matter.'

His eyes were red and his face smudged. 'It was because of my asthma, wasn't it? It was my fault.'

'No.'

'It was.'

And I tried to think of someone else to blame but I couldn't. 'It was bad luck, that's all.'

He turned to me. 'I'm sorry.'

I had never heard him apologize for anything before, not unless he'd been made to. He was growing up. He was taking responsibility. I said, 'I never liked Robinson's Lemon Barley Water anyway. It's yuck.'

Kate took Martin off me at the door and carried him in. 'Do something with that, will you?' she said, pointing to the dog turd on the pavement. The hound was back, and I hadn't even noticed he had gone.

She put Martin in our bed. She didn't look at me as she said, 'I want him in with me tonight. You sleep in their room.'

That seemed fair enough. I was too miserable to try to interpret what it might mean. I fell into the couch. With Martin safely in bed the brutal truth hit me hard. I closed my eyes and saw the Climbing Rose collapse like a house of cards.

Kate hurried from room to room with little steps, her head down, her mouth set, the way she was whenever I had behaved badly. I wanted to get angry with someone and she was nearest. 'You're blaming me for this, aren't you?' I followed her into the kitchen. She turned and hurried past me, pretending to be too busy to talk, and—it seemed to me—getting mileage out of the drama.

'You do, don't you?' I followed her back into the living room. 'I can tell by your disgusted face.'

'What?' She walked out again.

'Just stop moving around, will you?' I caught her arm and she snatched it back.

'I'm trying to make Martin comfortable,' she snapped.

'And you're blaming me for it.'

'You put him under this stress! It's always stress that brings on attacks, and you did it to him.'

'It was the cut grass that did it.'

'You should have known that. You should have known what would happen. But you were too keen to make some stupid money. You wanted this so much for yourself you didn't think about him.'

'That's not true! I wanted this for all of us! I was trying to make our lives better, I keep telling you.'

Now she spun and went for me. 'Listen to me, once and for all. You are not making our lives better! Don't convince yourself you were ever going to make our lives better, because you weren't!'

She was so flustered she started clearing up, picking up newspapers, tidying videos, anything. Then, abruptly, she left the room.

My head was boiling. I kicked the door shut after her. I threw the remote control across the room. It hit the wall and the batteries spilled. Then I marched into the kitchen and said, 'I'm not stopping now, you know! I'm not stopping here! I'll go crazy if I stop.'

And she turned and said quietly, 'Well, in that case, you're on your own.'

'That's what you think.'

I slammed the door and stamped down the stairs, then slammed the front door. I climbed into the car and slammed that door as well, and I would have driven away at speed but the thing wouldn't start. I pulled the choke out so hard it came off in my hands. I could feel tears rising again, and then I looked up and saw her gazing down at me from the window. I put my head on the steering wheel. I desperately wanted to do something to soothe myself, but I could think of absolutely nothing. I had no bottles to smash. The pool was closed. Vinod was shut and I couldn't buy fruit—how could he do this to me? He was my dealer and he'd let me down. In the end I wandered down to Hendon and found a place open. I bought some rotten grapes and stuffed them into my mouth.

Much later I crept back up the stairs of the flat and peered into our bedroom. There was my family. Martin was sleeping on my side of the bed, his chest rising and falling in time with Kate's, her steady breathing guiding him through the night. And there was Stephen on her other side, breathing whenever he felt like it, dreaming of life on another planet. They looked so vulnerable. They reminded me of that picture of the family of dustmites.

I checked my voice-mail and there were three messages: one from Vanessa asking me to return the trainers and tenniswear; one from Bryan Harper telling me he didn't want to represent me any more and I wasn't to return his call; and a second from Vanessa asking me to return the mobile phone.

I climbed into Martin's bed under a Thunderbirds duvet, and lay there with my feet sticking out of the end. I didn't feel comfortable in any of these rooms any more.

CHAPTER TEN

WINDSOR CASTLE, HAMPTON COURT, RUNNYMEDE AND THE KENNEDY MEMORIAL

I had a bad week. I wasn't good to be with. I did the Leeds Castle run (with afternoon tea included) and was rude to a Spanish woman. I took a tour to Oxford and got lost on a route I'd done a hundred times before. I found myself driving round and round a roundabout not knowing which exit to take. I felt rudderless. I refused to believe the Climbing Rose was lost to me, and yet I could see no way forward.

I took to scowling. I refused to wear a name-tag as a gesture of badwill. On an afternoon tour to Greenwich I heard someone say, 'That driver's a grouch.' The guide was a student, doing this as a holiday job, and he became so annoyed with my attitude he said, 'We'll get no tips if you carry on like this, you know.'

I put my face right up to his and said, 'You're speaking to me as if I give a shit.'

'What?'

'I hate people like you. Bloody students.'

'What?'

'What are you studying?'

'Why?'

'Just tell me what you're studying. It's languages, I bet. You lot who work with the tour buses are all studying languages. You walk in here and lick off the cream and then disappear after the summer. Some of us do this for a living, you know. I hate students.'

He looked as if he might burst into tears. 'I'm sorry, I didn't mean to . . .'

So then I became apologetic too. I knew I'd been mean to him. 'It's all right,' I said. 'I know you didn't . . . To be honest I wish I'd gone to university. I'd have studied languages if I'd gone to university.'

'It's not too late,' he chirped. 'It's never too late.' And I grabbed him by the collar and would have nutted him if it hadn't been for Herr and Frau

Glockenspiel climbing back on the bus and waving a Tower of London headscarf under my nose for approval. 'Look at this,' she said proudly. 'What do you think?'

'I think it stinks,' I said.

I thought my temper would calm. I thought I would be able to cope. But having had a taste of success I couldn't spit it out. I rumbled like a volcano about to blow. Little things annoyed me. On a trip to Arundel I heard an English accent among the passengers. I asked the woman where she was from, and when she said Bedford I said bluntly, 'What are you doing on a trip like this?'

She looked put out. She said, 'This is my birthday treat, thank you very much.'

'Why don't you just drive here for the afternoon? What do you want to come on a stupid coach tour with this lot for?'

'It's my birthday,' she repeated.

'But . . . you're English. This stuff isn't for you. This is . . . for them.'

Every evening I went swimming. I put my head down and ploughed hard through the water. Anyone in my way I hit like a steamer. One swimmer complained to the lifeguard and he called out to me. I pretended not to hear, so he blew his silly whistle, and when I stopped he told me I had to be more considerate in my swimming. I told him to fuck off and mind his own business, so he went and got the manager and I told him the same thing. Two more attendants were called, and I was thrown out of the pool and informed I was banned.

As I walked home I saw a dog having a crap outside our front door and something deep inside of me burst. I lost control. I yelled obscenities at

241

the animal from the top of the street. Men in suits stepped aside to get out of my way as I chased it and chased it and chased it. I chased it all the way to the park where it escaped me at a sprint across the playing field, leaving me panting on my knees. Had I caught it I really would have pulled its head off.

The best cure for my condition, I knew, would have been to climb into a king-size hotel bed with Alice, but I didn't see her for most of the week. I heard from another guide she'd been sent on the West Country Jaunt. When we finally were put together, on a day-trip down to Canterbury and Dover, she did her usual trick of ignoring me all day, just offering the occasional glance and raised eyebrow to keep me sweet. But there was to be no evening in a hotel on this trip, no sex to soothe me. I was a knot of frustration and I could see us getting back to London without so much as a touch.

I followed the group as she led it round Canterbury cathedral. 'The fine stone screens in the Chapel of Our Lady were a gift from the Black Prince,' she informed them, and I realized I didn't want any more play-acting. I wanted to take her in my arms in full view of the tourists and say to her, 'What do you want from me? I need to know!' I had this vision of us on the run together, spending our days travelling in carriages on bumpy roads, our nights in simple sixteenth-century hotels with four-poster beds in every room.

When she finished her guided tour she gave them ten minutes to wander round on their own, and I took my chance. I pulled her into an alcove where I kissed her so hard she struggled to free herself. 'What are you doing?' she said. 'Someone will see us.' When I let her go she tried to laugh it off.

'I don't care who sees us,' I said and kissed her again. The last few days had drained my strength; only she could invigorate me now. I put my mouth to her ear and said, 'I need you. I love you.' I felt her tense. I waited for her to respond but she didn't seem able. She looked away from me. She was trying to say something. She was trying to say, 'I love you too,' I'm sure she was, when a warden disturbed us, and she stiffened and folded her arms, then pretended to be looking at an oil painting in a gold frame entitled 'Thomas à Becket returns from French exile'.

At the end of the day, when we were back in Welcome, she came to me and asked, 'What's the matter with you?'

'Nothing's the matter with me. I want to see you tonight. I want to come to your house.'

'My house?' She seemed astonished I should suggest such a thing.

'Yes?'

'No.' And she turned smartly and walked into Graham's office.

I put my hands in my pockets and walked home from the centre of London, mouthing at the pavement all the way. At Brent Cross I looked up and saw the tangle of motorways and they summed up the way I felt. I was a confusion of plans and schemes.

I found walking gave me strength, so I walked home every evening, rethinking, unravelling, replotting, trying to make some sense of what had happened. I would come in late and Kate would shake her head at me. 'We've got to talk, Will,' she'd say on the occasions we passed each other in the corridor. But I didn't want that kind of conversation. I wanted action. We slept in the same bed, but I lay awake for hours and I think she did the same. In the middle of the night I would go and look at the children sleeping, and think how I couldn't bear to live without them, but knowing that the pain of staying here would one day soon overpower the pain of leaving. In the morning Kate would sigh and say, 'I can't take this much longer.'

'Neither can I,' I'd mumble.

Ted and Rita came round. Rita put her cigarettes and lighter down on the kitchen table and said, 'Nobody's passed comment on my new haircut.'

I grabbed Ted and took him to the pub.

We walked via Hamilton Road. Half of it was partitioned off now. Red and white tape fluttered from lamppost to lamppost. 'They've found another body,' Ted said. 'That's four now.'

'Yeah.'

'What did I tell you? I bet his place gets turned into a horror museum or something.'

'Horror museums are very popular with tourists,' I informed him.

In the pub Ted cheerfully bought the pints. I said to him, 'You're much happier now I'm a failure again, aren't you?'

'Oh, much happier. Much happier. Well, you can't go round changing things like you did. That's why I always vote Tory.'

When we got back home Rita and Kate were sitting in silence.

'We're going,' announced Rita, picking up her

cigarettes and striding to the door. 'I'm not being spoken to like that.'

When they'd gone I asked Kate what she'd said. It was the first conversation we had had in a week.

'I told her she was impossible; that she was a prude and self-obsessed, and if my brother had any sense he'd ditch her and find himself another woman.'

'That's not like you.'

'I've decided I'm going to act on impulse from now on. I'm not going to take a balanced view any more. I'm going to say and do exactly as I please. You're a complete bastard by the way,' and she swiped me across the face with a damp piece of laundry and left the room.

Everything I did felt like it was in desperation. Robinson's Lemon Barley Water had been my escape tunnel, but it had caved in on me. I felt myself gasping like Martin. I ate more fruit, and I began to believe that Alice was all I had. She was my core, and any bid for freedom I made had to be based around her.

I started to hang out with Vinod. I enjoyed talking to him, and he seemed grateful for the company during his night vigils in his shop. I'd go down on the pretence of buying milk or something, and then spend an hour there. I kept asking him about India. Didn't he want to go back and visit? And he kept answering, no he didn't; he had no interest in the place. So I'd say, 'But what about your roots?' And he'd laugh at me. 'This shop is my roots. You can't understand that, can you?'

Then one evening I went down there and he grabbed me by the arm and said, 'I've found a place.'

'What place?'

'To set up my florist's. My brother-in-law's coming in with me.'

'Where's the money coming from?'

'Savings. And a bank loan. We had to put together a business plan and a cash-flow forecast, but the bank was very helpful. They can see it's a good idea.'

I stood there holding a packet of rice, feeling sick. 'Well done,' I said. 'Well done. You've worked hard for it. Well done.' And I put the rice back on the shelf and left.

I tried so hard not to feel the way Ted had felt towards me, but the only way I could view Vinod's success was in terms of my failure. I felt a bitterness harden in me. I hoped his damned florist's would turn out to be a disaster, and I hated myself for that.

*   *   *

I could think of nowhere to go but to see my dad. I drove out there one evening into the setting sun. I had the handbrake on the entire journey and didn't notice. He saw me coming up the path and opened the front door as if he'd been expecting me. He offered me a cup of tea even though it wasn't the time for a cup of tea.

There was a new photo of Colin on the mantelpiece, on holiday somewhere, Florida at a guess. Dad came in with the mugs and saw me put the photo back. He began to wipe the frames with the old vest he used as a duster. When he came to the picture of Martin on his first day at school, he picked it up and held it to the light. 'He's a bright lad, your Martin.'

'Takes after his grandpa.'

He moved on to the picture of himself and my mother taken outside the *Cutty Sark*. He didn't look at me as he said, 'You're a good father, you are. You put them first. You're always there. They're lucky having you.'

I couldn't believe what I was hearing. The old boy was giving me approval. He was making me feel good about myself just when I needed it most.

He spat on the rag and cleaned the thirty-year-old snap of me and Colin taken on the garden swing. I said, 'Everything I know about parenting I learnt from you. You were a good dad too, you know.'

'I don't know about that.'

'It's true. You gave us ambition and strength. You taught me if I wanted something to keep going until I achieved it. Colin and I are the sort who never give up, thanks to you.'

He sat down. 'I'm sorry about that.'

He looked smaller and a bit pathetic sitting there in his shirt with the frayed collar and his cardigan with patched elbows. It occurred to me I had never asked him if he was all right for money. I was always too wrapped up in my own future, and he seemed so well organized in every department. I had been looking forward to giving him something extra to treat himself with, buy himself some new clothes pegs, but that had gone now too. 'You're all right for cash, aren't you, Dad? I mean ... you know.'

He blew on his tea. 'Me? Yeah. Don't you worry about me. It's you I'm worried about.'

'I'm all right. I'm doing overnights now. That's a

nice little bonus.'

'You can have your inheritance early if you want, you know.'

I could feel myself welling up again. This man who collected money-off pet-food coupons even though he had never owned a pet was offering to give me money.

I said to him, 'Tell me something, would you have given your life for your kids?'

'How d'you mean?'

'Would you have jumped in front of a bus to save us, knowing you'd get run over yourself? Would you have dived off that ferry to the Isle of Wight if one of us had fallen in?'

'For you and Colin? Yeah.'

Outside, a flock of starlings abandoned a tree, flew round in a circle and landed on it again as if they'd just discovered it. 'I'll tell you something else,' he added. 'I still would.'

'It's a bugger, isn't it?' I said.

I drove slowly home, wanting to make the journey last as long as possible. I didn't want to be in our flat. I switched on the radio for some distraction, and Harry Nilsson came on singing, 'I can't live, if living is without you', and I finally cracked, tears streaming down my face. 'You're a bastard, Harry Nilsson,' I said out loud, although it wasn't really fair to blame him. It wouldn't have mattered what song it was.

*   *   *

Then one afternoon I took the half-day excursion to Hampton Court, Windsor Castle, Runnymede and the Kennedy Memorial. The McCardles were on board again. They had just three days left of their holiday and they were going to do nothing else but take Welcome trips.

'Welcome looks after us so well,' said Cal.

'We feel we're part of a family outing with you,' agreed George.

They looked utterly bored with it all. They complained at everything. They were like children, wanting to touch all the things they weren't allowed to. At Hampton Court, as I sat on a bench in the gardens, I saw them moved on by an attendant for trying to pick flowers. When they spotted me they came and sat down.

'You wouldn't catch me going in that thing,' remarked George when he saw a sign pointing to the maze.

'My feet are itching,' said Cal. 'I think it's athlete's foot.'

'I bet you get people mugged in there,' went on George. 'If I was a mugger I'd mug people in a maze. Or if I was a rapist.'

Cal took off her shoes and I looked at her gnarled feet. What was it about tourists' feet that disgusted me so? I felt sick as she scratched one foot with the other. 'We're going on the tour of Robin Hood Country on Wednesday,' she said. 'It's our last trip before we fly home.'

'You taking that trip, Will?' asked George.

'No. Wednesday is my day off this week. My colleague Roy is taking that one, if I remember.'

'I kind of hoped it might be you,' said Cal. 'You and that nice Alice. You two are so good together. You looked after us so well with all those Japanese. We wanted you to wind up this vacation for us.'

'You'll be all right with Roy.'

249

Just look at all those chimneys,' she said, and took her video camera out to take a shot of the vast palace roof. And that was when I saw her wallet sticking out of her bag. I looked away instinctively, but it was too much to ignore. The clasp could hardly close, so many notes were jammed inside. Then as she sat back I noticed the ring on her finger, a stone in it the size of a nut; then her bracelet that gave a dull jangle of heavy metal whenever she moved her arm; her necklace; her brooch; she must have been wearing ten thousand pounds' worth of crap just sitting there. And that was just her. George was as valuable, with his bulging breast pocket and chunky watch.

She turned round to take a picture of me sitting next to George. 'You don't mind, do you, Will?'

'No no,' and I smiled for her with ease. I had just decided I was going to rob her.

At Windsor I followed them at a distance as they left the coach park with the group. I strolled up the hill behind them on to the main street, casually glancing at the shop windows. Suddenly everyone looked like a pickpocket to me. I had this fear that another thief would get to the McCardles before I could. How much had that mugger on the Jack the Ripper tour got away with? About seven hundred pounds. Cal McCardle had three times that amount hanging off her like gifts on a tree.

We reached the castle gates. George looked up at the turrets and said, 'This place is in pretty good shape.'

I would have followed them in but I couldn't afford the entrance fee. I was going to do it though; I was determined. Three months ago on that Jack the Ripper tour I had been appalled at the thought of robbing defenceless tourists, but now, as I watched them all walking round Windsor like panting dogs, I realized just how much I had come to dislike them. The way they wore shorts no matter what the weather; their stupid hats; their anoraks; their fat children; their utter lack of initiative; the way you took them to see the crown jewels and they yawned. I thought: They're all punters and they deserve what they get.

The last stop of the day was Runnymede. The guide gave the usual patter about the Magna Carta and grumpy King John, and then there was time to take a walk to the Kennedy Memorial.

I watched the McCardles in my mirror, hoping she might make it easy for me and leave her bag on the bus. But she humped it down the steps and then set out across the lawns, limping like a pilgrim. I got down and stretched, and walked nonchalantly after them.

They stopped at the Memorial and took video pictures of the plaque—they would read the wording later on their television. They shuffled around, wondering what else there was to do. Cal sighed and changed shoulders with her bag, and then there was the wallet, sitting up, offering itself like a piece of fruit. I could reach out and take it any time, and she'd never feel a thing. She probably wouldn't even realize until she came to pay for dinner, and then she'd say, 'Thank goodness we're so heavily insured, George', and they'd simply go to the bank the next morning and get some more money.

I was surprisingly calm. I almost felt justified as I slipped my hand out of my pocket, stroked my chin, took one last look around, and reached out . . . just

251

as George turned round and said to me, 'He wasn't all he was cracked up to be, you know.'

'Who?' I croaked.

'Old JFK. Nice guy, but you wouldn't want him running your country. Bit like that Robin Hood.'

I chuckled for him, and put my hands back in my pockets, then strolled back the way I had come. I had just decided not to rob the McCardles that afternoon, not because I had thought better of it or felt ashamed or anything like that, but because George had given me a better idea, much bigger and much more fun.

By the time we got back to the Welcome depot I had a grin on my face I couldn't lose. I went to look for Roy.

CHAPTER ELEVEN

NOTTINGHAM AND THE ROBIN HOOD EXPERIENCE

It was Roy's idea to dress up. 'When planning a crime,' he said to me, 'you can't pay enough attention to detail.'

I went round to his flat in Stoke Newington and tried the outfit on. 'It's proper Lincoln Green and everything,' he said proudly. 'I'll get you a pistol before the day.'

'I can't have a pistol.'

'Why not?'

'It's one of those . . . anachronisms.'

'A what?'

'Robin Hood didn't have a pistol, all right?'

'You can't hold up a coachload of tourists with a bow and bleedin' arrow, can you? You got to look convincing. I'll get you one of those theatrical ones that fires blanks.'

I flinched at the idea of anything being fired. 'The police might trace it back to you or something,' I said. I was trying to be professional about this, but he was way ahead of me.

'No one traces anything back to me. Don't worry about that.'

Roy was really up for it. I would probably have abandoned the idea without him. I would have looked in the mirror once too often, panicked and decided it was all beyond me. But not only did Roy have the contacts who would take anything we couldn't offload ourselves—credit cards and hardware like cameras and jewellery—he also saw nothing outrageous about the plan. Whenever I looked unsure he'd punch me on the arm and laugh: 'The punters will love it. It's like the Great Train Robbery all over again. Just don't go coshing the driver over the head, all right?'

I spun round in the mirror. I looked like someone about to go on stage in a pantomime. I looked quite good actually.

'Who's the guide?' I asked.

'Frank. He'll be under the seat.'

I noticed pictures of children in school uniform on the mantelpiece. 'Who are they?'

'My kids,' said Roy, matter of fact.

'I didn't know you had kids.'

'I've got kids.'

'They live here?'

'You're joking.'

They were six and ten. They were called Robert

253

and Holly. I never thought of Roy having kids. He didn't seem the sort who lived for anyone other than himself.

'Where are they?'

'Live with their mum in Tiptree.'

'You see them much?'

'When I'm not busy.'

I was hit by a wave of despair. I could see myself arranging to visit my children, taking them out to the pictures for an afternoon, delivering them back like something I'd rented. Then becoming too busy to see them; months going by; they'd be taller when I saw them next.

'I'm not sure this is right,' I said.

'No. You need a mask.'

I sighed. 'Robin Hood never wore a mask either.'

'Only 'cos they never had Identikit pictures in his day. Here.'

He handed me a rubber mask. 'Who's this?'

'Errol Flynn.'

I pulled it on and it snapped around my head. 'It doesn't look anything like Errol Flynn.'

He laughed at me. 'Course it does.'

'It looks like . . . Prince Charles.'

'They look alike, that's all.'

'Errol Flynn and Prince Charles do not look alike.'

'It's Errol Flynn, I'm telling you. It makes your voice sound different an' all. That's good.'

I turned to him. 'Has it ever occurred to you to ask why I'm doing this? I mean, doesn't it seem strange to you that I should do this?'

'No.'

'Don't you want to know why I'm doing this?

254

'No.'

'It's because I want to open a teashop, a teashop that serves homemade stuff and welcomes families and doesn't close just when you want a cup of tea and a piece of cake, a teashop that people will write home about. I want to open a teashop to be proud of . . . and this is only way I can do it.'

'Fine.'

I'd known Roy almost two years and I was finally getting to like him. He didn't question anything. I thought that was probably a good attitude to adopt.

*   *   *

I slept little the night before. I wasn't in the mood for highway robbery when the alarm went.

The first thing I did was go out and check the car hadn't been stolen. There were no problems starting it either. I had discovered that it was more likely to start with Radio 2 on, so I coaxed it with the sounds of 'Billy, Don't Be a Hero', and it coughed and spat and idled happily.

'It won't start,' I told Kate when I went back inside. 'It's playing up again.'

She called the Coopers down the street to ask if they could take the kids to school. 'I'll have a look at it this morning,' I said. 'Or we'll get the garage out.' She wasn't shocked by such extravagance. It was her policy not to be shocked by anything I did any more. She shoved the rest of her toast in her mouth and hurried off without a word. That was what she spent most of her time doing these days: hurrying off without a word.

Roy had got me two theatre pistols as promised. I wrapped them up in my costume and put the lot in a stuff bag with three black dustbin liners, then I went down to Vinod's for a big bag of fruit.

'You're eating a lot of fruit these days, Will,' he said.

'Five pieces a day.'

'More than that. Much more than that.'

He was right, of course. I was eating at least double the recommended dose. I inhaled grapes. I always had a papaya in my pocket. And now figs were in season I needed to turn to crime just to support my habit. If I thought about it, I lived off nothing but fruit.

'I've been under a bit of stress lately, that's all,' I explained. Vinod looked concerned for me, like a friend, as if he recognized a cry for help.

But I couldn't worry about it now. I would cut down on my fruit when this was all over. I filled up with petrol, then put on my sunglasses and set off up the motorway, north to the Queen of the East Midlands, north to Nottingham and Robin Hood Country.

*   *   *

The Robin Hood Experience was a theme park on the edge of Sherwood Forest, *a magical medieval world where staff dress in authentic period costume and re-enact everyday scenes from twelfth- and thirteenth-century life*, claimed the brochure. More importantly there was a good-sized car park, a souvenir and craft shop and a licensed bar and restaurant, and that was what drew the coach tours.

The Welcome excursion, with Roy at the wheel and Frank on the microphone, would call here for lunch at twelve noon, after a visit to Nottingham

Castle. They would have time to experience the Experience and then leave shortly before one-thirty. The plan was for me, in the guise of Robin Hood, to board the coach just before departure, 'overpower' the crew and fill the dustbin bags with loot before the unwitting tourists knew what had hit them. Roy would drop me near my getaway vehicle, and drive on. It would all be over in minutes.

I arrived at just past ten-thirty, but drove on for another mile or so and then turned down a B road and looked for a place to hide my car. Eventually I found a curved layby, the sort of tarmac backwater that gets created when a road is straightened. I could see the main road through trees and across a field, and there was access to it if I climbed a gate and scrambled through a hedge. It was good enough for a getaway.

From there I drove on a few miles to the nearest town where I waited in the anonymity of a supermarket car park and read the paper. A superdustmite, *Blomia tropicalis*, had invaded Britain, a virulent creature capable of producing asthma-inducing toxins even more powerful than those generated by our native dustmites. A senior scientist at the Building Research Establishment said the creature had probably been carried to Britain in the belongings of tourists travelling from South America. The numbers were small at present but studies showed the supermite was establishing itself.

I hadn't a moment to lose.

At eleven forty-five I drove back to the layby and parked, took my stuff bag and walked back to the Robin Hood Experience. A police car passed me and my bowels quivered. I wondered if I would go to prison for this. 'You're already in prison!' I shouted to myself above the traffic, a little too dramatically. I clenched my teeth and strode on.

There was the Welcome coach in the coach park, empty but for Roy sitting at the wheel eating sandwiches. I made myself visible. He came down the steps, and walked past me. He said, 'One-twenty departure.'

Twenty minutes. I found a Gents and locked myself in a cubicle where I put my costume on over my clothes. *I'd rather be in Ipswich with Bob*, was scrawled on the door.

Sixteen minutes later I emerged as Robin Hood. Under normal circumstances this would have made me look conspicuous, but here there was nothing strange at all about it. The place was crawling with actors dressed up as merry men and women. One visitor asked me the way to the craft shop, but otherwise I was ignored. Only once, when I walked through the foyer and bumped into Friar Tuck, did I think I might be rumbled, but he just gave me a bored nod and muttered, 'All right?'

'All right.'

I made my way to the coach park and approached the Welcome using the other coaches as screens. I could see the punters climbing back on board. There was Frank counting them all in. I took my pistols out of my plastic bag and tucked them into the belt of my Lincoln Green.

A jet from the East Midlands airport roared overhead. A squirrel disappeared inside a litter bin. My stomach rumbled because I'd had no lunch. I ducked behind a Golden Tours as a couple passed; the man asked, 'Who's the Duke of Kent married to?' I felt very alert.

'All aboard!' Frank called up to Roy and climbed the steps himself. I pulled my mask over my face and ran towards the Welcome.

Roy saw me coming. He did a double take and his eyes bulged as he tried to express shock and terror. I bounced up the steps and said firmly, 'Close the doors!' and I pointed a pistol straight at Roy's head.

'OK. Anything you sssssssay.' Roy started to stutter and shake. God, he was a crap actor.

The doors hissed closed and I turned to Frank. He was about to protest, but I pushed him into his seat. 'Don't be a hero, all right?' I spoke in a Birmingham accent and underneath my mask I had a curled lip. 'Don't be a hero and you won't get hurt. This won't take long.' I prodded his chest with the pistol and he sat back in shock.

'Drive!' I snapped at Roy, and he started the engine and moved off. I stood in the stairwell until we were at the coach-park exit. 'Turn left on the main road.'

When he had joined the traffic I turned my attention to the punters. I was sticky with sweat as I stood tall and announced, 'Your attention please. This is a highway robbery.'

'Speak up,' said a voice from the back.

I yelled down the coach. 'This is a highway robbery. Don't anyone move!'

They had no intention of moving. They had just settled themselves into their seats after a good lunch, and now they glanced up to see a character in fancy dress coming down the aisle, brandishing an antique pistol. They looked mildly curious.

'Who are you?' said an Australian in lime-green

259

golf trousers.

'I'm bloody Robin Hood! Who do you think I am? Stay put and nothing will happen to you.'

'Anything you say, Robin,' and the bastard laughed at me.

'Is this included in the Robin Hood Experience?' an American voice from the middle of the coach inquired. I spun round and there was Cal McCardle.

' 'Cos we're not paying extra if it isn't,' said George.

'No it isn't included in the Robin Hood Experience, you morons! It's a fucking robbery!'

'Language,' said Cal.

'It's Anglo-Saxon,' said the Australian.

'No it isn't!' I snapped at him. 'Just shut up and get your money out.' I pulled a black dustbin bag from my pocket. 'Put all your valuables in here!'

They smiled stupidly at me. 'Are you Robin Hood or Prince Charles?' asked a German across the aisle.

'He looks like Prince Charles,' said the Australian.

It was becoming clear to me that it was going to take a lot to convince this bunch I was anything other than part of the package, and I was tired of being part of the package, so I pointed my pistol in the air and fired.

It made a noise like a thundercrack. It frightened me and terrified the passengers. A woman screamed. A child started to cry. Roy jumped and the coach swerved. Frank slid down in his seat.

I coughed and regained my composure. Power was replacing fear now.

'As I was saying: I'm Robin Hood, all right? Forget Prince Charles. What was Robin Hood famous for?'

'His merry men?' answered the German.

'And what else?'

'Fighting Little John on the log over the river with sticks?' said an Australian woman.

'And what else?'

'Burning the cakes?' guessed Cal McCardle.

'Oh come on! He was famous for stealing from the rich to give to the poor. So, I'll have your money, your jewellery—unless of course it has great sentimental value—and your video cameras, and no one will get hurt.'

'Robin Hood didn't have a gun,' said the German.

'You shut your mouth,' I snarled. 'You're starting to annoy me,' and I shoved the end of the other pistol under his chin.

The bags went round; the loot went in. I had complete control. No one gave me any lip. Only one man looked at me with ideas in his eye, so I stood on his foot and said, 'Don't even think about it, sunshine; think of the insurance instead.' And that seemed to satisfy him.

We had quickly passed the field which gave me access to my car, but now we came to a roundabout. I called to Roy, 'Coachman, back the way you came.'

Frank stuck his head above his seat at this point and said, 'Now look here,' so I shoved the pistol up his nose and he paled.

I said, 'Look at this, everyone. The Sheriff of Nottingham here wishes to challenge Sir Robin of Locksley. What shall I do with him?'

'Shoot him,' said a kid from the back.

'Hear that?'

Frank closed his eyes and waited for the end. I said, 'Just give me your money before you wet the seat.' And he reached inside his jacket and took out his wallet.

There were over fifty people on board and they all gave very generously. 'Enjoying your holiday?' I asked the Italian family on the back seat as they poured in cash, credit cards and two nice watches.

'Yes, thank you very much,' they nodded.

'Jolly good. Visit the West Country if you have time, that's my favourite part.'

'And where are you from, sir?' I asked a man in a pure lambswool pullover, so new he had the label hanging down his back.

'We're from Norway.'

'Very nice. That bracelet please, madam, and your children won't get hurt. First time in England?'

'Yes. First time.'

'Good.'

'Can I take a photograph?' asked an American woman.

'No!'

'Oh, just a quick one?' She clicked her camera and I grabbed it off her and put it in the bag.

We were approaching the gate now, so I said to Roy, 'Driver, pull the coach up in a hundred yards and you won't feel the full power of my weapons.'

'Certainly, Robin,' replied Roy, and, terrified as he was, still remembered to look in his mirror and indicate in plenty of time. I carried the bags of swag to the door.

As the coach stopped I turned to face the

passengers. They were like children, so eager to please. 'Thank you, kind people, for your donations. You do not know what a difference they will make to the villagers of Lower Mendip who have nothing to eat but straw this night.' I fired the other gun and the blank went off and everyone on the bus screamed. This was fun.

'Well, open the bloody doors then,' I said to Roy.

'Yes, Robin.'

The doors swung open and I jumped down. 'Drive on, coachman!' And Roy pulled out and nearly collided with a Vauxhall Vectra.

I dived into the ditch and immediately vomited. I looked at the mess—nothing but fruit. Then I crawled along for a way, out of sight of the traffic, until I reached the gate. When all was clear I threw the bags over and clambered over myself. I took off my costume, wiped the sick off it and stuffed it into one of my bags.

There was the noise of a tractor somewhere, but no one saw me as I ran round the edge of the field. The bags of loot were much heavier than I thought they would be and I prayed they wouldn't break. I reached the wood and carefully climbed through the barbed-wire fence, then ran through the undergrowth to the edge of the layby, and my car.

I fumbled with the keys in the boot. I had to give the catch a thump to make it open, then I dumped the black bags inside. I just needed a quick getaway now and this was the perfect crime.

I put the keys in the ignition and switched on Radio 2. The Eagles sang 'Hotel California' to me as I calmly spoke: 'Now listen, it's not often a car gets a chance to be a getaway vehicle. It would be a shame to waste this opportunity.'

I closed my eyes and turned the key.

It fired first time. A tear of joy came to my eye as the little engine revved for all it was worth. I thought: This episode in my life was meant to be, and I laughed as I drove off. 'I forgive you for your past! I'll have you professionally valeted and serviced every six months from now on. I'm going to love you and talk to you, and even when I get rich I won't sell you for scrap. I'll restore you and keep you in a heated garage with a radio playing the station of your choice. You were there when I needed you. I won't forget this.'

And I headed back south, whooping and self-consciously punching the air, giggling as I thought of the ridiculousness of it all, how smoothly it had gone, and how composed I had remained throughout. 'Put your money in the bag, motherfucker.' That wasn't Disney. That was Tarantino.

I stopped just once, to fill up with petrol near Luton. I had planned to dump my costume in a bin, but then I thought: No, don't do that; you might need it again.

*   *   *

Roy had given me the key to a lock-up in Hackney. I drove the car in and quietly closed the doors, then I emptied the loot over the floor on to a blanket.

I was amazed at just how much stuff there was. I counted £6,440 in sterling; a wad of foreign currency—I didn't know how much, but the dollars alone came to more than two thousand pounds. There were over five thousand pounds' worth of travellers' cheques—no good to us as such, but Roy had said if we got them to his contact quick enough he would give us a deal, the same applied to the haul of seventy-eight assorted credit cards.

I counted thirty-four watches. I couldn't estimate their value, but there were a number of Rolexes and Cartiers. Then there was the collection of camera equipment, everything from top-of-the-range Panasonic camcorders to pocket compacts, a few thousand pounds' worth at least. Spread over the floor like this it was a treasure trove. I picked up handfuls and it glittered.

I felt delirious. What I wanted more than anything was to go out to a café and get a cup of tea and a big cake. But there was nothing I could do except wait for Roy. I sat and listened to the sounds of the city change as the afternoon became evening. It seemed an age since I had left home. I hadn't let myself stop to think of what would happen to me when the job was done. If I had committed a crime like this a hundred years ago I would have been hanged and my remains displayed as a warning. Everyone at Welcome would be questioned and would need to account for themselves. I put my faith in my reputation. After all, I was the employee who tackled robbers, not the sort who did the robbing.

At seven o'clock I switched on the radio and I felt my heart gallop when the story of a 'bizarre hold-up in Nottingham' was featured. But it was the kind of item that was designed to arouse curiosity rather than outrage. One of the tourists, the Italian man, I think, was interviewed and he said: 'He was very polite; he had very good manners. He came from Lower Mendip.'

An Australian said, 'He claimed he was Robin

265

Hood but he was dressed up like Prince Charles.' I wondered how much effort the police would put into something like this.

A knock on the door made me freeze, but it was Roy at last. He looked tired but excited, and then when he saw the spoils he fell to his knees and laughed like a pirate.

'What happened?' I asked, desperate for news.

He put his arm round me. 'Don't you worry your little head. They think it's someone local. Frank told them you had a Midlands accent.'

Another knock on the door, and I was convinced it was the police.

'Relax,' said Roy. 'That's Vince.'

Vince said very little. He wouldn't look you in the eye. He flicked through the credit cards, took a glance at the hardware, chucked out the travellers' cheques—'they're no good to anyone'—and one of the camcorders—'and that's marked'. I noticed a security number was stamped on the side and a name and address underneath: *Cal McCardle, 2210 W. Beaver Loop, Des Moines, Iowa.* Finally Vince scratched his belly and said, 'Give you two grand for the lot.'

'Fuck off,' protested Roy.

We settled on three. Roy and I weren't bothered; we wanted the cash in our pockets. Vince peeled it off in big notes. When he left Roy and I divided it up with the rest of the haul, forty per cent for him, sixty per cent for me, as agreed. I was left with a padded envelope containing over eight thousand quid in tight bundles. I felt light-headed. Roy said, 'You can have the video camera. Let's go to the pub.'

We sat in a pub off the Balls Pond Road. Roy

chuckled: 'This is just the start, Will. You should do a number of these. I can fix you up with other drivers all over the place. They don't have to be Welcome coaches. It's a piece of piss. And the punters loved it. Gave them something to write home about. You should have heard them afterwards. Coach companies will be booking you to rob their buses before you know it.'

'I'll dress up as Dick Turpin next time. Do the A1.'

'That's it. Or Florence Nightingale.'

'Florence Nightingale didn't hold people up.'

'Didn't she?'

'She was a nurse in the Crimean War.'

'The punters would be quite happy to be held up by Florence Nightingale or Thomas Cromwell of any of the buggers, believe me. You're on to a winner here.'

I drove back across North London in the driving rain. I felt invincible. I'd give the cash to Ted and he'd give me a cheque. If he asked me where I got it from I'd say, 'I was creative, Ted, like you told me to be.' The bank would just think it was the money from the advert. They'd set everything in motion like they promised. If I did two more hold-ups I'd have enough for the Climbing Rose. Three more and I could do the place up. Four and I could buy Anne Hathaway's Cottage.

The envelope was bulging and beating in my bag. My escape route was open again. I couldn't help myself as I drove on past the turning that would have taken me home and kept going, heading for Alice's house.

*   *   *

Fourteen-a Tremayne Rd, London N4. I had never written her address down but I remembered every detail from the one time I had seen it on her suitcase. Our affair was never supposed to come to this, I knew that, but if I was honest I had always imagined myself walking down a tree-lined street to her house, up steps to a black front door and into a flat with bowls of fresh fruit everywhere; a bedroom with nothing but a bed in it; a fridge stocked just the way she'd described it. Our relationship had been bound by the corridors, fire doors and full English breakfasts of the coach-tour hotels, but it was about to leave all that behind.

I thought Tremayne Rd would be round the back of Highgate, but it was a long way down the hill from there. I really wondered if I had read the address wrong, maybe got the wrong Tremayne Road, because she couldn't live here. There was a car without wheels stranded on the pavement; dogs were fighting over rubbish; there were no pretty town houses with window boxes and railings, just a dark terrace fronted by forlorn privet. At the far end, the road petered out into blocks of brick council housing. I was about to turn back when I saw number 14.

It was a dark house with bars on the downstairs windows. I sat in my car for a minute and looked for some life inside, then I saw the word *Flat* written on a gate that led down a passage. I zipped my precious envelope up inside my jacket and got out.

Night was falling and the whole street looked grim. The passage was ill lit, but it led to a door with 14a on it. I knocked and waited. Rain dripped on to my head from a blocked gutter. No lights came on. This couldn't be right; this was too much like where I lived. I started back to the street but then I heard a car door and some voices, kids' voices, and then footsteps coming my way, hurrying because of the rain. I nipped back and hid behind a low fence that screened off the dustbins.

I heard children's steps come running down to the door. Then I heard Alice say, 'You hang the laundry up, I'll put the fish fingers on.' A man mumbled a reply and they went inside.

Lights came on. I could hear them moving around the rooms. I could hear doors slam. The TV came on; the kids screamed; the adults screamed back.

'Don't get on the couch with your shoes on, for God's sake.'

'You're not doing anything before you're in your pyjamas.'

I lifted up a dustbin lid and peered inside: crumpled frozen-food packets, wrappers of own-brand biscuits. No sign here of crème fraîche or exotic ice creams. No sign of Italian breads or Marks & Spencer's delicatessen counter, just tins of spaghetti hoops and dented tubs of spread, and kitchen rubbish stuffed into an old sliced bread bag. The stuff was so boring it didn't even smell. There was even an empty packet of macaroni.

A toilet flushed and the drainpipes roared, then a light came on and illuminated the back garden. They'd made the best of it. There was a small patch of grass, a little sandpit and a flower bed with something pink in it. In the corner were two diamonds of light, the eyes of a rabbit in a hutch munching on carrot scrapings.

I peered round the fence. Now I could see into the kitchen, and there were two people. I was looking straight at them but such was the light they wouldn't have seen me. It took a while to realize that one of them was Alice. She was wearing glasses, and her hair was tied back which made her nose look big. She was bent over a sink scraping toast, her face a blank. Behind her a man was hanging up laundry on radiators. He shook out a pair of blue knickers I recognized, and he hung them on a radiator corner without any interest. He had a high forehead and he wore a jumper just like mine—British Home Stores January sales, £11.99.

I crouched there, not feeling the rain now, and stared in at the familiarity of this room. I could make out the drawings of spaceships on the fridge. I recognized the cereal boxes stacked on a shelf. I could even hear the TV from across the hall and I knew it was *Mary Poppins*. There was no communication between Alice and her husband or partner or whoever he was. They worked methodically; this was a routine night. He finished hanging up the laundry. The sound of 'Let's Go Fly a Kite' came from the TV room and he started to sing along. He knew all the words. He did a little dance and left the room.

With him gone I edged closer to the window and stared in at her as she filled a pan under the tap. I must have changed a shadow or made a noise, because she suddenly looked up and peered through the glass, then stared right at me. I didn't back off. All I could think of was how I was going to save her. I smiled at her as gently as I could. She reached out and tugged the blind down. Then I heard her call: 'I'm just going to get something from the car.'

I ducked back down the passage and crouched by the dustbins again. 'Here,' I whispered as she came out. She had her coat draped over her head and shoulders.

'Where?'

I stood up and let her see me. I wanted to put my arms around her and kiss her wet cheeks. But she ripped into me: 'What the fuck are you doing here?'

Before I could answer she had pushed me out of the passage and into the street. I said, 'You've got a husband! You never said you had a husband.'

'Have you got a car?'

She wanted to run away with me, leave all the burnt toast and laundry behind. But when we got into the car she turned to me with her face and hair dripping, and screamed, 'Are you crazy!'

'What?'

'Are you really crazy? You should never have come here! Don't ever come here!'

'Why not?'

'Because this is my home! I don't want you here.'

'You've got a husband.'

'So? You've got a wife.'

'And kids.'

'So have you.'

I watched a drop of rain glide down her face. I went to wipe it off but she backed away. I said, 'I thought you lived on your own in a little flat.'

She started to laugh at me. She made me feel stupid. She screwed her face up. 'What have you come here for?'

'I want to know what we're going to do.'

Her face became more serious; she was

271

wondering how things ever came to this. 'We're not going to do anything.' She spoke to me as if she was speaking to one of her children. 'Listen to me. Everything that went on between us when we were away was different. You know that.'

'Why does it have to be different?'

'Because it's . . . not me when I'm away, that's why. It's a different me, in a different world. Surely you know that. It's a fantasy land.'

'But I can make that land a real one. I can do it now. We can do it.'

'What?'

'I can make it real. We can leave all this . . .'

'I don't want it to be real.'

'Why not?'

She stopped and thought. 'Because I won't have a fantasy then, will I?'

'You said to me, if you have a dream you should chase it.'

'I said that?'

'Yes. When we were in the Lakes.'

She couldn't even remember. She shrugged. 'That's the kind of thing I say when I'm away somewhere beautiful with someone I'm attracted to.'

I tried to answer her but couldn't. She said, 'Do you understand what I'm saying?'

I just wanted some contact with her. 'All I understand right now is I want you . . .' and I reached out to take her hand, but she stopped me.

'Don't. We're not on some excursion now. This is my home. This is my family, and you don't belong here. I could keep our affair going only as long as you didn't interfere with this, as long as you didn't try to cross over. But now you have.'

272

'I want you to go away with me.'

She looked pained. 'Go where?'

'I don't know. We should be together.'

I grasped her hand and held it firmly, and then I could see fear seep into the corners of her eyes as she recognized desperation in my voice. But instead of fighting me she put her other hand on mine, to calm me, and she said quietly, 'I'm not leaving my home for you or for anyone. And if you had any sense you wouldn't leave yours. Go back to your wife and children. Don't ever come here again.'

And when she'd made sure I wasn't going to grab her and put my hands around her neck, she got out and closed the door quietly. I heard her steps running away down the wet concrete.

The car wouldn't start. All the excitement of the day had finally got too much for it. I didn't care. I walked home in as straight a line as possible. I walked through gardens. I crossed roads without looking. I was like someone sleepwalking. Cars blared at me, but I just kept going, head down, nose dripping. I ignored the rain. I felt hot, in fact. I stripped down to my T-shirt and kept on walking.

There was no one in when I got home. I'd been expecting to come back one evening and find the place empty, and now it had happened I felt nothing. I had no idea where they'd all gone. There was no note.

I sat down hard in the living room in the dark and didn't move for thirty-three minutes. My wet clothes made me shiver, but I just sat and watched the digits on the video change. The telephone rang but I didn't answer it. I didn't care who was after me. I didn't care what they did to me. I heard a siren in the distance and assumed it was the police coming. I resigned myself. The siren faded.

The light from a vehicle caught something sticking out of my bag, the McCardles' video camera, a small but expensive-looking model in a smart leather case. Inside with the camera were leads and attachments for playback on television. After a few tries I put the right lead in the right socket, then pressed rewind and play, and on to my screen appeared George McCardle posing in the Robin Hood Experience, his hideous shirt looking the colour of vomit in the vivid shades of the camera. Little John and Will Scarlet stood on either arm, and from behind the camera you could hear Cal: 'You look like one of his Merry Men, George.' George folded his arms and tried to look legendary as Cal continued her commentary. 'So here we are in the Robin Hood World ... Experience. It's hard to believe, I know, but we are right here in Sherwood Forest where Robin Hood and his Merry Men lived and fought with the Sheriff of Nottingham whose castle we've just visited.'

This was better than TV. This was voyeurism. I laughed and laughed at George as he stood there with his inane grin. Little John next to him said, 'Can I go now?' But Cal wasn't through yet. There was a crackling of paper as she began to read from something.

'Robin Hood and his Merry Men fought against repression and gave hope to the common people, bringing romance and adventure into our historical setting.'

She zoomed in on George as he pretended to grapple with Little John. 'We've just had a very nice lunch of egg salad, and George had some apple pie and . . .'

I pressed rewind. There was Cal at Windsor talking about health insurance. Rewind again and there was George with his shirt off in a hotel room, trying to hold in his stomach. Rewind again and there was a close-up of their cream tea at Leeds Castle with Cal's voice-over. 'Here is a typical English cream tea,' and she cut to George with jam on his nose.

There they were at Stonehenge and Bath, then at Warwick Castle with George creeping round the dungeon: 'Look, Cal! Special disembowelling instruments. They thought of everything!'

Fast forward and they were in the Lakes, on the trip Alice and I had taken them on. There was the slate-clad hotel. I could smell Alice's body just looking at the building.

Then we were at the model village we'd visited on the second day, and the camera just loved this place. Cal followed the steam train as it twisted and turned round the prefabricated landscape, through tunnels and goods yards, pulling in at the cream and maroon station. On film it was easy to be fooled by the scale, so that this was like watching a newsreel from fifty years ago. We followed the road up from the station past the Station Hotel to a little town where the butcher wore a jolly striped apron, where grocery and bread vans called door to door. There was the vicar with his jacket off pruning his roses, and there was the farmer with his workhands labouring in fields where shire horses pulled wagons piled high with hay.

Along a road with only the occasional car the camera tracked, over a perfect stone bridge under

275

which a fisherman cast his fly; down a river to the town port where a sizeable workforce was employed loading vans and swinging cargoes wrapped in tarpaulins from dock to hold.

Further up-river an impressive castle stood on a hill with guardsmen patrolling battlements. From there you got a fine view of the funfair that lined the road back into town along the seafront, and of the beach with its white cliffs at each end, and the lighthouse with a jolly lighthouse keeper standing on his deck smoking his pipe and watching sailboats ride cresting waves.

Cal's voice-over whined, 'The great thing about England is it's just the way they say it is in the brochures.'

She panned to the left, and said, 'Oh George, look at that.'

There on a piece of grass, next to the cricket pitch, the camera had found a figure in a pale blue shirt and striped tie, lying on the grass, dozing in the sunshine, arms across his chest, shoelaces undone. 'It's Will,' said Cal. 'He's having a snooze.'

'Better wake him up; we got to go soon,' said George.

'No. He looks so peaceful. He looks like part of the scenery.'

I hit rewind.

'It's Will. He's having a snooze.'

'Better wake him up; we got to go soon.'

'No. He looks so peaceful. He looks like part of the scenery.'

She was right, of course. That's exactly how I did look. I was Gulliver in this Lilliput, but I was still part of the scenery. I was the man snoozing in the meadow in this model England, this throwback to an era when the trains ran on time and summers were warmer; when people were polite to each other and no one grassed on their neighbours; when children could go out without fear of abduction, and everyone was poor but happy, and proud to do their duty. Lying there in my Hush Puppies I had slipped seamlessly into the landscape. I was a resident, on first-name terms with the baker and grocer. I played for that cricket team. I took my kids to that village school. I said good morning to the vicar whenever he passed on his bicycle. There I was in the Olde Teashoppe across the road from the tobacconist's, serving up hot cross buns to occasional visitors.

I pressed the stop button and it was gone.

I sat there for another eighteen minutes. Nothing moved in the room, just the dustmite family scampering across the hot, blank screen. I wanted my own family back. I wanted to hold my wife and hug my children. I felt as though I had spent a long period macheting my way through the jungle and finally emerged on to a path.

On top of the television I noticed a package. It had *Help The Aged* written on the front. Inside, with a return envelope, were details of the Adopt-a-Granny scheme, including a short personal history of a woman named Nanki Devi, a seventy-three-year-old Indian. *Nanki was born in the village of Chatore. She has seven children and lives with one of her sons. She is becoming increasingly frail and suffers from tuberculosis. She can no longer work and is worried she is becoming a burden to her family. Please help supply this elderly person with food, clothing and medical care.*

And there was a picture of her—toothless,

277

wrinkled, one-eyed, but dressed smartly in her best shawl. I took my padded envelope with the eight thousand pounds in and sellotaped the Adopt-a-Granny return envelope to the front. Outlaw to prince of thieves in one easy step.

I stood up. My leaden legs were suddenly full of energy. I wanted to run through the night. I wanted to paint something from top to bottom. I wanted to build something with my own hands. I wanted to throw everything out of the window and replace it. I wanted to take Nanki Devi out for a night on the town. I had a strong urge to survive. I had an even stronger one to vacuum.

I reopened the envelope, took out seven hundred pounds and resealed it. Then I telephoned Toby Jones. He answered with his mouth full.

'Toby. I've decided.'

He was silent. I could hear the TV on. 'Who is this?'

'It's Will Green. I've decided. I want to buy a Turbo Vac.'

The TV went mute. Toby swallowed. I imagined him standing up and straightening his tie. He said, 'I'm very pleased for you, Mr Green. Pleased you have made one of the best decisions you have ever made. You'll be pleased to know we're giving away a free bottle of champagne this month with each order.'

'I am pleased to know that, Toby.'

'Great. Well, I'll be round in the morning and—'

'No. I want it now.'

There was a pause, a chuckle and a . . . 'Actually it's almost eleven-forty-five.'

'I know what time it is.'

'I'm watching the athletics from Oslo.'

'If you want to sell me a Turbo Vac bring it round my house tonight or the deal's off.'

I stuck a book of stamps on to the front of my padded envelope and went out and posted it to Adopt-a-Granny. I had to squash it in the pillar box. When I got home Toby Jones was waiting at the door. He said, 'The great thing about the Turbo Vac of course is the after-sales service—'

'Shut up, all right?'

'Right.'

We went upstairs and he gave me the big box containing the Turbo Vac and all its accessories, and then he handed me a bottle of champagne. I opened it at once and poured two cups. Toby seemed a little uneasy. 'Are you alone?'

'Entirely.'

'Where are the family?'

'I haven't a clue. Relax. Sit down. I want to drink a toast. Did you know, Toby, that a recent report on dustmites suggests that asthma and many other allergen-based diseases are the direct result of a more affluent lifestyle?'

'No, I didn't know that.'

'It's encouraging, really. I didn't know I was living a more affluent lifestyle but apparently I am.' I clinked cups and looked him in the eye. 'Death to dustmites.'

'Death to dustmites.' He took a sip and watched me as I downed my cup in one. I poured another.

'I've just had an epiphany,' I told him, already feeling slightly drunk.

'I'm sorry to hear that,' he said and edged towards the door. 'Oh well. I'll get back to watch the pole vault, if you don't mind. Can I have the money?'

'Ah yes, the money.'

I took the seven hundred quid out of my back pocket and handed it to him.

He laughed nervously. 'Haven't you got a credit card or something?'

'No.'

'Fine. Fine.' He looked at the notes in the light. 'Well, thank you very much.' He put his cup down and backed out.

I started vacuuming at twelve-thirty. I put the Turbo Vac through its paces for two hours. I marvelled at the way it rinsed the carpet pile with air, at the way the deep-cleaning head probed the corners of the staircase, at the way the orthopaedic design enabled me to vacuum without damage to my spine. I drank the rest of the champagne. It was the first time I had vacuumed over the limit. I vacuumed things one wouldn't normally vacuum, like crockery and shoes. It was war on dustmites and there was nowhere for them to hide. They screamed as they were sucked into the bag, and I sang songs from Disney films as I exterminated them. I felt relieved of my burden. I was in detox. I had entered the equivalent of the Betty Ford Clinic for people who are obsessed with buying tea-rooms and gift shops. I wanted to come out and talk about my addiction. I wanted to let people know that I would, in my subconscious, probably always harbour a desire to own a teashop in the Cotswolds, but I had learnt that it was an unrealistic urge and developed a means to control it. After two hours' work with the Turbo Vac I really believed that. This was vacuuming as therapy.

I had no idea Kate had come home until the Turbo Vac went dead, and I turned to see her bending by the plug socket.

She looked pale and fraught. Something was wrong. She said, 'Where have you been? I've been phoning.'

My stomach dropped away. My body prepared itself for a shock. There was that tone in her voice, the urgency and the emphasis. There was the pain in the eyes. I'd known her for eighteen years, for God's sake.

'What's happened?' I said softly. I could hear the diesel rattle of a taxi waiting outside.

And her eyes began to fill, her face sag. 'It's your father,' she said.

CHAPTER TWELVE

THE HEART OF ENGLAND

He'd been hit by a car. He was having the chimneys swept and the sweep told him to go outside and watch the brush come through the pot; it would bring good luck. He walked backwards into the road and was clipped by a delivery van.

He never regained consciousness. Two days later he died from internal injuries. I phoned round and broke the news to his friends. 'He can't be dead. I only saw him down the supermarket on Tuesday,' was the typical response.

Colin came over from America and stayed at the Moat House Hotel on a roundabout in Borehamwood. He gave the speech at the funeral.

281

Kate said I should have done it—I was the one who had looked after Dad in his old age—but Colin was the first child, and he could speak in public better than I could. His accent had become noticeably more American since the last time he was over, and that seemed to give the occasion added solemnity. He told stories from our childhood. He told of the pleasure my father had in his family, of his love for his wife, of his happy career as a groundsman. He finished with a parable about a monk going to see a wise elder and asking what the secret of happiness was. The wise elder replied, 'Happiness is grandfather die, father die, son die.' The confused monk said, 'But how can this be happiness?' And the wise elder said, 'In that order.'

Colin was only over for four days. We didn't speak much, but we arranged everything together and we were each mindful of how the other felt. I thought about asking him if he wanted to stay up late one night and get drunk. I didn't in the end, but just being on the verge of asking made me feel closer to him. When he was saying goodbye to catch his plane I shook his hand and said, 'It's good to see you looking so well.'

'And you.'

'You look as though things are going all right for you.'

'They are. How are things going with you?'

'Fine.'

'You should all come over and visit. I've just moved into a new house.'

'I know. I'd like that.'

He stood there, nodding, not knowing how to say goodbye. Then he smiled sadly and said, 'You know the thing that used to really get me about

Dad? The way he used to talk about you all the time. Whenever I spoke to him he'd go on and on about how well you were doing. How proud of you he was. It really used to piss me off.'

Then he was waving to us from a taxi window.

Later that afternoon the phone rang and it was Graham. He said, 'Now, listen, the police want to speak to you tomorrow.'

*　　　*　　　*

It was the call I had been expecting. I'd had this nightmare image of them bursting into the funeral and dragging me out. Now at least I could sit back and let them talk me into a corner and confess. It would be a relief of sorts; an inevitable end perhaps, the end I had been heading for ever since I saw the Climbing Rose. It occurred to me that behind all my effort had been a need to impress my father, and now he was gone it didn't matter. I could face the truth.

Graham called me into his office as soon as I got to work. He made a point of closing the door. Then he quizzed me about the day of the robbery. He never thought for one minute that I did it, but he was annoyed that I had no alibi.

'They're giving everyone who wasn't working that day a hard time,' he said to me. 'They'll want to know what you were doing.'

'I wasn't doing anything; it was my day off.'

'Come on, Will. You've got to do better than that. I don't want any of my staff under suspicion. Particularly not you. They won't like it upstairs.'

'What's so special about me?'

He didn't want to tell me. 'They want you on the

cover of next year's brochure, that's what's so special.'

'What?'

'Don't look at me. It's 'cos of that Jack the Ripper business. They want you as the face of Welcome. So this doesn't look good, does it?'

'No.'

He studied the schedule for the day of the robbery. 'Listen. You were driving the Diana tour that afternoon, all right? I'll fix it. That's what you tell 'em. You got it?'

'Got it.'

And that was what I told the young detective with tattooed knuckles. He wrote it down and I heard nothing more on the matter. That evening I dumped the video camera and my Robin Hood outfit in the bottle bank, in the hole marked green.

On my next day off I went to my dad's house and started sorting through his hoards: his collection of greaseproof paper; his boxes of assorted elastic bands; his envelope containing used envelopes; his tins of string marked *Long, Short* and *Misc.* I spent every evening for a week over there, working into the night, filling dustbin bags. On the Sunday morning I took a pile of stuff down to the car-boot sale. Until then I wouldn't have been surprised to have heard a flush and discover he wasn't dead at all, he'd just been on the toilet for a longer period than usual; or to look up and see him walking up the path with a suitcase and remember he had just gone on a visit somewhere. But when I set up the stall in the playing field, and stood there on my own selling his crockery, I knew he was gone for good, and I couldn't stand it. Selling his collections would have been like losing touch with him and I

284

wasn't ready for that yet, so I decided to keep them all.

I returned to his house—I felt more at home there than in my flat—and continued sorting. It was about two o'clock in the morning, as I was tackling the last room, his bedroom, that I looked under the bed and pulled out a cardboard box marked *Finance*. At first all the brochures and certificates were a mystery to me, but then I realized they were all saving and investment accounts; they were stocks and shares, and treasury bonds. Then I came across copies of the deeds to the house, and they were in his name. He owned the place, for God's sake! He'd talked of buying it when my mother was alive, then seemed to forget about the idea. But he'd just gone ahead and not told us. I sat on his bed and couldn't stop myself crying, so that tears dripped down on to his policies and certificates. I left the house with the birds singing and the sickly London dawn spilling over the sky, and the knowledge that Colin and I had inherited in the region of £140,000 each.

I climbed into bed next to Kate. Dad's death had overshadowed what had gone on between us; it had put everything into perspective. She had been there for me. She had offered support in the way she would have done for a refugee seeking political asylum. She had held me; she had looked sorry for me. But no questions were asked; there were few words at all.

Now, though, as I watched her sleeping, I knew the time had come to face each other, to be bold. I stroked her cheek and she woke. Her limbs moved instinctively towards me before she could stop herself. 'Where have you been?' she whispered.

'I'm back now.'

When I told her about the money she was immediately defensive. Money was trouble. She lay there quietly. I was enjoying the rise and fall of her breathing. She said, 'What are we going to do?'

'I want us to do something together.'

'So do I.'

We both knew that we could recover from this one way or another. 'We have to think ahead,' I said.

But at that she grabbed me and shook me and yelled at me. 'No! Forget about thinking ahead! We need to think of the here and the now. It's the only way I'm prepared to go on!'

From that moment I knew what I had to do. I had to stop behaving like a tourist. I had to understand that I lived here.

*   *   *

Six months after my dad died we bought a house on Hamilton Road, a few doors down from where Mickey with his ponytail and his skip lived with his cemented corpses. We would never normally have been able to afford a house on that street, even with our inheritance money, but, as Ted said, you could never second-guess the property market. Mickey's house plummeted in value rather than skyrocketed, and so did the rest of the properties on the road. Residents were all keen to sell; no one wanted to move in. It was a buyers' market and we got our house for a snip.

And it was a beautiful house, with four bright bedrooms, a modern kitchen, lots of living space, a big garden, a cellar, and an attic to store my dad's collections. Stephen loved it because it had three times as many doors to slam, and Martin was convinced the moment he saw the tree-house perched in an old sycamore at the bottom of the garden.

If you looked out of the top-floor window you could see into Mickey's back yard, where the remains of the fourth body were found, but we could live with that. People used to die horrible deaths on the motorway outside our window at the flat all the time. I used to see Mickey at the bottle bank for a while after we moved in. He told me the police reckoned the appalling history of his house was all the work of a previous owner who had died himself twenty years ago. Mickey told me he was coping with the trauma of it all, but I knew he was drinking a lot just by his boxes of empty bottles. He'd gone back to drinking Virgin vodka, and his blue glass dilemma was becoming an obsession. I met him sitting on the pavement by the bottle bank one afternoon, looking pained, looking like he'd been there for hours. 'Is blue nearer to brown or green in the rainbow?' he asked.

'I don't think they have brown in the rainbow.'

As we sat there a truck pulled up, and we watched as the driver attached his hydraulic hoist to the bottle bank, lifted it and emptied the contents into his tipper, all the bottles crashing into one multicoloured mash.

The driver winked at us and drove off. I never saw Mickey again.

Kate and I had enough money now to start a business as well, although not in Stratford-upon-Avon, of course. We looked for something local, and something we could both feel involved with, nothing to do with catering. When a good premises became available on Station Road I was half joking when I suggested we open a vacuum-cleaner shop. Kate laughed, but the next morning she cuddled up to me in bed and said, 'I like the idea of us working with vacuum cleaners.'

I back-peddled. People went to department stores to buy those kinds of things now. High street shops belonged back in the model village. But Kate's gut reaction, coupled with her complete lack of business experience, intrigued me. Customers got no service in those big stores, she argued. They hated going there. And we would do repairs; we would sell everything to do with cleaning. We would become known locally and then further afield. 'It would be a useful business,' she enthused. 'A good service. It's the kind of thing we could do well.'

I could certainly do it well. Vacuum cleaners were my specialist subject. I knew all the decisions potential buyers had to make. I understood their needs. So we bought the leasehold. We employed a man to do the repairs, and we were all set for business.

The kids still went to the same school and we still went to the same shops, but life became different. 'It's because we got rid of the dustmites,' I said to Kate. 'A recent research paper published by Southampton University claims that dustmites have a debilitating effect on mental health.'

Hamilton Road was tree-lined and parking was easy. I found it hard to sleep at first without the motorway, but I left the windows open at night and if a west wind blew I could hear the gentle hum of traffic. After the newspapers had lost interest in

288

the events at Mickey's house, the Borough Council initiated a programme to try to change the road's associations. It was one of Kate's colleagues at the library who discovered that the nineteenth-century poet Christina Fairfax was born at number 36 in 1875. A plaque was put up. The name was changed to Fairfax Road, and the Heritage Walk was diverted to include us. Notices went up threatening fines for owners who allowed their dogs to foul the footpath.

We spent a long time trying to think of a name for our shop. Ted suggested Suckers. In the end we chose Clean Machines. We opened for business in March, the day after the clocks went forward. The first person through the door was Vinod with a bouquet of flowers. His florist's was nearby and after a dodgy start he'd found his feet. We both advertised in each other's windows. He offered me the bouquet and said, 'Daffodils are good for calming nerves.'

But I had no nerves. On the first day we sold four vacuum cleaners, including a top-of-the-range Electrolux. Twenty people came in with repair jobs. Within a fortnight we were branching out into floor scrubbers and polishers. We quickly established a reputation as cleaning consultants. Kate was only going to help out to start with, but she quickly became more involved. We ran the shop together. A week or so after opening Toby Jones walked through the door. He saw me and grinned. 'I knew you were in the business,' he said.

I work hard. I pick the kids up from school. I go running now instead of swimming. I keep sun-dried tomatoes and free-range eggs in the fridge. We're going to have a holiday in Florida this autumn and then visit Colin. Vinod and I have a cup of tea together whenever we can, and once a week we'll try and get to the pub. We talk problems through, business and personal. He's my mate. He said to me the other day, 'The bank always stresses long-term planning, but I reckon the success of a business is the day-to-day stuff.'

I nodded. 'Keep the customers satisfied and the future looks after itself.'

'That's right.'

Sometimes I look around me and wonder which I would rather have: my dad back, or the money he left me. And of course I say I would rather have my dad. Well you have to, don't you? But I really wonder what would have happened to me if something hadn't come along. I had fallen off the edge and my dad caught me, as all good dads do. I don't mind that all I own now was handed to me on a plate. I'll do the same for my children—that's all I'm going to do with this inheritance, nurture it and pass it on.

I do think of my dad a lot. I tell the kids, 'Grandpa's a cloud now,' and we search the sky for one we like the look of, and that's him. Sometimes I find myself doing it when I'm on my own. I can always find one that has his silhouette. Although, if I want to see him all I have to do is look in the mirror and see the way my chest is barrelling out; or look at my feet and see how my toenails are beginning to grow horny the way his did. When I was clearing out his drawers I found pictures of myself as a young child. They show a boy with knitted eyebrows and a worried face, gazing off camera, and I look just like Martin. His hair, his posture, his pout. My dad's gone but we're all busy recreating him.

Nanki Devi became our adopted grandmother. The kids wanted to call her something else, and we had to remind them this wasn't like having a pet where you got to name it, and if it got run over you got another. This grandmother was a member of the family. We put her picture on the mantelpiece next to my dad's. We were sent a regular newsletter, *Adopt-a-Granny News*, which gave details of the many projects donations went towards: day-care centres, minibuses, the rethatching of houses damaged in monsoons. George and Cal McCardle, and all the passengers on the excursion to Robin Hood Country that day back in July last year, could be assured their money was being put to good use.

Ted and Rita separated on Valentine's Day. It was Ted's present to the woman he had been having an affair with for six months. He moved in with her and said to me, 'It's a dream come true. We can talk about anything, washing machines, Bosnia.' But within a month he was calling round our house and taking me to the pub. 'She farts in bed and blames it on me,' he moaned, appalled.

I never went away with Alice again. I kept working at Welcome until Christmas, but I told Graham I wasn't prepared to do any more overnights, and I think she fixed it so that we weren't ever on day-trips together. The first time we saw each other after that evening when I went to her house, she said to me, 'I think we'd better . . . you know.'

'I think so as well.'

'These things get out of hand . . .'

'You're right.'

'People are starting to . . . you know.'

'Yeah.'

We were so polite to each other. I thought we were going to shake hands. A German came over and asked her if she knew Harrods' late opening days, and I slipped away.

She started to do conference work shortly after that, taking delegates round, and only occasionally came in to work for Welcome. On the day I quit I saw her come out of a hotel reception as I waited in my coach. I ran after her and touched her shoulder. She turned and when she saw me she almost screamed. It was hard to imagine we had once been so intimate.

'You startled me,' she said.

'Sorry. I wanted to tell you, I'm leaving.'

'I thought you were going to be on the brochure, the face of Welcome.'

'I didn't think that was a good idea.'

'Where are you going?'

'I'm going to work with vacuum cleaners.'

She nodded. 'I never thought you were cut out for this business, to be honest. I always got the impression you hated tourists.'

I caught the train home and missed my station by three stops.

*   *   *

One evening in March Kate climbed into bed and said, 'About this baby.'

'What baby?'

'The baby we've been trying to have for the last year. I've decided I don't want it any more.'

The curtains fluttered as something flew out of

the open sash window. I said, 'Why?'

'I think we should concentrate on ourselves. And on our boys.'

We lay there in peace, just the gentle wheeze of Martin's breath from the next room.

'I've dusted out my diaphragm,' she whispered.

'That old business again.'

On my birthday she gave me a blank-for-your-own-message greeting card. Inside her message read: *Good for one vasectomy.*

My appointment was 23 April. When the day came I got up in the dawn light, and from a recipe I'd cut out of one of the weekend papers that gave suggestions for food to be eaten in bed, I baked cherry muffins. I placed them in a preheated oven as instructed, and as the daylight grew stronger a wonderful aroma filled the kitchen and then the whole house. I opened the window and it filled the garden, and then wafted through letter boxes along the whole street. I placed the muffins in a basket and made a pot of tea. I sliced a nice pink grapefruit in two and segmented it, and then placed it all on a tray with a freshly picked tulip. As I carried it upstairs the cups and saucers rattled gently.

I placed the tray on the bed and Kate turned with surprise: 'What's this?'

'Shakespeare's birthday.'

'What? Oh no, I forgot.'

'You always forget.'

I drew the curtains and looked out over our lawn. A trail of molehills had arrived in the night.

I had my vasectomy at ten-fifteen a.m. The vasectomist said, 'I'm an Arsenal supporter,' and he asked me which team I supported.

'Arsenal,' I said.

In the evening, despite my aching and swollen genitals, Kate and I went out for a curry. 'Happy Birthday, Mr Shakespeare,' she said and clinked my glass.

I sat back and a twinge of pain shot up my crotch. 'This time nineteen years ago you were walking into the Blinking Owl in your black jeans and that low-cut brown T-shirt with short sleeves that made your arms look sexy.'

'You even remember what I was wearing.'

'And you drank a vodka and bitter lemon without any ice because you didn't like it diluted. And your friend Yvonne drank Pernod because she didn't like the taste and so she wouldn't drink it so fast.'

She said, 'I like going out with you. We should do this more often. We don't need special occasions.'

I leant forward and a twinge of pain ran down my crotch. 'Nineteen years ago. That means, from this night on, we've known each other longer than not.'

'That's right.'

I squeezed her arm and said, 'You know what we've got? We've got history, that's what we've got.'